PRAISE FOR

House under Snow

"This artful first novel by the poet and editor Jill Bialosky is a quiet stepsister to Rick Moody's *The Ice Storm*."
—*The New York Times Book Review*

"Lucid, finely crafted...Captures the purity and desperation of adolescent love in thick, sensual descriptions tinged by the wisdom of distance...An elegant debut." —*Los Angeles Times*

"Stunning." —*Glamour*

"Evokes the complexity of familial relations and the way they put their inevitable stamp upon our own future relationships."
—*Elle*

"An elegiac novel of a father's sudden death and its lingering effect on the family he leaves behind." —*The Washington Post*

"Well crafted...The book's pacing is refreshing and brisk, and Bialosky demonstrates a remarkable ear for emotional rhythm as well." —*Chicago Tribune*

"Jill Bialosky proves that good things can come from poets who turn to prose. She works a poet's sensibility into an intricately plotted novel about a mother-daughter relationship that contains a core of anger." —*The Plain Dealer* (Cleveland)

"A nicely satisfying end." —*Kirkus Reviews*

"With lyrical acumen, Jill Bialosky explores a family hothouse of maternal, filial, and sexual love in which the needs and desires of a mother and her daughters become fiercely entangled. A provocative and unsettling novel."
—Suzanne Berne, author of *A Perfect Arrangement*

"Such lyrical heartache awaits the reader in this lovely first novel. Here is a poignant page-turner that reminds us of the enormity of our first love, and reveals to us along the way—with a sharp and compassionate eye—the desperation of mothers and daughters and men."
—Elizabeth Strout, author of *Amy and Isabelle*

"This is story-telling from the toughest organ of them all, the heart, in prose distinctive as much for its music as for its muscle. Hers are characters—that witchy siren of a mother, those damaged children—who rise up out of the page to take up permanent residence in mind and memory."
—Lee K. Abbott, author of *Wet Places at Noon*

"Stunning for its depiction of the destructive power of love. Reading it one feels the competitive bonds between mothers and daughters, the awful echo of need and desire as it slips from one generation into the next."
—A. M. Homes, author of *Music for Torching*

"A passionate, sensually written tale of a daughter's struggle to wrest free of her mother's fitful and destructive influence."
—Jennifer Egan, author of *Look at Me*

"A coming-of-age story that is as wise as it is sensual. Lilly, one of the great, frightening mothers in contemporary writing, is as powerful as she is weak, and as maddening as she finally is mad. She is a nightmare figure, beautiful and terrifying, like something out of the paintings of Munch. She is impossible to forget." —Frederick Busch

"Rarely has a mother and daughter relationship been so haunting. The dangers vibrant, sexy, and selfish Lilly pose to her memorable soulful teenage daughter are only part of what makes Jill Bialosky's debut so astonishing." —Helen Schulman, author of *The Revisionist*

"A jewel of a novel—perfectly crafted and all the more brilliant for the sharpness of its edges. The story it tells is tragic, but Bialosky's prose is so beautifully restrained and her protagonist, Anna Crane, so resilient that this is not just a transfixing but an uplifting read." —Elizabeth Gaffney

House under Snow

ALSO BY JILL BIALOSKY

Subterranean

The End of Desire

Wanting a Child
(coedited with Helen Schulman)

House under Snow

JILL BIALOSKY

A Harvest Book • Harcourt, Inc.

Orlando   Austin   New York   San Diego   Toronto   London

www.HarcourtBooks.com

*This is a work of fiction. Names, characters, places, and incidents either are the products
of the author's imagination or are used fictitiously, and any resemblance to actual persons,
living or dead, events, or locales is entirely coincidental.*

Library of Congress Cataloging-in-Publication Data
Bialosky, Jill.
House under snow/Jill Bialosky.—1st ed.
p. cm.
ISBN 0-15-100685-7
ISBN 0-15-602746-1 (pbk.)
1. Mothers and daughters—Fiction. 2. Paternal deprivation—Fiction.
3. Fathers—Death—Fiction. 4. Young women—Fiction.
5. Sisters—Fiction. 6. Ohio—Fiction. I. Title.
PS3552.I19 H68 2002
813'.54—dc21   2001007435

Text set in Garamond 3
Display set in Dali
Designed by Cathy Riggs

Printed in the United States of America
First Harvest edition 2003

C E G I K J H F D

To my family

*"Taint not thy mind, nor let thy soul contrive
Against thy mother aught. Leave her to heaven..."*

—FROM *HAMLET* BY WILLIAM SHAKESPEARE

House under Snow

✦ ✦ ✦

The day my sister Ruthie left home, in 1973, my mother was upstairs in her bedroom in front of her vanity with a cutout of a model's face from *Vogue* pinned to the oval-shaped mirror, experimenting with her eye makeup in an attempt to replicate the exact fusion of eye shadow, lipstick, and eyebrow shape. Our mother was obsessed with the curves, shadows, and cast of light across a face, the many moods the combinations evoked.

She had been this way most of our lives. And when she wasn't preoccupied with her looks, she scoured the society pages of the *Plain Dealer* and *Jewish News,* to fish out the latest Cleveland society gossip—who had attended the art museum opening or the evening symphony—and what newly eligible men might be available. This was when she was still looking for a husband. She once had one of our relatives track down the phone number and address of a man she had dated in high school, after she read his wife's obituary in the evening paper.

But on the night my sister left, my mother was still ensconced in her room tweezing her eyebrows and experimenting with lipsticks, even though her long and complicated history with men had dried up. It seemed to calm her, her endless fascination with mascara wands and nail lacquers; her perpetual need for reinvention. It was the way she dealt with what she'd lost, a means of finding solace and safeguard from the tumult of the world outside herself. She was one of those women who believe that if her hair is the perfect shade, the ideal softness, she can control the chaos of her inner universe. That day, while my mother powdered and played with eye shadow and eyeliner pencils, Ruthie sequestered us in her bedroom for a conference.

"I can't take her anymore," Ruthie said. She had just turned sixteen that fall of 1973. She wore a winter scarf wrapped around her neck and a pale blue wool sweater that reflected her blue eyes. She had long, dark hair she parted in the middle, and white skin. A draft snaked through the house. Ruthie's one Samsonite suitcase was already packed. "She drives me crazy."

"I know," I said.

Ruthie fingered the tassels on the curtain against her window. "It's better if I'm out of her hair."

"You don't have to explain it."

Even though I would miss Ruthie, part of me felt relief that she was leaving. It would mean that my mother would quit pacing the floors at night wondering when her daughter would come home. I was willing to tolerate Ruthie's absence, if it meant her happiness. I knew my sister's mind had gone to a thick and complicated place that had proved dangerous. Ruthie's boyfriend, Jimmy Schuyler, had been busted for dealing pot. His parents sent him away to a boarding school in Pennsylvania. Then Ruthie had filled the hole left in her life by locking herself up in her room like a Buddhist monk in solitary confinement, and getting high.

"We'll be fine," Louise, the youngest of us three—we were each born barely a year apart—tried to reassure her. Louise was tomboyish, with a short haircut framing her face, and knowing eyes that looked older than a girl of fourteen.

"I don't want you to think I'm deserting you. If she gets weird you have to promise to call me. Maybe Aunt Rose will let you come, too." Ruthie cracked her knuckles, pulling at each one of her fingers in a kind of perverse determination, a recent habit.

Unlike Ruthie, I couldn't comprehend leaving my mother alone. I couldn't imagine how our mother would survive without the armor of protection we provided. But later that night, after I heard the hired car come rolling into the driveway to take my mother's firstborn, it dawned on me that Ruthie and I weren't so different: Most of my waking hours, I realized, were concentrated on devising plots to escape the seclusion of our house.

When our mother watched the car move down the driveway, she pressed her nose against the window of the front door, a handkerchief balled up in her fist, and waved good-bye. The makeup she had spent hours working on had smeared. She stayed by the window long after the car had left its tire tracks behind. Her breath fogged up the pane, and she stood there on tiptoe, as if she expected the car to turn around and bring her daughter back. All that night I was kept awake by the sounds of my mother, Lilly, rummaging around in her bedroom, opening drawers, turning on the television, climbing up and down the stairs, restless as a sleepless child.

Ruthie's absence that year was palpable. We felt it in the emptiness of her room without her dark silhouette against the window and her vacant chair shoved against the supper table. The atmosphere in the house was like a threatening cloud that promises precipitation but never erupts. Frozen snow from weeks of chilling cold covered the ground and formed a layer over our roof, buried our shrubs, and blanketed the front stoop leading to the house. The wind caused the branches of the tree outside our window to thrash like someone waking from anesthesia.

+ + +

*N*ow I live hundreds of miles from my mother's house in Chagrin Falls. Decades have passed since that one long winter. But the minute the snow begins to fall over the tall buildings of the city, everything comes back—the shudder the winter chill sends through the body, the reluctance to have your footprints be the first to taint the snowbound streets, the lack of separation between falling snow and sky, the sense that winter will never end. But what stays with me most is a feeling I carry of being *responsible,* as if by leaving home and creating a life for myself I abandoned my own child.

In a few months I will be coming home for my wedding. After all these years, I still have to steel myself. The thought of returning is bittersweet. Half of me wants to celebrate this occasion with my family, and the other half wishes we'd decided to run off and elope.

After I return to my apartment from work for the evening, I obsess over the details of the wedding, and then I think about how far I've come. I remember our house in winter—the endless white madness of the snow and the rush of cold air as it moved into the living room, circulated through our narrow rooms, blew the door shut behind it—as if to remind me how fragile happiness is, how easily it can shatter like a pane of glass. That's why I'm compelled to tell this story—don't we all have one secret that has shaped us we are burning to reveal?—to convince myself that I'm entitled to my own life.

We never forget childhood. It is always planted there like a white house on top of a steep hill. My memories are harsh but necessary. I imagine the wind, uncontrollable and crazy, coiling around the trees, whipping off branches, pushing cars off the road, and in one powerful gust setting in motion an unstoppable avalanche capable of destroying everything in sight.

✦ ✦ ✦

In the long-awaited spring after the winter Ruthie left, the smell of lilac and forsythia overwhelmed. All the windows in the house were open. Children ran across our yards in cutoffs and T-shirts, suburban lawns glistened with promise. It was as if, because the winter had been long and bleak, God decided to bless us with a fruitful spring. In Ohio the trees are rich and bountiful, and sitting beneath a huge maple or elm waiting for a cool breeze to whip through the maze of leaves and branches to save us, we could barely make out the sky, wanted only to lift its mantle of heat.

That spring there was magic in the air. Often, in the distance, was the smell of rain and lightning, and the light roll of thunder. All it would have taken was an outstretched hand and warm lips to kill the heat. Or a bluebird to put out her wing and cast the spell over my body, and I'd sink onto soft grass, into arms and tangled legs, then be gone like a puff of smoke. And all that would be left was a boy's aura, pungent, strong enough to bring tears.

The end-of-school parties began in April and lasted until late June. I was going into my senior year. The fact that Austin Cooper had invited Maria Murphy and me to *his* party was a sign we'd made the inner circle. On the night my relationship with Austin Cooper was sealed, the crowd was thick, making the rooms of the house feel cramped; the air was layered with smoke and the dark haze of pent-up energy and recklessness.

Austin Cooper had moved to Chagrin Falls from Denver, Colorado, three months before the party. He was tall with long, thin legs, broad shoulders, and a square-jawed face that made him look older than seventeen. The spaces underneath his cheekbones pulsed with intensity when he spoke. When I saw him walking down the halls of our school in his black work boots and faded jean jacket, and his eyes fastened on mine, it was as if a door had opened; there was no glass, no screen of protection. I walked into the open bloom of him and was trapped.

The rumor was that in Denver, Austin Cooper's mother had screwed around with the husband of the family next door, and then after she'd taken off with him to another state, he dumped her. After the affair, Austin's father, who was a partner in a national accounting firm, relocated to Cleveland in the middle of Austin's senior year of high school. Austin was exactly the kind of boy I'd dreamed about. Catherine, the great and tragic heroine of *Wuthering Heights,* the book I had studied like a bible my junior year, said this of Heathcliff: "My love for Heathcliff resembles the eternal rocks beneath—a source of little visible delight, but necessary." The visceral persuasion Austin Cooper had over me was there from the moment I inhaled my first breath of him.

That first day, Maria was whispering the rumor about Austin Cooper's parents when our math teacher, Mr. DeMott, was turned to the blackboard to write out the formula for finding the area of a right triangle. It was the first day after spring break. Any time there was a new kid in our school it was cause for celebration. We looked forward to a new face to break up the monotony of our ordinary existence. That day Austin sat for a few minutes in the last row of Mr. DeMott's classroom, having read his schedule incorrectly. Once he realized he was in the wrong classroom, he packed up his notebook and stack of books and left, but not before his eyes passed through mine.

When I saw Austin's bowlegged walk move down the corridor after class, I dawdled near my locker as if I were looking for a misplaced book. He stopped, and his eyes ran along the length of my body, lingering over each curve. I had to catch my breath. After I turned my back, I felt his eyes again, the press of them, like a wind, on my neck.

He walked me home from school that day, and immediately he consumed my imagination, the way an overgrown cherry tree in blossom overtakes a yard. Then, a few weeks before his party, he invited me to his house after school. Austin had the house to himself each afternoon until six-thirty or seven o'clock at night, when his father came home from work. After he put a new Jefferson Starship album on the turntable, he caught me off guard and kissed me. My body went liquid to his touch. We went up to his bedroom and rubbed against each other, in our clothes, for so many hours that the skin on my legs was raw. The register of his hands on my skin felt like a tattoo grafted into my body. But after that late afternoon I still hadn't been sure whether I meant something to Austin. I didn't know how to gauge a boy's interest. The invitation to his party I took as a good sign. That maybe we were going out.

Austin's father was out of town on business that weekend. The party was scheduled for the first Saturday night in May. I had worried about it all week—how I would get out of the house, what I would wear, and then what would happen, once I was alone with Austin.

In front of his house, five cars were parked bumper-to-bumper in the driveway. A caravan of parked cars wound its way down the street and around the bend. It was a warm late spring night. The smell of lilac was in the air. A streak of heat lightning ignited the sky. In the backyard a group of boys huddled around the keg. Bruce Webster was doing the honors of pumping Styrofoam cups full of Miller. The hard-core partiers brought their own mugs. Austin led me to the keg, handed me a cup of beer. His eyes looked wet; sweat beads had begun to form on his face; not even nine o'clock and he was already toasted. He sent heat through my body when he brushed up against me; then he disappeared.

I was drawn to a damaged and wild streak in his character. I liked the wildness about Austin, because it was familiar. My mother had that streak inside her, too. It flared up when a man was around: Her eyes caught on fire. She couldn't quiet her body. Her knees bounced up and down so that she had to place her hands on her thighs to contain herself. Sometimes I felt that my very being was what kept my own mother alive and grounded in the world, that without me she was like one of those falling stars that dissolves as it crashes to the earth.

Looking back, in some ways Austin and I were the perfect match. We provided what the other lacked. I had learned to allow another person to consume me so much that I could become invisible; Austin needed the open field of unconditional love to survive.

In the Coopers' garage that night, a joint was being passed.

I looked around for a familiar face. But most of the kids at the party I really didn't know well. They were seniors from our school. I had convinced Maria to come to the party with me, but after a half hour she took off to go cruising with Todd Levine in his mother's Lincoln. There was that spring-fever madness in the air. Anything could happen.

From the backyard I could see into the windows of the house. People were in the kitchen, huddled in packs, propped on the granite counters, or standing around the table. The air in the room was a maze of hormones. The sky outside electric. I tried to join a small crowd talking about what they were doing that summer.

"Party! Party!" Danny Keller chanted, as he walked through the crowd, his shirt tied, like a sheik's headdress, around his head. He gave me the high five, and pushed his can of beer against the slice of skin on my back that showed when I raised my arms to fix my hair. As he brushed past me, he sprinkled my shirt with beer.

On the way upstairs to the bathroom, I passed girls standing on the staircase. They flicked the ashes from their cigarettes into Austin's father's flowerpots. I found myself getting angry, as if I already had a stake in the Coopers' private territory. Nancy Singer and George Weisberg were making out intensely on the landing. After waiting my turn in line, I closed the bathroom door against the party. The sounds siphoned off to static buzzing in my temples. I had never felt comfortable at parties, around large groups of people. I was always the girl who stood in the sidelines, outside of a group, looking on. It took so much energy just to be present. I longed for a time when I could forget myself. Ever since my father had died, a part of me went out of the world and floated, lost and disconnected.

One hand held my mother's, the other the dark ethereal leaf on a tree you could snap off in a single gesture.

✦ ✦ ✦

My father, Lawrence Crane, had been a builder. He designed our house in Chagrin Falls, and with the help of his construction crew, dug the basement, poured the cement, and built the frame. They leveled and laid the floors, plastered, Sheetrocked, and stroked on the paint. Lilly had told us the story so many times, I knew it by heart. He was so strong, my mother said, so smart. When she spoke like that, it was to the wind, or the weeping willows. She was swept away by the current of her memory. Lost. Her words were like long sighs.

Our house was the only one in Chagrin Falls with a gazebo in the backyard, she liked to boast, her expression full of pride. When my father died in the spring of 1961, he was standing on a ladder leaning against the gazebo to replace one of the little white lights that he kept lit all year round. One by one, over the years after he died, they had burned out, but no one bothered to replace them. The ladder lost its grip. My father fell, hit his head dead center on a rock, and never regained consciousness. I used to wonder what his last thought was, whether he held it inside his skull, freeze-framed, when all the lights shut down.

I was four years old, Ruthie five, and Louise barely three. I was too young to remember my father exactly, but on the cold winter mornings when my mother was asleep and I was playing in my room, I felt his timeless spirit through the house. Sometimes, now, sitting in my own tiny kitchen, I can feel it, the warm wash of love. But at night, when my sisters and I were alone, and my mother was out, I thought the moon must have iced over when my father died, casting a cold glow over the house of his dreams. We were left to live in his haunted place.

When I go back home, the house is still all filled up with him. I wonder if that's why my mother has stayed in it all these years. My mother doesn't talk about my father anymore, but it floats in the air around her, what his death has cost.

+ + +

*I*n the Coopers' bathroom I looked in the mirror on the medicine-cabinet door, and steadied myself against the sink. My hair had grown longer that year, and rode the middle of my back. My round, baby face had finally chiseled itself into a shape I was no longer embarrassed of. I saw the difference, the way boys stopped on the street to look at me. It felt good to have their eyes on mine if it meant I could become remade from one of Lilly's daughters into a girl someone desired. My mother taught us early how important it was to make sure a man couldn't live without you. She based all of our lives on that notion.

+ + +

*A*fter my father died my mother, who was only twenty-five, woke up each morning, put on the same white sweatshirt and ankle-length black stretch pants that clung to her thin legs, and tied her hair back with a black string. She wore not a stitch of makeup. This time was when I felt connected to her, when I snuggled up next to her on the couch before bed at night and she dreamily stroked the top of my hair.

My sisters and I played in the deserted winter field at the end of the street and came back with chapped red cheeks and dirty fingernails to find Lilly sitting cross-legged on the couch watching the snow begin to build outside her window. She held a magazine in her lap, though the pages were rarely turned. The same pained look would be in my mother's face when, sometimes, with no warning, at the supper table, or standing in the grocer's checkout line, a memory would seize her and her eyes would cloud up. She'd take a deep breath, will back her strength, and smile at us.

My mother's grief was mostly unspoken, only a slow, steady throbbing that permeated the body of the house. She sometimes spent an entire afternoon indoors doing crossword puzzles or staring into space. In the morning she made bowls of cereal for us and then watched the day begin, completely unaware that another year had passed since her husband had died. But her eyes were soft, filled with part daylight and part darkness.

After Lilly rinsed the bowls and set them on the rack to dry, she'd prod us upstairs to dress in whatever we could find, and paid no notice when our socks and sweaters began to fade.

Nobody came to the house and nobody called. After my father's death, we had been cut loose of the world and our connections. When my father's family was face-to-face with us, we seemed to reflect back what they had lost; our presence was too painful. My mother—she was still a young woman then—was pitied more than loved. We felt as if we were a pack of girls to stay away from. Still, those were days when we were still connected as a family, in the three or four years after my father died. Even though my mother was ensconced in her grief, my sisters and I were a part of it. Nothing had happened yet to hint that we would not be saved.

In those years my mother would sit on the couch all day clipping pictures from magazines and newspapers while the TV ran. *Gilligan's Island* or the other mindless shows she watched would be interrupted by a news flash. More troops were being sent to Vietnam; each day thousands of American soldiers were killed. Meanwhile my mother occupied herself with cutouts while my sisters and I played on the floor making flimsy houses out of a deck of cards. She clipped prints, photographs, pictures of certain objects she liked: furniture, gardens, bouquets of flowers, women in exciting, fashionable dresses. She had acquired a peculiar passion for snipping and saving. Soon she had shoe boxes and hatboxes and folders overflowing with samples of things in the world she loved. When I asked what she was doing, she said, "I'm trying to capture something," and then drifted away again. Before my father died she collected old pictures and postcards she'd find at local flea markets and junk sales and she took them out from the baskets where she stored them. She made scenes of garden parties, blond children playing in the sun, men and women embracing. Sometimes she'd clip African mothers from *National Geographic.* She brought the outside world inside our house so she would never have to leave home.

When she felt particularly blue, she'd snip black-and-white photographs of catastrophes. A woman who had lost a son in a boating accident; a picture of a family mourning a plane crash. Sometimes she'd clip articles from the obituaries. I watched her make this paper menagerie of dreams and nightmares, which was stuffed and folded at night's end, and tucked under the couch.

One day Lilly slept until late afternoon. She finally came downstairs to find us transfixed by the television. President Kennedy had been shot. My mother grew hysterical. She crumpled a Kleenex in her hand as Walter Cronkite reported the tragedy. The day of President Kennedy's funeral Lilly was still beside herself. She opened a new box of Kleenex and hunkered down in front of the television and watched the processional. Her eyes were glued to the screen as Jackie stepped out of the limousine holding the hands of her two small children. "That poor woman," Lilly said over and over, as if she were guardian of Jackie's fate.

When I picture those years when my mother was a widow, it's like this: my mother in her bedroom fast asleep all day, or working on her cut-outs, Ruthie staring out the window, her long braids wrapped around her head in contemplation, and Louise and me playing tic-tac-toe in the cellar.

The summer before I entered second grade, something changed. My mother seemed to realize that we could no longer live in seclusion, that the world expected more from us. Maybe my mother was getting bored, clipping and sorting all day, stuffed in our house like dirty, used-up socks in a drawer. Maybe she simply needed to be touched by another person besides her daughters to feel vital again. Nevertheless, once she stepped out of our isolated cocoon, nothing was the same. It was no longer just the four of us bundled together like a package.

My mother had decided she had to do something to change our lives. At first, she changed her cutout world. One day I was watching her, as usual. The purple light of dusk had crept through the windows. I looked down from the couch at my mother's newest composition. The entire living room floor was laid out in elaborate festive party images. I remember the cutouts of men and women dancing, and a long buffet table covered with a lace cloth. On top were crystal wineglasses filled with champagne. In the center of the scene was a grand piano topped with a lilies-of-the-valley bouquet. Up above sailed colorful butterflies and powder-white clouds. Paper doilies cut in the shape of furniture were carefully arranged around the garden on my mother's imaginary canvas. By this time I never questioned what she was doing day after day, alone in the house; that in her grief she had become eccentric.

As I looked closer the scene came more strikingly into focus. While it was impossible to remember every detail from the cutout world she was creating, there was one image I'll never forget. My eyes rested in the right corner on a black-and-white photograph: It was a picture of my father and mother cutting a three-tiered wedding cake. All that evening she lingered with a pair of scissors in her hand, sipping cups of tea and reflecting, as though she were trying to savor her memories of her wedding, my father, her happiness, to store them in a place she'd never lose them.

✦ ✦ ✦

My mother grew up in East Cleveland, on a block where houses were two and three stories high and lined one beside the other. It was a community of Jewish immigrants from Hungary, Poland, Lithuania, and Russia. Lilly told us stories of how her father's friends used to play cards in the basement while Aunt Rose made big meals of stuffed cabbage, borscht, noodle pudding, and sweet and yeast breads for everyone who happened to stop by on a Sunday. Aunt Rose and my grandfather were siblings. My mother was eight years old when her mother, Dora Rosenberg, died of a brain aneurysm. Afterward, no longer able to live in the house his wife had inhabited, my grandfather and mother moved into

Aunt Rose's two-family. Aunt Rose became my mother's second mother.

Sometimes in the evenings Lilly would stretch out on the couch and take down her photo album, which seemed sacred to her, like a bible. In one picture my father and mother are inside Aunt Rose's house. My mother is dressed in black loafers and stretch pants, leaning against my father. Her hair is irregularly parted, and her eyes are burning with happiness. It's one of the few photographs of my parents together.

Before my father died, we used to go to my great-aunt Rose's house every Friday night for the Sabbath.

"Hi, Daddy," Lilly flirted with her father, as if she was still a young girl, the minute she opened the heavy storm door to their house. When we walked in the door, my grandfather was usually sitting in his leather recliner smoking his pipe. The cherry scent of his favorite tobacco was on his breath, and the prickle of his six-o'clock shadow scratched our cheeks when he hugged us. If we listened we could hear the sounds of Lilly and Aunt Rose already chattering in the kitchen.

When I recall my childhood, I'm not sure if I remember an actual event, or whether what seems like a memory comes from a story my mother or one of my sisters or Aunt Rose told me or whether I've blurred events together. But if memory can also be a feeling, I can still feel the extravagant warmth of our Sabbath dinners at Aunt Rose's house before my father died; the smell of Aunt Rose's brisket simmering in the kitchen, mingled with the powdery smell of the rouge she brushed on her cheeks; how my grandfather squeezed my hand, sometimes so hard I felt my knuckles crack.

After we had sat at the long table and Aunt Rose served us bowls of matzo ball soup and plates full of brisket, potatoes, broccoli, and farfel with onions, our grandfather took us into his study and gave us each a shiny, brand-new copper penny. To us it was worth a hundred dollars.

From the kitchen we could hear Aunt Rose talking to Lilly while they did the dishes. My mother and Aunt Rose could not begin a conversation without rehashing the stories of my mother's family in the old country before they'd been decimated by the war. It was a connection they shared strong as the current of a river. My father would be in the bedroom watching the news on Aunt Rose's portable television.

My mother told us that after her mother died, my grandfather did not allow his wife's name to be spoken in his presence. He dealt with his grief by routine: Every day he went to work at the bank where he was a bank teller; at night he returned religiously at five-fifteen to have dinner with Aunt Rose and Lilly. On Saturdays he meticulously manicured his lawn and garden.

Aunt Rose was the only person Lilly dared talk to about her mother. I remember catching snippets of their secret conversation. (If my grandfather happened to walk into the room, it was as if a door slammed shut. The room went silent.) One Friday I had crept into the kitchen to tell my mother something, and stopped in the hallway.

"An aneurysm?" Lilly was saying. "But, Aunt Rose, she was so young. It doesn't make any sense."

"Your mother and I were so close. We were like sisters." I could make out Aunt Rose, around the corner. She always dressed modestly. Her skirts and blouses were ironed perfectly, her hair braided on the top of her head and held together with one long hairpin. "She had no one in America, except us and your father.

"None of the doctors would confirm it, but what do doctors know anyway?" Aunt Rose finally said. "The aneurysm was caused by what your mother endured in the war. How could it not catch up to her?" She shook her wet hands before wiping them on her apron, then brushed a wisp of salt-and-pepper hair from her face. "Imagine, all those months living in a basement alone, in hiding."

"What was my mother like?" Lilly asked. "It's hard to remember."

"Like you, Lilly," Aunt Rose answered in her sturdy voice. Her eyes brimmed with tears.

Aunt Rose had never married. My mother told us that she was once engaged to a man who was in the army. They planned to marry when he returned on leave. But years went by, and she never heard from him. Aunt Rose eventually tucked away his photograph, which used to sit on the nightstand by her bed, but when I grew older I could tell, when I went out to visit my aunt and we watched a sad love story on television and her face filled with shadow, that her heart was broken. When it became clear she wasn't to marry, my grandfather arranged a job for her as a secretary at his bank. After Lilly's mother died Aunt Rose had devoted her energy, when she wasn't working, to making a home for my mother and grandfather. Like other immigrants, she lived modestly, never expecting more from the world than enough money for a hot meal on the table and clean clothes for her family. In her presence I always felt like I had room to be myself, because she demanded so little of me. Maybe she expected so little from others because she liked herself.

Dora Rosenberg, my mother's mother, had endured the invasion of the Nazis in Lithuania. She was the only member of her family to survive. After the war the priest who had kept her in hiding arranged for her to live with a family in Switzerland. Eventually the family orchestrated Dora's passage to America. She met my grandfather on the boat to America. Their first home was in Hoboken, New Jersey.

I remember, as the Sabbath candles burned low in the dining room, listening to my mother and Aunt Rose talking. I couldn't take in the reality of the Holocaust. I couldn't believe that Lilly had lost her mother when she was eight.

When it was time to go home that Sabbath evening, my father turned off the black-and-white television with the bent rabbit ears in Aunt Rose's bedroom, gave her a kiss on the cheek, and came to collect us from the living room. I was very young, and looking back, it seems impossible that I could remember the details of that evening at Aunt Rose's house with my father. Perhaps I had fused together the story of how Lilly's mother had died with one of the only memories I had of my father. But still, the memory of the evening seems so vivid, as if I'd sealed it into my consciousness and willed myself to always remember.

In the winter, snow had often accumulated in the few hours we were at Aunt Rose's. My father would get in the car, turn on the heat, and then carry each of us from the side door to the car if we had forgotten to wear our boots. Squished in the backseat, our mother yawning in the front, my sisters and I waited while my father cleaned the snow off the windshield. I felt sleepy and dozed against Ruthie's shoulder. The winter could have lasted all year for all I cared. There was no reason to stay awake or keep alert, no fear or danger. There was no reason to want, or try to hope, or have to pray.

Lilly was nineteen when she married my father. She went from her aunt and father's grief-ridden house to her husband's without learning how to pay a bill, iron a shirt, make a pot of soup, tidy a room. After her mother died, she had been treated like a little princess. Everyone, I suppose, tried to make up for the fact that she had lost her mother. Maybe you never recover from a loss like that. Maybe you're always damaged.

After my father died we lived off the blue Social Security checks Lilly received from the government each month, a small life insurance policy, and occasional handouts from Aunt Rose or Nonie and Papa, my father's parents.

I know that I had lost my father, but I couldn't imagine losing my mother. Maybe because my mother was all that I had. After all, even if Lilly forgot about us for an hour, a day, or two, there was always the gentle sound of her voice humming at the sink, her different smells, her footsteps on the wood floor. I had learned to believe the mere physical presence of another person was enough. Sometimes at night after my father died, before I fell asleep, I used to worry that something would happen to my mother to take her away from us.

Lilly's father had passed away from lung cancer the year before my father's death. Aunt Rose had boarded up the house in East Cleveland, packed her bags, and moved to California to be with one of her girlhood friends who was recently widowed. With my mother married then and her brother gone, she felt free of her responsibilities. How could she have expected my father to die so suddenly, at the age of thirty?

We all missed Aunt Rose's Sabbath dinners after she moved. Without them it felt as if a piece of our lives had fallen away. And after Aunt Rose had settled in California, at her age it was too much for her—the Cleveland winters made her arthritis flare up—to pack up again and move back, to help look after Lilly and us girls, when my father died.

My mother must have figured that we'd survive somehow.

It didn't occur to her that it was up to her to put our lives together. She just preferred to drift off into a quiet, godforsaken place where nothing was demanded of her. She favored dreams and wind and sky.

✦ ✦ ✦

*O*ne summer day Lilly was again cutting out things from magazines, laying them on the floor of the living room, as if she were a young girl playing with paper dolls. Again she was re-creating with her cutouts her own wedding scene, when Ruthie and Louise came barreling through the front door and the wind sent my mother's menagerie flying.

Lilly laid her head in her hand and breathed heavily.

"Look what you've done," she said. "I thought I told you to come through the back door."

"Why do you cut things all day?" Ruthie asked.

"There's nothing wrong with using your imagination," Lilly answered defensively. Her hand reached down for the wedding photo, and she stuck it inside her brassiere. "But you're right," Lilly said. "I'm going to have to pull myself together." She took us in her arms and hugged us, but we hadn't any idea what she meant.

In that gesture I remembered another hand. A cool, coarse hand placed gently over my forehead. A hand that massaged my temples as I lay under the stars, on his lap, and he pointed to Ursa Minor, through the crown at the roof of the gazebo, not knowing this was what he might be remembered for. It was a touch I carried with me, wore like a second skin.

"Come on, I'll make supper," Lilly said, stepping over the remains of the wedding party, which adorned our carpet like scattered leaves.

Lilly's dinners were simple: tuna fish or grilled cheese sandwiches and bowls of soup she brought into the den on trays. The fancier meals had been boarded up in a past more spirited.

After supper that night Lilly said, "Girls, things are going to have to change."

She walked into the living room and in a manic heat began to pull out her boxes from the hall closet and folders of clippings from underneath the couch. "Here, you take this," she said to Louise, and piled her up with a stack of bursting folders. I carried three shoe boxes, one on top of the other. "Come on," Lilly said, and walked out the back door, down the grass, past the trees, to the rocky path that led to the gazebo.

It was nearly dusk. I could hear the familiar creaks coming from the wind in the rafters. After we put down our load, my mother drew us girls into a circle. We heard the sound of Chagrin Falls crashing in the distance. Lilly closed her eyes and inhaled. In the air I tasted the spray from the white water. She had us all hold hands, and motioned for us to sit down in a circle on the wooden floorboards of the gazebo.

"Something has happened to us," Lilly said. "And we've got to change. We can't continue to live like savages. Look," she continued, holding out her hands. I noticed how pale they were, how lovely my mother's unpainted nails appeared in the light of approaching dusk. "Look at us," she went on. "When's the last time you girls changed your clothes? You're filthy. We can't go on like this. Do you understand?"

Our eyes were planted on her.

"What I mean is, you have to start learning how to act like other children. Otherwise, we'll always be alone." Lilly's voice was gentle, but it hurt to listen to her.

"Inside, you can be whoever you want. You can imagine yourself floating on a cloud, or that you're part of the darkness when you're sitting in the shade, but on the outside you have to talk like other people, and pretend you belong with them."

Not one of us said a word.

"I don't want to see those sad eyes," Lilly said. "We have to learn how to become dignified, all of us."

"What's that?" Louise asked.

"Being dignified means holding your head up high, no matter how terrible you feel. It means taking care of yourself when all you want to do is play in the fields and lie in bed dreaming. It means having lots of friends, and never letting anyone know how lonely you are."

She paused. It was so quiet you could hear the sound of the river in the distance, its lap of endless promise and desire.

"We have to start acting like Aunt Adrienne, Uncle Ben, and your cousins. We have to pretend we're like them," Lilly said. "Even if we're not."

Lilly was referring to my father's brother, his wife, and their children. They lived in Cleveland, in one of the very newest sub-urbs, not far from Nonie and Papa. After my father died we saw them only once or twice a year, for Rosh Hashanah or Passover. It wasn't until I had long left home that I learned from Aunt Rose that, a few years after my father's death, Lilly had refused a job that Uncle Ben had arranged for her, through a friend of his who was a dentist. Uncle Ben had offered Lilly a position as a receptionist in his friend's office. Aunt Rose said that Nonie and Papa thought it was ungrateful for Lilly to refuse, but Lilly, she said, was intimidated by them, by their wealth.

That evening out in the gazebo, Lilly continued. "That's the only way to grow up, to pretend you're like other people." Now I see she was trying to ignite her past into flames and pretend it had never existed, so she could move on. My mother tried to build us up, because inside she felt so small. But then

I was simply engaged by the purposefulness with which my mother spoke and the newfound confidence in her voice. She coaxed herself by coaxing us.

"Do you think your father would have fallen in love with me if I had sat around all day moping and didn't brush my hair or wear a smile on my face?"

"Is that why he loved you? Because you were dignified?" Ruthie asked. From the very beginning, when it came to Lilly, she was a skeptic.

"Ruthie, when you don't come from money, all you have is yourself. You must focus all your energy on becoming as beautiful as a blossom, as perfect as a piece of fruit. You must smell as fresh and clean as grass after a summer rain. I was raised to believe that for a Jew to fit in you had to make sure not to make your own needs or presence too visible. You'll see. I'll teach you how."

"But what if we don't want to?" Louise said.

"You don't have any choice."

"Who says?" Ruthie questioned.

"It's my own fault," Lilly said. She looked off, her face fine and girlish, in the watery wind. "You'll see, darling. From now on everything will be different. I'm going to pick myself up and start a new life. After all I'm not yet even thirty." I had no idea then what my mother meant. I was perfectly content with the life we had. But for the first time it dawned on me that my sisters and I weren't enough for our mother: She needed a different kind of love to make herself feel alive. To insure she wouldn't disappear.

By then the sky was nearly dark. Lilly stood up and turned on the lights around the gazebo. "Now we have to make a fire," Lilly said, walking toward the woodpile. She came back with an armload of kindling and ordered me to lay it campfire style, with a few logs, in a clearing beside the gazebo. Lilly rolled up some old newspapers from the garage and placed them around the logs. She took a book of matches from her pocket and lit the paper and kindling, and the logs caught fire. Together we fanned the flames with folders full of Lilly's paper cutouts, then sprinkled their contents into the growing fire before we stepped back. Lilly poked the dying embers with a stick. Then she threw in the rest: boxes and boxes of cutouts, pictures, faces she had obsessed over and saved. I watched them all curl in the heat and slowly smolder into shards. Firelight reflected in my mother's hair.

"Ring around the rosy, pocket full of posies, ashes, ashes, we all fall down," Lilly began to sing. She reached for our hands, and we formed a circle around the fire. "Ring around the rosy, pocket full of posies, ashes, ashes..."

When it was time for sleep, Lilly opened her bed to us. We all three cuddled around her and tried to fill the empty space where our father had once slept. Lilly turned off the lights, except for the dim flame of the kerosene lamp she kept at her bedside. I awoke in the night to find my mother staring at the ceiling, wide-awake, with a smile on her face. She was far gone then, far from the river that surrounded our town, far from the falls, her garden, and her house. I didn't realize that night how safe and peaceful it was to be alone with our mother, because once she began to go out with men we lost a part of her forever.

✦ ✦ ✦

*O*nce I was in the Coopers' tiny upstairs bathroom, the party in full gear, I took a packet of Marlboros from the pocket of my jean jacket, held the firm, square box in my hand, took out a cigarette, and lit it. The window had a view to the backyard. It was dark. The only light came from the orange tips of cigarettes, blinking on and off, like fireflies.

Someone banged on the bathroom door. I dropped my cigarette into the toilet, flushed, and walked out past a girl waiting to get in, down the stairs. The floor vibrated to the sound of the bass coming from the living room speakers. I quickly downed the rest of my beer and moved outside toward the keg. As I filled my cup again, I looked for Austin in the hazy blackness. The beer, the color of urine, was warm and came back up my throat after I pounded back the full glass.

I watched the moon slip over the tops of the trees. Danny Keller took the empty cup from my hand and filled it once more. In that brief pause, bass throbbing through the open windows, I felt for one moment the courage I had been waiting for.

I marched confidently through the crowd, looking for Austin. He had invited me to his party, and now I was going to cash in on it. I followed a path of people, peering through bare legs, hands crossed on hips, a girl's arm around another boy's back, groups huddled in twos and threes, laughing and talking loudly, until all I could hear was a rumbling of voices.

Brian Horrigan cornered me before I had a chance to get to Austin. He was the first boy I had ever let kiss me. Once, during a hockey game, I had gone back behind the bleachers and made out with him, until his hand went down my shirt and cupped around my breast like a claw. But as soon as the lights went on, after the game was over, and I looked at him, the spell was over. Even though I used to think about him sometimes in class, wondering what it would feel like to be kissed by him, in the bright lights of the skating rink that night, all

I could focus on was the zit that had appeared on his chin. He was from the other side of town, lived in an old mansion, went to Aruba for winter vacation, drove a BMW. At one time he had gone to private boarding school, where he learned Latin and French. I was completely enthralled with the interpretation of *King Lear* he presented in a paper in our English class. But in spite of the fine polish and education his money offered, and the look he wore in his eyes that said *you just say the word*, there was no intersection on our emotional maps. Or if there was I hadn't discovered it yet.

After I ditched Brian, I looked for Austin. He was leaning against the rail of the porch with his arm around Rita Fox. He was whispering something in her ear. Rita had long legs and dark brown hair straight as the mane on a horse's back. She was the first girl we knew about that had let a boy go all the way. The first to get her period, to wear a miniskirt. Over the sound of *they Stone you when you don't come home*, I heard Rita's high-pitched laugh. Austin lifted a strand of hair that had fallen in her eyes and pulled it behind her ear. It looked as if he kissed her.

I turned around and walked into a crowd, into the lawn littered with empty plastic cups, hoping Austin wouldn't catch me wandering alone. I had thought, during those weeks leading up to his party—when Austin walked me home from school, flirted with me in the cafeteria, tucked a strand of my hair behind my ear and kissed me on the neck and close to my breastbone up in the attic room, where there were no sounds save the sound of his pounding heart underneath the dampness of his shirt—that I had meant something to him.

Throughout my mother's dating career, I often stumbled upon her kissing a man on the couch, or worse. Watching Austin with Rita I felt the same way I had as a child, as if I had wandered into someone else's dream, a world filled with dim ceilings, dark windows. I remembered my mother with her pumps kicked off. And then she was taken from us, into the arms of a stranger, a man who could do anything to us because she had given up her power.

I looked back to the porch, where Austin stood with his arm propped over the banister, cornering Rita. They were still laughing. Sharing a cigarette. Only, by then, my eyes were blurry from the beer, my head floating like the fuzzy tip of a dandelion into the air. I told myself that I would be as strong and resilient and self-sufficient as the thick roots dug into the earth belonging to an ancient tree, that I would never let myself need anyone. To me, need was associated with powerlessness, with a woman taken to her bed. But even as I vowed to be strong, I heard a branch breaking above me, like my resolve.

✦ ✦ ✦

In the weeks after the night of the bonfire, Lilly began to go out with men. I was then in second grade. My mother went out with a different man almost every night. Soon these dates would dominate the rhythm of our house. One afternoon we heard her on the phone to Aunt Adrienne who had set her up. "Steve Kennedy? Well, what does he look like? Has he been married before?" she drilled.

I stood in wonderment, watching how excited my mother got before a date. She spent hours in a crazed whirlwind preparing for her evening out, as though her very being depended on this candlelight dinner at the most expensive, most elegant restaurant in town.

"What are we having for dinner?" Louise asked Lilly. We were used to having our mother with us, if not her undivided attention. It was hard at first for us to believe she was leaving us, even for a night.

"She doesn't care if we starve," Ruthie said, pulling out a few strands of her hair.

"Ruthie, stop that," Lilly told her. "You're going to ruin your gorgeous hair. Come here and help me get ready. I'm going to be late."

Lilly twirled her hair in a lazy French twist and pinned it against the back of her head. "Anna, run down the basement and bring up my stockings. They're hanging on the line. Louise, see if I have any clean panties in my top drawer. Little angels," Lilly added, impatiently, "I'll stay home tomorrow night. I promise."

"Cross your heart?" said Louise.

"You said last night that you were staying home tonight," Ruthie said.

"Well, that was before Steve Kennedy called," Lilly said.

I watched as my mother looked at herself in the mirror, as though she were examining a hidden scar she had not wanted to remember, then motioned for us to sit down on her bed. As she stood over us, her robe opened and revealed the tops of her full breasts.

"Girls," she started. "I have to go out. Don't you understand? Your old mom won't be able to meet anyone if she stays home every night. Don't you want me to be happy? Don't you want a father?"

"So, are you going to marry Steve Kennedy?" one of us asked.

"We'll see," Lilly said.

My mother's nipples, surrounded by dark circles, were erect and so hard it seemed as if they must hurt.

Louise sat on the bed. She looked like she was going to cry.

"Let me see my smiles," Lilly said, drawing a line across our lips with her finger. "Wait till you meet Mr. Kennedy. He's so handsome. You're going to like him. I can feel it."

"But what will you do?" Louise asked.

"We'll have a nice long dinner with wine and candlelight."

"What will you talk about?"

"Oh, all kinds of things," Lilly said. "Some men like it if you just sit back and listen and smile and tilt your head; and others like it if you're bubbly and can't stop talking. You learn to figure out what a man wants." Lilly stopped herself. "Look at the time. If I don't hurry we won't have time for my exercises."

Lilly walked to the closet, took out a padded mat, and spread it over the faded olive carpet in her room. She went into the bathroom, slipped off her robe, and put on her bra and panties. My sisters and I sat silent on the bed, watching her through the half-open bathroom door.

The flowery smell of our mother's soaps and oils enclosed us. When she was washing the dishes or had her hands gripped around the steering wheel of the car, she stopped what she was doing to lift up her hands and hold out her slender fingers, admiring her polished nails against the light. She wore her dark red hair, the color of autumn leaves, to her shoulders, with the ends curled up in a flip, and on her lips, which dipped in the center like a heart, scarlet lipstick. It left its impression on our cheeks after she kissed us, or on the crumpled Kleenexes that were strewn, like paper flowers, all around the bathroom sink. She had the kind of beauty that people stared at. It was nearly impossible not to feel invisible next to her. My mother had full breasts, a slender waist, round hips, and long curvy legs. Most men, married or not, weakened in my mother's presence.

Lilly came out of the bathroom and switched on the radio. She centered herself on the exercise mat and began to do her stretches. She reached down to touch her toes. Then she pressed her calves back by pulling her toes against her buttocks. I had never watched my mother exercise before. It seemed to take so much energy for her to do our supper dishes or wash our clothes, and there she was, waving her arms from side to side, jogging in place, her neck stretched toward the ceiling, her forehead beaded with perspiration. The last of the afternoon light shone in her face. In what would become her getting-ready-for-a-date routine, Lilly could forget herself.

"Louise, come sit on my feet so I can do my sit-ups," she said.

"One, two, three, four..." Louise counted to one hundred.

Ruthie crept off the bed and kneeled by our mother's side.

"Do you have to go out, Mom?"

"Ruthie, don't make me feel guilty," Lilly said, struggling to do another set of sit-ups.

I hopped off the bed and followed my mother as she began her jumping jacks. "One, two, three, four," I counted, each time I heard her clap her hands together in the slowly dimming room.

We circled around our mother, absorbing her light.

In the chair, by the last rays of sunlight through the window, Lilly polished her nails. Afterward she went into the shower, washed her hair, and splashed body oil on her skin. She came out dripping wet, her sleek hair shining. I sat on the toilet seat watching her every move. On my lap I held a small basket of bobby pins that I handed to her, one by one, while Lilly rolled her hair. The smell of the steam from the shower, the lilac fragrance of her soap, and the scent of her shampoo filled the room. I knew what Steve Kennedy was going to see: I felt intoxicated and giddy, just being next to her.

After her hair was set, she opened the double doors of her

closet and took out dresses, one by one, holding them to her body while she looked in the mirror. Then Lilly still believed the world held all sorts of possibilities and all she had to do was be ready. She was filled with excitement and hope when she was making herself up and fantasizing about the night ahead. It was a rich and complex project, and so it was painful to see my mother deflate when she found herself face-to-face with a man. The men she dated were rarely what she'd dreamed about or hoped for.

Ruthie went into the closet and took out a trailing white lace dress wrapped in yellowed plastic. "Why don't you wear this one?" Ruthie said.

"Ruthie!" Lilly shrieked. "What do you think you're doing?" She lunged toward Ruthie, knocking over the perfume bottles on her dresser as she shot out her arm. "Put that back this instant. Who said you could go through my things?" Lilly grabbed her wedding dress from Ruthie's hand. "Are you trying to hurt me?" Lilly said. She shoved the dress back into the closet.

But then Lilly softened. "Girls, I don't know what I'm doing," she said. "I don't know if I'm coming or going. Who do I think I am? Just what do I think I'm doing?"

"Don't cry, Mom. Ruthie didn't mean it," I told her.

"Of course she didn't." Lilly patted the bed, motioning for Ruthie to sit next to her. "I sometimes forget you girls are only children."

"There's an old fable that goes like this," Lilly said later, before she left that night. "When a baby is born, an angel comes down from heaven and kisses it on one part of its body. If the angel kisses him on his hand, he becomes a handyman—a gardener or a mechanic or a plumber. If he kisses him on his forehead, he becomes bright and clever—a lawyer or a doctor." Lilly paused for a moment before finishing. "I've been trying to figure out where the angel kissed me, so that I can take care of you."

I tried to see how this story applied to my mother. "You take care of us, Mom," I told her. "We don't need anyone else." But while my mother was fixing herself up, I momentarily entertained the idea of having a new father. I wondered, if she married, would our mother get out of bed to get us ready for school? Would I be able to get a pair of new shoes, instead of having to wear Ruthie's old pair?

"Oh my stars, look at the time, he'll be here any minute," Lilly said. But her eyes still looked worried. She stood up, detached from us, and straightened her robe. She sucked in her cheeks and pursed her lips together when she looked in the mirror, as if to convince herself of her own seductive power. My mother was confronted with two choices, to stay home and live in her grief, or to bury it in a semblance of pleasure.

"I think that old angel kissed me right here," Lilly said, fatalistically pointing to her heart. We all laughed along with her, in spite of the eerie feeling the image left us with.

As my mother put on her lace slip and garter belt, and fastened her ivory stockings, I looked on in admiration. I couldn't wait to catch up to her. It all seemed like some kind of dress-up game, like the games we girls played down in the basement.

"Darling, you look ravishing," I would say to Louise as she tromped around in my mother's high heels and a fake fur stole.

"Oh, you're just being kind," Louise flirted back.

"Why do you have to put on so much makeup?" Louise said, as Lilly sat at her vanity.

"Well, it's not easy being a woman," Lilly replied, in a knowing tone. "But men know if you let your hair grow and use makeup and dress to please them. Ruthie, you choose my lipstick," she went on, as if awarding her firstborn a grand prize.

Once Lilly had put on her makeup, the natural shine to my mother's face dissolved underneath the powders and creams. She became someone else entirely; she was no longer our mother then, her familiar face concealed in the glamorous, distant, utterly confident face she displayed to the men in her life.

She applied shade upon shade of lipstick until her lips became a deep red, pulsing over the dark secret heart of her mouth. When she was finished she looked as beautiful and unattainable as the models on the covers of the women's magazines she had strewn all over her bedroom floor.

When the doorbell rang, the room went silent. I braced myself.

"March," Lilly said, shoving us out the door. "I need a minute to myself."

We ran downstairs and opened the front door. Mr. Kennedy was tall, handsome, and wore an expensive suit with a starched white collar and striped tie. His aftershave hung in the air around him. He handed a box of candy to Ruthie.

I eyeballed Mr. Kennedy from top to bottom. It would become a game with us. Each time Lilly dated a new man, we would try to guess whether he would be the one Lilly would choose as our new father. I liked Colin Harris, the dentist. He had pearly white teeth and a British accent. Louise was partial to Tom McVeigh, who promised her he would get us tickets to an Indians game. Of course, Lilly dumped him before the season began. Ruthie preferred Tony O'Brian, who claimed to once have been a lead in the Cleveland Playhouse performance of *Macbeth*. Sometimes Louise liked one that Ruthie and I disapproved of. And then we would fight about it, about which of my mother's men would be awarded the honor of becoming our new father. The truth was that Lilly liked the least fatherly types the best: men with slick cars, money, flashy clothes, and no patience for children. The handsomer they were, the crueler the spell they cast over her.

From upstairs we could hear our mother's high heels walking back and forth in her room, which made Mr. Kennedy more and more restless. He took out a handkerchief to wipe his brow, crossed and uncrossed his leg, straightened his tie. Lilly kept him waiting a good half hour.

Finally I ran upstairs to get my mother. Steve Kennedy made me nervous.

Lilly was sitting perfectly still on her bed, staring at the clock.

"One day you'll do the same thing," Lilly said.

"But, Mom, he's waiting."

"Anna, you don't want a man to think you're too eager," Lilly said. "Just tell him I'll be right down." So I ran back to the living room.

Finally we heard our mother's bedroom door open and the sound of her heels on the stairs. She carried herself as if she were royalty. Mr. Kennedy rose from his corner of the couch while the three of us sat side by side at the other end. He walked into the hallway to greet her. A gasp came from his lips, as if to acknowledge that it had been worth the wait. Lilly elegantly held out her hand, turned her face to the side, and allowed Mr. Kennedy to kiss her cheek. She was composed and in control.

I listened as my mother put on the new voice that was reserved exclusively for her dates.

"Now, you girls be good. I'll call you with the phone number. Come give me a kiss." I watched as Mr. Kennedy looked on, nearly salivating as Lilly bent down to kiss us.

"Don't they need a baby-sitter?" he asked.

"My angels? Why, they're nearly more grown up than me. Be good," she called to us, blowing a last kiss. Then she turned her head to her date and looked into his eyes, and he escorted her out.

I could feel the room's emptiness when she had closed the door and left, clutched against Mr. Kennedy's arm. All the energy and verve went out of the house with her.

The three of us went upstairs to watch television on Lilly's bed.

"When do you think she'll be home?" Louise asked. Usually I let her sleep with me on the nights Lilly went out.

"Who cares?" Ruthie said.

"Why did she let him kiss her?" Louise said.

"She's allowed," Ruthie said. Then, "I don't want to talk about her anymore."

"We always talk about her." Louise looked at Ruthie searchingly.

"I liked the way he smiled," I said, searching for something positive to say.

"I liked his dimples," Louise continued.

"Be quiet," Ruthie ordered us. Ruthie seemed not to have any hope or belief in anything, except in the cold wind she had turned toward our mother. But after we had all gotten under the covers, I saw a smile spread across her face, and imagined she was also fantasizing about the many possibilities we could invent for our new father, the shapes we could cast him in, as if we were building him out of clay.

We fell asleep on our mother's bed. When I heard the creak of the front door and the whispers of our mother and Steve Kennedy, I elbowed my sisters awake and we flew into our separate beds.

I always felt safe when my mother came home. When she was gone I worried about her. When I was older, I tried to imagine what my mother must have appeared like to her dates. Her face was sad and lovely, with bright things in it. She had dark, pain-filled eyes and a full smile and a vulnerability in her voice that men seemed to gravitate toward. The way she moved and laughed promised she had done careless, reckless things, I imagined. But all the gaiety had been taken from her when our father died. I wondered if men felt her weakness, and moved toward her in what seemed to me, as a child, a powerful and frightening way. I felt I had to protect my mother, only then I wasn't sure what I was protecting her from, exactly.

I tried to stay awake until I heard my mother say good night, until the door shut, the key turned in the lock; until my world closed in the safe and private darkness of the house. But Mr. Kennedy stayed for hours.

I trailed downstairs and stopped at the landing to see what was going on. On the stereo Lilly had on a sultry blues song. Through the windows dawn was beginning to break.

"Steve, you have to leave now," I heard Lilly say.

Eventually I heard Lilly get up, and Mr. Kennedy followed. The door closed behind him. I quietly crept up to bed.

We had hope for Steve Kennedy. He and Lilly dated for more than a month, and every time he came to pick her up, he brought us paper dolls, bags of M&M's, or coloring books.

The last night Steve Kennedy took my mother out, I again sneaked down from my room to the landing of the stairs to watch them say good night. But this time Lilly didn't send him home.

"You can't cut me off now," Mr. Kennedy said.

"Come on," Lilly persisted. "There's always tomorrow."

"I know you want it," Mr. Kennedy said.

I quietly tiptoed into the hall. Lilly and Mr. Kennedy were sitting at the very end of the couch, so close together, it seemed as if Lilly couldn't breathe. I watched Mr. Kennedy's large shape engulfing my mother. I could hear the sound of the furnace kick on. It was the dead of winter. I saw Mr. Kennedy's hands slip underneath Lilly's dress and heard the sound of my mother's breath, like a reluctant yet powerful wind, as she slowly succumbed.

The next morning Lilly showed up with a new strand of pearls dangling from her neck.

"He's no gentleman," my mother said. "But at least I got this out of him."

We never saw Steve Kennedy again.

✦ ✦ ✦

The party at Austin's house grew louder as the night wore on. Everyone was getting buzzed. The keg of beer had run out, and Danny was collecting money to make a beer run. It was a warm, humid night. My shirt was sticking to my skin. I walked back into the house, through the hallway, into the vestibule, stepping over empty Styrofoam cups. A net of smoke hovered over the dimmed lights. I hoped I'd catch someone heading out to his car who might give me a lift.

"Have you seen Austin?" I asked Robbie Reinhert. He shook his head and held up a bottle of tequila. "Want to do a shot?" he slurred, his T-shirt sticking to his sweaty chest.

I nodded.

After clinking glasses we threw the tequila back. The liquor warmed my throat and shot up my veins.

At the top of the stairs, some senior girls were whispering and, I thought, pointing at me.

"That's the one," said Jocelyn Foster, her eyes made up dark as Cleopatra.

I lifted my head, returned a fake smile, and pushed open the screen door. I'd walk home.

In the bushes Dickie Livingston was getting sick.

"Anna," I heard Austin call.

I walked quickly down the driveway, pebbles kicking up into my sandals and nipping at my ankles. My body a rush of adrenaline.

"Hey, wait," he called after me. "Where are you going?"

"Home."

"This is my fucking party," Austin said. "You can't go yet."

I looked down the block. A row of cars: Corvettes, beat-up sedans, and a VW Bug were parked along the street. For almost two hours Austin hadn't said a word to me, and now he was pissed off that I wanted to leave? I kept walking, knowing that this was my only chance, that if I ignored Austin just at the moment he was finally paying attention, I would have him in the palm of my hand.

"Stop," Austin said. He wrapped his arms around me from the back. I tried to shimmy away. He hooked one arm around my neck and pulled me smack up against him, in a judo hold.

"Tell me why you're leaving," he whispered in my ear. I felt my body relax.

"It's late," I said.

"What's the matter?"

"Nothing."

"Come on," he pleaded, thinking I was half kidding. He turned me around, lifted my chin so I'd meet his eyes. "You're not rejecting me, are you?" He smelled like beer and cigarettes.

"Don't," I said.

"Jesus, Anna. What the fuck's the matter?"

I looked at him blankly.

"Okay," he said. "You want to go home?" He pulled the keys out of his pants pocket. "I'll drive you."

Once in the car everything was quiet. Under the street lamps, the summer lawns were the color of limes; green, calm, and stretched out like sheets of plastic. Austin chewed the inside of his jaw. He wasn't speaking.

When Austin pulled up my driveway, I turned to him. But he looked straight ahead and drummed his fingers on the steering wheel. "Thanks," I said. I had no idea whether I'd ever see him again. I studied the throbbing of his pulse in the curve of the hollow of his cheek and almost weakened before I slammed the door and walked up the driveway. Before I got inside the house, he revved the engine. His tires screeched around the bend of the driveway, leaving a skid mark on the lawn.

Inside, the house was dark. My mother and Louise were asleep. I was still buzzed from the party, and whipped up from being in Austin's presence. Downstairs I walked from one room to the next to still myself. I touched the vase of flowers on the mantel, picked up the newspapers on the couch, fingered the waxed apples sitting in a bowl on the dining room table. I couldn't sit still.

Two weeks before, on the night we'd first made out, Austin took me to his house on the pretense of showing me his secret passion: He was into impressing girls with card tricks and other sleights-of-hand. He drove his beat-up black Mustang along the sidewalk as I was walking home, cranked down his window, and offered me a ride. I remember the exact hue of the late spring sky slowly giving in to evening. He insisted I come over. He had something to show me. In his bedroom he had a deck of cards and a drawer full of coins. I sat on his bed, leaned against the wall, barely saying a word, watching him make coins vanish from one hand to the other. He slapped cards down in rows and turned up the jack of hearts, the ace. He pulled a colored handkerchief out of the sleeve of my shirt. Later, I learned this was his trademark. He slipped handkerchiefs out of the shirtsleeves of the girls he wanted to impress at school. It had become a kind of joke. But while it was happening to me, I was totally transfixed. The handkerchief, like a colored flag, spiraled in the air. I grew so tired my eyes almost closed, waiting for him to finish and begin on me; touching my eyes, nose, mouth, with his lips, pulling me onto his bed; making my body disappear.

At last he got up, put on a Jefferson Starship album, and with the touch of his lips against my own, I forgot who I was, where I came from. All the tension between us from flirting in the halls for months now had built to this crescendo.

I had imagined love was a cure for the parts of myself I found fault with. The attention of a man always, at least for a brief time, restored my mother, gave her the sustenance she needed to get out of bed. But in Austin's bedroom I welcomed the oblivion, where all I had to do was lie back and let him roll on me into blackness. Right away I knew I'd go to any length, do anything, to keep him. His magic was light and airy, like a wizard's; mine was dark and gloomy.

I pictured Austin reading in his bed late at night, putting the marker in the book, going to sleep. I saw him awaken, his eyes slowly accepting the morning light, saw him stretch as he pulled the covers away. I had not known that a person could consume one's entire imagination. I wondered if he thought about me, as I did, before he fell asleep at night, if he pictured me when I got out of bed, when I pulled off my nightgown, when I made the endless long walk to school and home again. If my face was the one he returned to after he completed a history test, when he was stopped at a traffic light, as he tried to focus on conversation.

Roaming the house after Austin's party, I kept playing that first night we'd made out over in my mind, wondering if I had invented it all.

The living room was dark and I stumbled over a pan of dried paint my mother had left in the middle of the floor. That year, which marked Ruthie's going to live with Aunt Rose, I had turned sixteen. My mother had sworn off men. For years men had come in and out of our house as if it were some kind of salon. But by the time I turned sixteen, there hadn't been a single man around. Lilly couldn't balance how much she required from a man with the disappointment she felt once she had one. When Austin happened into my life, Lilly had had her fill.

"I'm turning over a new leaf," she said to Louise and me on that snowy, arctic day, after the car that came to take Ruthie to the airport had vanished into the winter storm. "I want no more men in this house." I was just beginning to appreciate how the presence of the opposite sex could light up a life, give it purpose and meaning. My mother couldn't see that maybe she had picked the wrong men for her, or that her expectations were out of whack. Maybe she was afraid that Louise and I were going to leave, too, if she didn't shape up and get her act together. But when I stopped to think about what she said, it made absolutely no sense. It was another one of my mother's private conversations with herself that sometimes filtered out, unconsciously from her mouth. There hadn't been a man around in three years.

Instead of finding some constructive way to prepare for her future, now that she'd sworn off men, she found a new obsession: painting our house. She used Ruthie's old room for a place to store paint cans and brushes. She hounded me for days with color swatches. In the living room her brushes and rollers were soaking in a bucket of turpentine on top of newspapers. I switched on a lamp and looked at the walls. The far wall was still faded white, contrasting the right wall, which Lilly had painted a disturbing shade of green. And bunched in a ball was an old cobalt blue shirt she had used as a rag. I moved to the couch, laid my head back, and closed my eyes. They burned from the paint fumes.

+ + +

Shortly after Lilly dropped Steve Kennedy, I came downstairs one Saturday and found my mother still dressed in the clothes she had worn the evening before, curled up in a ball asleep on the couch. After Steve Kennedy she dated Robert McBride. He took us to Euclid Beach and let us ride the roller coaster three times while he made out with my mother on a nearby bench.

On the floor in front of the couch lay a pair of high-heeled black pumps, and Lilly's silk stockings and red garter belt were slung over the arm of the couch. A bottle of crème de menthe, two cordial glasses, and an ashtray filled with cigarette butts sat on the coffee table. The sticky mint smell of the liqueur hung in the room.

"Mom, Mom, wake up," I said. Even as my mother slept the unconscious sleep of intoxication, I knew her thoughts were threaded to the broad shoulders and slicked-back hair of Robert McBride, whom she'd said good-bye to barely an hour before.

Dressed only in a tight black evening dress hiked up to her thighs, Lilly huddled further into the couch.

Louise trailed downstairs rubbing her eyes.

"Something's the matter with Mom," I said. I must have been eight by then.

Louise touched my mother's cheek. She shook her shoulders. Lilly's body was warm and limber, but when I picked up her hand and let it go, it fell smack down on the couch.

"We better wake Ruthie," Louise said. The sound of her bare feet stuck to the cold wood floor as she ran up the stairs.

"She's drunk," Ruthie said, as soon as she saw our mother in a lump on the couch. "Anna, make some coffee."

I filled the percolator with ground coffee and water and plugged it in, as I had watched my mother do nearly every day.

Ruthie turned the television set on full volume. Louise sat next to our mother on the couch, pressed her lips into an O, and blew her breath over our mother's face. "Come on, Mom," she said. "Get up."

I brought in a tray with a pot of coffee, a cup, a bowl filled with warm water, and a washcloth.

Louise began to hum *the hills are alive* from *The Sound of Music.* She did that when she got nervous.

"Help me sit her up," I said.

With some effort we propped our mother to a sitting position against the back of the couch, but her body was as floppy as a rag doll's.

"Wake up, Mother," Ruthie said, shaking Lilly's shoulders.

I dipped the washcloth into the bowl and sponged my mother's forehead.

"What's going on here?" Lilly said, in a tiny, cracked voice. She shook her head and practically slapped me in the face as she stretched her arms.

"Why couldn't you wake up?" Louise said. Sitting with her legs propped against her chest, she pulled her nightgown down from her knees to cover her bare feet. To save money, during the night Lilly kept our thermostat on low.

"Because I'm tired," Lilly said, irritated. "Isn't that allowed? I'm going upstairs to lie down. I'm not feeling well."

Lilly hiked her knit dress to her hips, cradled her head against her shoulder, and shuffled up the stairs to her bedroom. "Don't get into trouble," she called behind her.

I sat on the couch and looked out the window again into the glacier sky. My eyes moved to the grass on the front lawn. It was covered, like a truth you knew was there, but didn't want to see, with icy dew. I wanted to believe this was just a temporary thing, an accident. That Lilly would get up in a few hours and return to us as our mother, not the mysterious woman who went out at night as if she were expecting to bring back heaven. But I was wrong. That mother we had known seemed so far from us.

In the afternoon, when our mother woke up, I caught a glimpse of the old Lilly, the one who sat in our house and sighed or daydreamed by the window most of the day, and that gave me hope. After lunch we went out to the yard to play. Lilly was studying her crossword puzzles or staring out the window, watching. When she caught our eyes, she tapped her nails against the glass and gave a wave. Then we showed off for her: Louise was good at handstands, and Ruthie could turn three cartwheels in a row. Lilly liked to watch our gymnastics on the soft lawn.

It was quiet in the yard, and time went on and on. The day

nearly lasted forever. When the sky darkened and Lilly changed into her yellow robe, she opened the screen door and whistled for us to come in. Upstairs, Ruthie supervised while Louise and I washed our hair in the sink and scrubbed our ears, followed by the usual fight over who got to wear the prettiest nightgown. Lilly came upstairs with the bedtime snack, and we were quiet and good for her. We crawled into our cool beds and said our prayers. Lilly sat on the rocker and sang her tired song in the twilight.

But as Lilly continued going out, nearly every night of the week, the times we had our mother with us grew fewer and far between. The men that came and went swarmed together like bees, turning our house into a hive of seduction and betrayal. Lilly rarely treated them any differently from each other. I began to hate the way she primped and groomed for them; how much attention she paid to herself, as if she were a work of art.

Not only was she out most nights, but she slept in most of the morning, sometimes the entire afternoon, until around four-thirty, when we'd hear our mother's bedroom door creak open. I dropped whatever I was doing and ran up the stairs, Louise at my heels.

"Hello, angels," Lilly said, unaware that we were still in our nightgowns; that the entire Saturday had passed. "Should I make cream-cheese-and-jelly sandwiches, or grilled cheese?" she asked, as if this was all perfectly natural.

Not only did our mother forget about making our dinner or making sure we were up in time for school, she seemed to turn her back on God. My mother had neglected all the Jewish holidays once our father died. I remembered our Friday-night dinners at Aunt Rose's before the Sabbath. The smell of the doughy challah fresh from the oven, the lighting of the candles, the prayers all had disappeared. Lilly no longer went to synagogue, not even for the High Holy Days. On Saturday mornings she dropped us off in front of the synagogue, and picked us up after services in the parking lot, sometimes an hour late. I surmised she was angry with God because he had taken her husband away. But, unlike my mother, I sought comfort in the rabbi's sermons. I let the deep and guttural sound of his voice, which echoed in the hollow synagogue, float over me. The Bible stories of Abraham, and Moses, and the ancient Jews from a lost land having to endure droughts, famines, and plagues meant that we were put on earth for a higher purpose. What the Jews had suffered made what my family had lost seem less important. I thought that maybe if my mother came to synagogue she could learn how to banish her black moods with faith. But my mother was firm on the subject. She said whenever she entered a synagogue she began to cry.

I wish my mother could have found sustenance, if not in religion, then somewhere inside herself. The only place she found it, briefly, was with men. I noticed how her cheeks looked sunken, her complexion waxy in the morning, and then rosy and full as soon as the sun went down. My friends' mothers spent the day shopping for groceries, cleaning, preparing long suppers. But in my mother's spare time, when she wasn't on a date, she daydreamed, tended to her bath, or slept. I wished for the normalcy of a freshly plowed driveway, the busy sounds of cake mixers, eggshells grinding in the disposal. The hum of a healthy life.

Sometimes I stared at the gazebo and convinced myself that if I willed it, I could conjure my father there in the icy circle the sun made through the rafters. I imagined us all sitting on the floor, my father with his arm draped around my mother's shoulder, my mother holding Louise in her arms, all of us dressed in our winter coats. If I closed my eyes and concentrated hard, I could still hear it, my father's voice, telling us about happiness. About how the trees, and the grass, and the flowers he would plant once the frost had lifted were all blessings, and about how fortunate he was, to be with the woman he loved most in the world, my mother, and these fine daughters. I could hear the words, *these fine daughters,* and told myself it was enough.

✦ ✦ ✦

I was distracted by a small tap on the screen of our living room window. At night, in the late spring, the hot air was like a layer separating you from the rest of the world. Nearly an hour, maybe more, since I got home from Austin's party, I was still downstairs, lying on our couch, doing a play-by-play of the night. I sensed that Austin would come back for me. Even then, before we'd ever made love, it was the way we communicated, in silence, by touch and scent.

I sprang up and peered outside. My mouth felt dry from the aftertaste of diluted beer. Austin was crouched in the bed of rhododendrons, staring back at me with lustful eyes; I felt a pinch in my chest. I quietly opened the front door, let in a swallow of air.

"What time is it?" I said.

"Around two o'clock."

"*Shhhhh,*" I said, when he practically tripped on a bucket of Lilly's paint, motioning with my eyes upstairs. I didn't want him to wake my mother.

I stood with my back to him. He lifted the hair up from my shoulders. I was still mad about Rita. I remembered watching the way Steve Kennedy looked at my mother with that same hangdog look, and then how quickly he vanished. "What are you doing?" I quipped. "Why do people think they can just touch you?"

"I shouldn't have come, is that what you're saying?" Austin turned me around and searched my face.

I wasn't an extraordinarily pretty girl, but I knew I would do. There was vulnerability in my eyes and shyness in my walk, but I wasn't timid enough not to invite a boy's attention. I had brown eyes and long, wavy hair a boy could twist through his fingers. My signature pair of silver hoop earrings dangled from my earlobes. I thought I wore my desperation on my face where everyone could see it.

As Austin looked into my eyes, then reached for my hand, I felt the hollow place I imagined his mother left in his heart like an opening in a tree, the kind a scared animal wanted to burrow inside for the long, bleak winter.

Outside, a late-night storm pressed against the sky. Wind whipped up the hot, muggy air and cut through it like a knife. It sent a chilling, owl-like sound through the house. The sound of rain against glass.

"No, I wanted you to come," I said. "I'm glad you're here." I moved back to the living room, toward the couch, and closed my eyes for a moment. In his presence I felt the world stop.

"Sit down," I said forcefully. Now I would tell him what to do. What *I* wanted.

"Anna?" Austin moved closer. "Do you want me to leave?"

"I just don't understand why you're here." I arrogantly ran my fingers through my hair. Of course I knew. "How was the party?" It came out harshly.

"It's still going on," he whispered. "It's just that once you left, I didn't want to be there anymore." He moved to the couch next to me. His blue jeans were faded, and worn at the knees. "How come you wanted to leave?"

I was speechless. How could I confess that it was because I felt irrelevant and blank without the thumbprint of his attention?

"Okay, so now comes the part where I have to pry everything out of you? You know what your problem is? You walk around thinking you're better than everyone. You could have at least tried to have a good time."

It wasn't that I thought I was better than anyone. He had read me all wrong.

"How would you know about it?"

"About what?"

"About me."

"I know everything about you. I got the goods."

His shirt hung out from his jeans, and was open at the neck. His chest was the color of porcelain and sweaty, same as his face. And after he'd made that comment about me, his eyes registered an emotion I hadn't interpreted before: I saw how vulnerable he was.

"I said something wrong," I said. I touched his face. "I'm sorry. I'm glad you're here."

He shrugged in that offhand way that boys do. He didn't hold anything against a person for long. Or at least I thought so. "So do you forgive me?" he said.

"For what?"

"For ignoring you at my party."

I pushed away the image of him and Rita together, at least for the duration of the night. Instead, I felt the dark heat of him, of the wild and partly drunk boy beside me on the couch.

Austin propped his head against the sofa's arm; he slouched so he was half lying down, his legs hanging over the cushion. He reached for me. I folded myself into his arms, felt the baby fluffs of hair at the back of his neck.

"I saw you talking to Brian Horrigan," Austin said. "He's got the hots for you."

"Does that surprise you?" I tasted the salt of sweat on his skin.

"Fuck, no," Austin said. "But it doesn't mean I have to like it."

I fit myself against him like the last piece to a puzzle, for-getting Lilly was upstairs. He was warm and damp. He opened my arms, and unbuttoned my blouse. I traced the blue vein up to the inside of his elbow with my finger and back down again; pressed my finger against his pulse. Again, the spatter of rain against the window. The caw of birds just before dawn.

"I know you. I know what I love about you," he said. He rolled me off the couch with him, onto the carpeted floor. "Isn't this enough?" Austin said, kissing me again. "Let's not ever fight. Can't we be happy?"

Happiness was a word that had no meaning, I had decided, years before, without ever knowing it. I had watched, and felt, even when I wasn't watching, how my mother's dates fed her with scotch and sweet talk, and saw how the force of their presence for that short time made the rest of the world disap-pear. Happiness was not the issue. I simply wanted to vanish into the other misty and distant world, never wanting to be pulled back.

"I'll make you feel better," Austin said, as if he were com-forting a child who had awakened in the middle of the night from a nightmare. "Close your eyes." He gently moved his fingers over my face, closing my lids as if they were a doll's. Like a kind of sly sorcerer, with his soft breath, he had the power to make me disappear into his earth-cool dark room; possessing my body, the way men do.

I knew when something out of the ordinary was about to happen, just like Aunt Rose used to tell us she could sense a storm coming because her arthritis began to act up; I felt it hovering like a heat cloud. The sun seared bright with possibility, but inside our house my mother was cooped up, obsessing about the color of paint she wanted for each room.

In the days after Austin's party, I played the night over in my head like a scene in a movie: the minute I heard his knock on the window of my house, the sandpapery feel of his lips against mine. It was as if a door had creaked open, just slightly, exposing the white crest of his soul. When the phone rang I practically leaped out of my skin.

One morning I awoke early and found blood splattered against the window. A bird had flown into the pane, broken its neck, and fallen onto the windowsill. It was a bad sign, I thought. I was like that then. If it was raining the day I was supposed to take a history test, I was sure that meant I would fail. I read my horoscope every morning and analyzed its meaning as if I were deconstructing the allusions in a Shakespeare play. I opened my underwear drawer and took out the robin's egg wrapped in tissue that Austin and I had found one day when we were getting high in the woods behind his house, rubbed it as if it had powers, and prayed.

Austin cleaned the stalls at the harness track a few days after school and on weekends. I knew when he'd been in the stables; the stench of the manure in his clothes and in his hair was a dead giveaway. But it was something besides his love of horses. The track life was different from the upper-class world he had grown up in. Most of the guys I knew were into sports and partying. Austin's passion for horses made him different.

"When you first start training a horse, you can't control her," Austin said the first time he took me to the track and showed me the horses he cared for. "It's like developing a relationship. She has to learn to trust you. Once you develop the trust, she'll do anything you ask. It's that strength and power in a horse's body that gets to me," he continued, as he reached out his hand and let one of the horses eat a handful of oats from his palm. "When a horse is in her rhythm, she's on fire."

He was employed by a man named Howard White, who owned a slew of racehorses. Once school ended Austin worked in the barns full-time. When he wasn't at the track, he sometimes rode his own horse, which he boarded at a stable off County Line Road in Chagrin Falls. Austin rode with Jane Smart, one of the girl grooms who worked in the barns. Jane had dirty blond hair, greasy near the part, and a face cut like a diamond. Sexuality seeped from her pores.

One Saturday Austin was working at the track. Even though I had no interest in hanging out with Skippy Larsen and his entourage that night, I told Maria I'd go with her to Skippy's party. Maria and I had the reputation at school as being joined at the hip. For my tenth birthday she had given me a friendship necklace, with one of those hearts perfectly split in two. We each wore one half, tucked into our blouses, close to our skin. But since I'd begun seeing Austin, he became my heart's cool and silent keeper.

Shortly after we arrived, the party spun out of control. Maria and I made our way to the keg, passing a joint back and forth between us. A neighbor called the police; the party broke up for a while, then resumed, full force, once the cops had left.

I went outside on the patio to smoke a cigarette. The night was mute, no hint of birds in the backyard, not a sound from a cricket; just the bare world at night gazing down on me like a loving father. My arms and legs had that pins-and-needles feeling, that numbness I got when I was buzzed.

Most of the evening Maria was perched on the top of the kitchen counter sucking up to Billy Fitzpatrick, who was one of six brothers. Three of the Fitzpatrick brothers played on our high school hockey team. Maria had lusted after Billy for as long as I could remember, but Billy was hanging out with Lucy Brownwein, who had thick red hair and perfectly sculpted breasts. Early that year we had learned that Billy's brother Josh was diagnosed with leukemia and would not make it to Christmas. How could Josh, with his soft, curly brown hair and dark eyes, who at sixteen was already an amazing artist—his self-portraits bedecked our art room walls—wake up one morning and learn that he had months to live? While the rest of my friends seemed content to flirt and gossip, I stared at Billy wondering what it was like to know your brother was going to die.

Brian Horrigan passed me a joint. I took a toke. "Where's Austin?" he asked.

I was glad word had leaked out that Austin and I were together.

Skippy and his entourage were doing shots of peppermint schnapps. Johnny and Daniella were practically having sex on

the living room couch. On the coffee table Robbie and Steve
were doing lines of coke with a rolled-up dollar bill. Steve
divvied it out from a vial's worth that probably cost about as
much as my family's monthly grocery bill. The twins, Franny
and Mindy Klinger, were describing their identical summer
wardrobes, which they purchased on a shopping trip with their
mother in Paris. I was in one of those moods where I questioned the point of existence.

I cornered Maria as she was coming out of the Larsens' per-
fumed bathroom, and begged her to drive me to the track.

"Now? It's after midnight."

"You owe me," I said, because I had come with her to the
Larsen party so she could see Billy. Maria glanced into the
kitchen. Lucy and Billy were making out against the refrigerator door.

We drove to the track in her father's Lincoln.

"Do you think Austin will be pissed off that I'm showing
up unannounced?" I asked, and lit up a cigarette.

"Does he have a reason to be?"

"What's that supposed to mean?" We were stopped at an
intersection. I knew Maria wasn't going to cut Austin any
slack now that he was the focus of my attention. But, still, the
remark got to me.

After we parked and walked back to the stables, we found
Austin sitting on a hay bale across from Jane Smart, sharing a
beer with her. Maria and I looked at each other. Jane's cheeks
were flushed. Turned out they had been riding together that
afternoon. Austin had gotten someone to cover for him at the
barn. Austin came toward me and lit up like a Christmas tree,
half excited and half shocked to see me. But why hadn't he
tried to find me at Skippy Larsen's party, where I'd told him I
was going, instead of hanging out with Jane? He asked me to

go riding with him the next day, and there was no way I was going to say no and allow him to take Jane instead.

Austin saddled up the horses, made a step with the interlocked fingers of both hands, and boosted me onto a horse called Night. Austin assured me that she was calm and gentle. He walked Night slowly around the fenced-in paddock by holding on to her bridle until I got used to the feel of the saddle, the weight of the reins in my hands. Austin showed me how to pull her back, how to coax, and cluck, and give the horse encouragement.

"They know if you're afraid, Anna. They sense it," he said, as if he was talking about himself, as if he and the horses were interchangeable. He promised we would take it slow. We left the paddock and walked the horses down the driveway behind the barns. We entered the field. I relaxed as the sun shone on my back, and gradually I fell into the up and down of the horse's rhythm.

But Austin wasn't satisfied.

"Not through the trees," I said. I saw where he was headed. We were halfway across the field before we entered the narrow trail through the forest. The sky that day was as blue as I'd seen it.

"Trust me. Anna. Jane and I found this trail the other day."

"I'm not ready for this." My voice was quivering.

"Do you think I would let you get hurt? That I'd let anything happen to you?"

He kicked his horse with the heel of his boot, turned his horse around, and motioned for me to do the same. But it was too late. I was losing control of the horse. Austin pulled back on his own horse, slowed down, and waited for Night to pass.

Then he swatted Night's rear end with his crop to get her moving.

The trail, parallel to a running creek, was muddy and thick with forest on each side. My hair caught the bottom branches of a tree. Burrs attached to my jeans. My heart throbbed in my chest and threatened to outsound the rhythm of the horse's hooves knocking against the ground, spitting up dirt and dust. The trail took us farther into the thick of the woods, over a small ravine, until it seemed we had vanished far into the forest. My legs and buttocks were sore. My fingers, from clutching so tight on the reins, hurt if I opened them, but slowly I began to relax, until a splinter of sun burst through the trees. Light bloomed in front of us, and suddenly we moved into an open field like a beautiful dream, but when Night saw the treeless expanse of grass, she broke into a run. I heard the soft chunks of mud breaking underneath her hooves and felt deep roots below us loosening from the ground.

"Pull her back!" Austin shouted. "Anna, hold tight on the reins and get her under control. You take the lead, goddamn it," he ordered. "Can't you for once be in charge?"

The comment cut into me, but my mind and body were at odds. I wobbled to the side. I clutched my calves harder against the sides of the horse, pressed my buttocks firmer into the saddle, trying to regain my balance, as Night raced through the field.

When she threw me to the ground, the wind was knocked out of me, but I wasn't in pain. I simply couldn't move. It was like the time Lilly crashed into a car in front of us at a stoplight and I went flying back against the seat. For days I had heard the inside of my head rattle.

Austin hopped off his horse and whistled between his fingers for my horse.

Night ran back through the field and circled around us. I was flat on my back. When I tried to move, I couldn't get up. The fall had happened so fast, it was hard to put the events together. I tried to raise my head and realized Night's hoof was standing on a long lock of my hair. I was facing into the back side of her, my face between her two back legs.

"I can't get up," I said. If she moved an inch, that would be the end of it. My face was that close to her leg.

Austin coaxed the horse by stroking her mane and slowly moved her forward. I felt my hair come loose. Austin reached for my hand, and helped me up.

Against his chest, I felt his pulse race in his neck.

"Anna, you fucking scared me," Austin said.

"I'm okay."

"But what if..."

"I'm fine," I said, quieting his lips with my own.

As day solidified into night, it grew quiet, except for the sound of the cicadas and the crickets. No one was there to hurry home to, no one but us, and in our shadow the heavy breathing of the horses, under the thick white summer clouds, where nocturnal animals were awakening. There were no compromises to be made, no one to please or take care of. The two horses put their necks down to feed in the grass, and Austin's smell stuck to my clothes.

Maria blamed me for Billy Fitzpatrick's lack of attention. It was irrational. We both knew it, but nevertheless, I woke up the morning after Skippy's party friendless. Maria refused my phone calls. I would have to choose between her and Austin. I would probably have felt the same way, if the situation had been reversed. But I couldn't change anything now. I had driven into a fog so thick everything slid out of focus and disappeared.

When I was a child, the two most important people in my life had vanished, first my father, and then my mother, when she lost herself in her dates. Love to me was always sheer, something you could see right through. I longed for a kind of love that was impenetrable, that was tough and enduring.

✦ ✦ ✦

By the snowy December the year my mother started her dating career, she was going out almost every night and sleeping all day. She forgot to wake us up for school in the morning, to leave money in an envelope in the milk chute for the milkman, to call the snowplow to dig us out. Sometimes the snow drifted so high that our house looked like an animal burrowing in the ground. My mother lost all sense of time and place; all sense of herself, except for an obsession with her figure. She went on liquid diets; for a week, she ate only three grapefruits a day.

While Lilly busied herself with her makeup and creams, Ruthie heated cans of Campbell's soup for supper. Meanwhile, Lilly looked as elegant as royalty, the way she carried herself down the stairs in the late afternoon. Yet there was often little in the refrigerator except a stack of frozen dinners or a doggy bag from one of Cleveland's elite restaurants filled with gristled filet mignon or leftover slices of prime rib.

By the time Kent Montgomery came to call, my mother's flirtations had gone beyond playfulness and she had grown anxious.

That afternoon, I watched Lilly try on cocktail dress after cocktail dress, complaining that not one looked right. After she finally decided on one, she worried over the color or wave of her hair. She became irritable at these times, snapped at us over small things—if she ran her last pair of panty hose—then begged our forgiveness.

I pleaded with my mother to stay home. She looked worn down and haggard, like a slab of meat hanging in the butcher shop. With panic in her eyes, she answered, "Don't you see? I have no choice." She continued to cream her tired face. Later, when Lilly glided down the stairs to meet Kent Montgomery, I saw her forced smile as she gazed into his eyes, and my heart plummeted.

When she got home from her date, the front door creaked open. Lilly fumbled with the lock; Kent's voice echoed up the stairs. He stomped his feet on the front doormat to clean the snow from the perfectly polished leather shoes I had noticed when he had come for Lilly.

"*Shhhhhh,*" Lilly whispered. I heard both of them laugh. The front door creaked shut again. Loose paint from the hall ceiling outside my bedroom fell in chips to the floor. My heart gradually slowed from quick, anxious beats to a more normal pace.

My mother's high heels clicked up the steps and stopped outside our door. "I thought I heard you two talking," she said to Louise and me, opening the bedroom door a crack. "How come you're still up?" Her voice was slow and thick like syrup. She slipped inside the room and sat down at the bottom of my bed. She stretched out one leg and slipped off its shoe with the other foot; her red polished toenails shone through her nude stockings. Her body was warm and floppy. That's how she got when she drank. Sleepily, she laid her head down and curled up her body. She let out a long sigh. She was absorbed in something dark and secret.

"Isn't Kent adorable?" she asked at last, pushing herself up. She tossed back her head and laughed. "You liked him, didn't you?"

"He's got a beard," Louise said.

"I like a man with hair on his face," she said defensively.

"Maybe he can come to my school?"

"What are you talking about, Louise?" Lilly snapped out of her fantasy.

"For Father's Day. Missy's father works for Channel Five," she said.

"Let's not talk about that now," Lilly said. She reached over to Louise's bed and squeezed her hand. "I think it's too premature to ask Kent," she continued, in her out-of-body voice. "Girls, he has the softest hair," she said. "Did you see the size of his shoulders?"

The tortured look on Lilly's face, so clear earlier, had faded away. She grew soft and wistful. She was under one of her lovesick spells. She laughed a private, no-good laugh. "Kent's sweet, isn't he?" she said to no one in particular.

I didn't think so. But I was slowly learning that my mother's moods could be determined, like changing weather, by the kind of man she was with and how he treated her.

"Tell me the truth," she continued. "I'm your mother. You can tell me." Her eyes darted back and forth from me to Louise and back again. "What's wrong, Anna?"

"Nothing."

"You didn't like him, did you?"

"I barely know him," I said impatiently.

"Well, he's very nice," Lilly snapped. "Besides, he offered to fix the leak in the garage roof." She dragged her body up, and with her shoes slung over her shoulder by their straps she closed the door behind her.

After Lilly had gone into her bedroom, I heard the telephone ring. I could hear my mother talking.

"Kent, is that you?...I don't know, it's so late."

The spring on my mother's bed creaked as Lilly rose to go into her dressing room. Then I heard the *swish-swish* from her lace nightgown as she passed our bedroom door on the way back downstairs.

"Where are you going?" I called through the door.

"Anna, go back to bed," Lilly said.

"But where are you going?"

"Kent forgot his keys." Lilly's voice sounded defeated and tired.

"If he forgot his keys, then where was he calling from?"

"Anna," Lilly said, exasperated. "There's a hole in the garage about two feet wide."

I wished I could travel far into space, like the astronauts who'd gone to the moon. Then my spirit would be safe from the world where my mother lived, with her assorted men and sultry music, her makeup and sexy dresses.

Throughout the years of my mother's dating, she often sat at the foot of my bed and quizzed me. I didn't understand why my opinion mattered so much—perhaps she just needed to hear herself talk. But I didn't want to hear her. I had my own problems. I would have liked her to help me.

Soon I would start third grade. I couldn't concentrate on the math equations on the board that year. I had worried about what my mother was doing in the house all day alone. If Lilly had too much time on her hands, she grew vague and transparent as if you could slip right through her.

"Robert told me he was seeing other women," she'd said

once. "Anna, is there something wrong with me? I thought we connected. Should I call him?"

I didn't think so, but I knew she wanted to hear the opposite. My mother seemed to have an endless desire no man could fill. "When we were at the Reinsteins' cocktail party, he said he loved children. Don't you think he was trying to tell me something? When a man touches you...well, I thought it meant something."

✦ ✦ ✦

After the night of Austin's party, my body didn't feel mine unless he was next to me; I felt if he wasn't in my vision he didn't exist, or more to the point, I didn't exist for him.

That spring and summer there was hardly a place to be alone. Like everything else in Chagrin Falls, my house felt incredibly small. When I wasn't working or out with Austin, I sat in the living room and in the stream of sunlight I watched specks of dust slowly float into the air, and I wondered about the meaning of life until the sound of a lawn mower or the phone ringing drove a wedge into the silence and pulled me out of my thoughts. Upstairs I could hear the drone of the TV in my mother's bedroom. Her melancholy overtook the air in our home like the smell of rotting fruit. Sometimes I retreated outside and sat in the gazebo reading a book, or laid out in the sun on a lounge chair working on my tan before it was time for me to go to work.

My mother had swung back to isolating herself in our house the way she had during those years right after my father died. I worried that my mother might decide to stay shut in our house forever. I suppose she could have if she had wanted to. She had enough money to squeak by on from her monthly

Social Security checks, occasional help from Aunt Rose's pension, and handouts from Nonie and Papa.

After my father died Nonie and Papa were always after her to take some classes, get an education. But Lilly managed to skirt the issue.

Every time Aunt Rose came back to Cleveland for her yearly visit, she, too, pleaded with Lilly to get a job or an education. But Lilly always defended herself, saying, "The only thing I know how to do is take care of my family."

"But, Mom, maybe Aunt Rose's right. Maybe you'd be happier if you worked," I'd say after Aunt Rose left.

"I don't have Aunt Rose's constitution," Lilly reasoned. "Imagine me, working at a bank."

That kind of logic had an awful effect on me. I wanted to jump through the roof. But if you stepped into those waters with my mother, it was as if you had walked into an inner argument she was having with herself. She sucked you in like an undertow, and then spit you out again, carrying her burden.

✦ ✦ ✦

When Lilly went out on dates, we worried when she would come home or what kind of mood she'd be in once her date deposited her back inside our front door like an opened package. The winter I was in third grade, if I wasn't at Maria's house playing Barbies or Monopoly underneath the alcove in her attic while her father worked and her mother chain-smoked in the den, I hung out with my sisters in the yard building snowmen and making snow forts until it got late. We tried our hardest to stay busy, so we wouldn't have to wonder when our mother was coming back.

One icy night she had gone out with Kent Montgomery,

and when she was with him we never knew what time she'd be home. When our hands grew cold and our cheeks stung, we went inside and had hot chocolate with marshmallows and slices of toast spread with butter and sprinkled sugar. Then we climbed up to our rooms. I cleared off the schoolbooks, trousers, and balled-up sweaters that were always piled in a heap on Louise's bed. I untangled the blankets, tucked and dusted clean the flowered sheet. "Why are you such a slob?" I turned to Louise, and scolded. Louise, as a child, was disorganized and anxious. When I looked into her face, I could see the weight of sorrow she carried in her eyes. I knew her body, like mine, missed feeling the hands and warm lips of our father on her; showing a daughter what it meant to be loved. I was only four when my father died. My memories of him were vague, but poor Louise confessed she had no memories of our father at all.

I helped her pull the sweatshirt over her head and handed her a nightgown. There was dirt in her fingernails, and I made her go into the bathroom and clean them off. Soon we both slipped into bed, but later Louise went to Ruthie's room and summoned her. Then Ruthie came and climbed into Louise's bed with her. Before we fell asleep, we waited for Lilly to come back home. When Louise couldn't sleep, Ruthie read *The Adventures of Pippi Longstocking.* I liked Pippi's red braids, her skinny legs, brave adventures, and the sound of Ruthie's voice creating the scene for us.

When we grew tired of hearing the story, we played a game where we bought three horses and had to name them. Sugar was a good one; Henry, Midnight, Star, Strawberry, Red Stallion, and Chester were some of the favorites. Ruthie liked Grand Canyon. We said the names until one fell asleep, then the other. Then the last one.

In the morning after Lilly's date we heard the shrill ring of the telephone. I wasn't sure my mother was home yet, but after two rings, Lilly picked up. I went downstairs. Lilly was still dressed in the navy blue dress she had worn on her date with Kent the night before.

I went back upstairs. "Something's the matter," I told my sisters.

We trailed downstairs and lingered in our mother's shadow.

"Who was it, Mom?" Ruthie finally said.

Lilly sat up and wiped wisps of hair off her face with her sleeve. Snow had come in the night and was building faster in the yard, scratching out the last sliver of sky. There would be no school that day.

"Oh, it was no one you know, darling. It was nothing. I'm just tired. I was up all night." Lilly was edgy. She had canceled her next date with Kent. When the phone rang again, Kent no doubt pestering Lilly to change her mind, she asked Ruthie to answer and say she wasn't home. She stared out the window, biting the cuticle skin around one thumb. Her makeup from the night before was smeared under her eyes.

"Why do I have to lie for you?" Ruthie barked. But when she looked into our mother's tired eyes, she gave in.

Lilly tied her hair back off her face in a ponytail. She began to move about the house, washing dishes, doing laundry, still in her tight-fitting evening dress, as if she were following a routine she'd carried out for years.

The doorbell rang. Lilly moved the curtain and peered out the window. It was Mr. Hopkins from down the street with the immaculate lawn that looked smooth as carpet or golf-course grass.

Lilly opened the door.

"Mrs. Crane, the block association has signed a petition,"

he began, clearing his throat. He shoved a piece of paper into Lilly's hand. "You've got to do something about your house. It's affecting the value of the neighborhood."

Lilly looked at him the way sad widows do.

"I'm sorry to be the bearer of bad tidings," Mr. Hopkins stuttered. "But we've got to consider our children. I wish we could do something to help."

Lilly took the petition, crumpled it in a ball, threw it back at him, and shut the door.

"You'll be hearing from our attorneys," Mr. Hopkins called.

Lilly went to the kitchen and swallowed down three aspirin. "No one understands," she sighed.

Around three o'clock she shoved us outdoors. "I need peace and quiet," she explained. "My head's throbbing."

I looked down the block. The front lawns of the houses on our street were covered with snow. Our neighbor was shoveling his driveway. I looked at our own yard. The old snow was covered three or four inches high.

The paint on our house had begun to peel, and the wood was buckling. One of the shutters on the upstairs windows hung crooked. The gutters sagged with packed, frozen snow. The broken attic window was held together with masking tape. The hedges surrounding our house had long become overgrown and uneven. The other houses on the block were freshly painted. An acorn wreath with a red ribbon hung on the door across the street. It dawned on me then, though I had walked our block hundreds of times, that next to the other houses on our street, our house, the one my father had built for us, looked neglected and old.

My sisters and I took out the rusted shovels and began to shovel a path along the front walkway. Down the street the Magilicuttys must have lit a fire in the fireplace. The burnt smell hovered over our roof. I watched as the smoke created patterns in the sky. It began to turn from afternoon to dusk. The winter storm enveloped us in a frozen cocoon.

A shiny black Mercedes pulled up by the side of the street to our house. "Hello, girls," Kent called out through his rolled-down passenger window. "Is your mother home?"

We pointed inside.

"I think your mother is really special," he said. "And I'm looking forward to getting to know you. Which one of you is Anna?"

We had been introduced to him more than a handful of times.

"I am," I said.

"I understand you and my son Mark are in the same class."

I just stared at him. I couldn't help but wonder if Mark Montgomery, who looked a little bit like the Pillsbury Dough Boy, knew his father was obsessed with my mother. Sometimes, before school, Kent came to our house dressed in his business suit to see my mother before heading downtown to work. She'd make coffee for him in our narrow kitchen. He sometimes showed up again, unannounced, in the middle of the afternoon. I once saw Mark with his mother at the grocery store. She was overweight and had the look of a divorcée who knew she was no longer desired. Mark flipped through a comic book he tore off the rack near the cashier counter so as not to catch my eye.

When Kent emerged from his car we smelled a blast of liquor on his breath. He waltzed into our house, as he always did, without ringing the bell or knocking. Once Lilly had begun seeing Kent regularly, he became possessive and forbade her to see other men.

"How can she go out with that greaser?" Ruthie said.

I wandered up to the front door and opened it. Kent had Lilly in a tight hold. His beard was pressed against her neck.

"Why don't you and your sisters go to the corner and buy yourself an ice-cream sundae?" Kent said, thrusting a crisp twenty-dollar bill into my hand, and closed the front door.

When we got home, our snow jackets soaked through, our hands and feet frozen, Lilly was still in the kitchen with Kent. Our hands and faces were burning from the cold. Kent was drinking a glass of whiskey from a bottle Lilly kept under the kitchen sink.

"It's time for you to go home now, Kent," Lilly said. She looked frightened. "I need to give the girls their supper."

"No one tells me what to do," Kent said. He wobbled and almost fell off the stool he was sitting on. "I don't care how big her tits are."

"Leave now," Lilly demanded. She began to reach for the phone.

"You bet your pretty ass I will," Kent said. "And you can forget about that loan I promised you. You're nothing but a goddamn tease."

Kent began to pour himself another glass of whiskey. Lilly took the bottle out of his hand. "Just get out!" she screamed.

After Kent stormed out of the house, Lilly burst into tears. "I don't know what I'm going to do," she said.

We pulled off our wet coats and boots and sat around the table. Lilly confessed that the phone call she had received that morning was from the bank. We were months past due on the mortgage on our house. She stared at the letter from the bank that she held in her hand. Then she opened the drawer where she kept her bills. There were unopened envelopes from the gas company, the grocery store where Lilly paid for everything on credit, the telephone company, Higbees department store, where she charged our school clothes and the wardrobe she updated each season to keep up with the competition from the slew of rich divorcées that had begun to plague our neighborhood.

"I can't let your father down," she said. "We have to find a way to pay down this mortgage. This house is all we have left. When we dated your father used to pick me up every Sunday, and we'd drive to Chagrin Falls to eat caramel corn or get an ice-cream cone and watch the falls. It always seemed to us that we were in some little New England town far away and not barely twenty minutes from where our families lived. When your father and I got married, we decided we wanted to live in Chagrin Falls. This house was our secret paradise."

Louise, in an attempt to cheer up our mother, dragged Lilly to the window to show her that we had shoveled the snow from the driveway. Lilly gazed out into the yard in a stupor. Lazily she picked the frozen ice from my sister's hair.

But new snow had furiously filled the driveway. In less than an hour, all our hard work had gone to waste.

Later that night I came downstairs and found my mother sitting on the couch thumbing through her old scrapbooks. Her eyes rested on a crinkled carnation ironed between sheets of wax paper. It was the corsage my father had given Lilly on their first date. I pictured my mother coming home that night, taking the corsage and the roll of wax paper, setting up the ironing board, heating the iron, oblivious to her fate.

My mother was slipping into her memories. When she did that, day after day would pass with my mother so deeply into her thoughts it was as if she were almost invisible, like the bushes in front of our house huddled under a casing of snow.

"When was that picture taken?" I pointed to a photograph

of my father and mother standing in front of Nonie and Papa's house.

"This was the first time I met Nonie and Papa." Lilly's eyes lit up as she spoke. "Your Papa was a shrewd businessman. He owned a pawn shop on 113th Street. I stayed up so many nights worrying that Nonie and Papa wouldn't approve of me because I was only a bank teller's daughter. But your father could have cared less."

Aunt Adrienne and my father's brother, Uncle Ben, lived just a few blocks from Nonie and Papa's house. When we visited my sisters and I dressed in our hand-me-downs, while our cousins were cloaked in the fashions of the moment. On their block the driveways were freshly tarred, and basketball nets hung above shiny white garages. By contrast, the houses on the block where Lilly had grown up were decades old. At Aunt Rose's house in Cleveland, before she moved to California, family photographs in sepia tones decorated the plaster-cracked walls. The plumbing and fixtures were creaky and rusted. Rugs from the old country covered the splintered wood floors.

After my father's death we visited his family once or twice a year. Around the modern glass coffee table, I listened to Aunt Adrienne and Nonie chitchat about upcoming parties, hairstyles, the color of someone's nail polish, events at the country club, the opening of a new restaurant downtown. The death of a family member, a mixed-up child, someone's unhappiness—these things weren't spoken about. They were like dark wounds, not to be touched, cared for, or reopened. The memories of my father, the war that claimed my mother's relatives, people I never knew, were whited out. Most people keep their pasts secret. Even I find myself doing it: inventing a future for myself separate from what I've lost. But I didn't understand then why everything had to be a secret, when at home it was obvious our lives were hanging by a thread. In the trapped air at Nonie's and Papa's, the unspoken truth felt impossible not to notice: If my father hadn't died, my mother and sisters and I would be living the same carefree existence as Aunt Adrienne and Uncle Ben's family.

The furniture in Nonie and Papa's house was sleek and contemporary. Wall-to-wall carpet covered the floors instead of throw rugs hiding scratches in the wood. With all their money they tried to cover up the suffering they had endured in the old country, but its shadows were stubborn.

"When your father proposed," Lilly continued, still looking at the photo of the two of them together, "there was so little money, my family had to rent an extra bedroom in Aunt Rose's house for a boarder. I couldn't imagine not having to think twice about spending money on a new dress or a pair of stockings. When I married your father, it was a step up, a key to all my family never had. My family was so proud.

"Come sit next to me, angel."

I begrudgingly snuggled up against my mother. I knew she needed the feel of a body against hers, so she could forget, at least for a few moments, that she now belonged to no one. I let her squeeze me, as if her life depended on it, before I went up to bed.

Later that night I awoke to what I knew as the sound of suffering coming from my mother's bedroom door. I took off the covers, crawled out of bed, and tiptoed into the hallway. Lilly was sitting in a chair by her window with a Kleenex balled in her hand. The heat was down so low that the air in the house felt damp and cold, like the inside of an old shed. "I can't take this anymore," Lilly whispered softly to no one, only to the long, slender branches of the oak that stroked her window.

"Mom, are you crying because of Kent?"

"That creep," she said. "I don't care ten cents for him. Go back to bed, darling."

Why couldn't my mother meet a nice man? Not the kind who looked at her too long and made her crazy, but a man like Nancy and Scott's father, who always walked them to school before he went to work and made sure their jackets were zipped, their heads covered. I thought that if my mother met the right man, she would return to us whole again, and have room to love us the way children ought to be loved.

The next morning was Saturday, and the three of us, like the dips, hues, and shadows of the same self, went out to play. We rode our bikes over the wet pavement on the snowplowed streets to the Chagrin River and skated with our shoes on the frozen patches of ice. Across from the river stood the old brick homes with colorful garden beds and black iron lawn furniture.

Once, when we had driven past one of those houses, Lilly said, "Can you imagine, angels? Isn't that garden exquisite? It's a palace, a home for a queen. If your father were still alive, that's how we'd be living." Now Ruthie had a plan to kill more time. She wanted to get inside and see how the rich people lived. We hid our bikes in the bushes and walked through the snow-packed grass till we came to one of Lilly's favorites.

I liked being with Ruthie when she was on a mission. She could tuck her own anger and feelings away, and with her in charge, I could step back and be a child again. Sometimes when Ruthie, Louise, and me were away from our house we could forget about our mother. I felt the still place in the center of my being when I was cut off from her frequency.

Ruthie rang the doorbell. The house Ruthie decided we'd try was the one Lilly adored most. My heart began to beat so loud I could hear it.

When the door opened everything in that house was lush and spotless. Red Oriental carpets, antique furniture, gold-framed paintings on the walls. But it wasn't the expensive furniture and huge house that impressed me. It was the sense of order and care. Not a glass or a pillow was out of place. The books lined in the bookshelf were arranged perfectly according to size.

"What can I do for you girls?"

The man who stood before us was different from the men who hung around my mother. An aura of contentment radiated from his being.

"I was wondering if my sister could use your bathroom," Ruthie said. She pushed Louise forward. "We're a long way from home."

Louise's mouth fell open.

"Charlie Dodd," the man said, holding out his hand.

"I'm Ruthie Crane, and these are my sisters," Ruthie said, like a grown-up.

"Lilly Crane's daughters. Well, I'll be goddamned. I knew your father. We played football together in high school. He knew how to make everyone feel important." He shook his head sadly, the way everyone did when they talked about our father.

After Louise came back from the bathroom, we said good-bye, and mounted our bikes. As we pedaled away beside the road that followed the banks of the river, none of us said a word. Across the water a school of baby ducks followed in their mother's uneven wake.

That night Lilly went out and didn't come home until after midnight. When we told our mother we'd met Charlie Dodd, Lilly said: "Oh my stars. Your father and I used to double-date with him and Sally Wasserman." She thought for a moment. "Is he single?"

"I don't think so," Louise said.

"Need I even ask," Lilly responded. "All the good ones are taken."

Frost had begun to form along the edges of the windows in the den.

"Why aren't you two in bed?"

Louise and I turned from the TV, where we were watching *The Twilight Zone.* Our mother's eye makeup was smeared, and her lipstick had melted off.

"I'm going to bed now," she said. "Don't stay up too late."

Almost another two years passed, marked by the long, languishing days we spent at school and the evenings at home watching episodes of *Patty Duke* or *Father Knows Best* while our mother went through the eligible bachelors of our community, picking and choosing as if she were checking out books from the library. It began to feel impossible to us that our mother would find the man she was waiting for. Ruthie took the defeat the hardest. By the time she was in sixth grade, she began hanging out with a fast crowd at school, sometimes not coming home when she was supposed to, instigating fights with my mother, bringing boys home she'd sequester in her bedroom. Her recklessness was like a quick high that for a brief instant took her away from us. I couldn't blame her. Over the years, it would grow more difficult to pull her back.

"Where's Ruthie?" Lilly said one night when she had come home after midnight. I was in fifth grade.

We shrugged.

"Well, where is she?"

Lilly walked briskly up the stairs and pushed open Ruthie's door. I don't know what my mother thought we did all those nights she went out. She must have assumed we'd be there frozen like statues exactly how she left us.

"She went out," Louise called from our room.

"At this time of night? Girls, get your coats on this instant."

As we drove around the neighborhood, Lilly nibbled at the sides of her fingers. "How could she do this to me?"

I tried to think of something to console her. "I'll never leave you," I said.

"Of course you will, Anna," Lilly paused. "One day you'll all leave me." She looked ahead at the dark, slushy street.

After nearly an hour Lilly began to get hysterical. "Didn't she say where she was going? How could you two let her leave? Do you think I'm having fun when I go out? Girls, do you? It's hard work," she said, perhaps remembering all those nights we had pleaded with her to stay home with us. Tears came to her eyes. "Ruthie, Ruthie," she called out the window as if she were beckoning a poor, pathetic lost dog.

"I just don't understand that girl," my mother said.

When Lilly pulled back up the driveway to call the police, Ruthie was sitting on the front step of the house in her jean jacket and blue jeans, smoking a cigarette. Her long, unwashed hair fell over her face.

"Get in the house right this instant, young lady," Lilly ordered. "And take that filthy thing out of your mouth."

From the driveway my eye fixed on the roof of the gazebo, where the wooden rafters came together. The gazebo lights were all lit, like they always were when my father was still alive. Overhead a cloud passed over the moon, and it went dark, racking the sky with hunger.

Once Ruthie was back in the house, Lilly settled down. She came upstairs with three mugs of hot chocolate on a tray. "Girls, I have a surprise for you," she said. "I've met someone

special." A smile spread across her face. "His name is Max Mc-
Carthy," she said. "Doesn't he sound presidential?"

For three years Lilly had pinned her hopes on each man
that had walked into our house. By this time we no longer believed her.

✦ ✦ ✦

/ found a job waitressing at a diner called Dink's once school
let out that summer, and when I wasn't at work I was usually
with Austin. What do we know of ourselves and the world
when we are sixteen? The suburban walls of our community
shielded us from the Vietnam War, hid the fact that our grandparents and great-grandparents had suffered world wars and
concentration camps. Even the racial tension, violence, and
poverty in downtown Cleveland seemed, from Chagrin Falls,
as if they were happening worlds away. That summer the universe I inhabited narrowed down to my mother, my sisters,
and Austin. I rarely ventured any farther than my house, the
diner where I worked, or the racetrack. I suppose that was the
purpose of the postwar suburbs: to separate and protect us
from all that had been lost and return us to the private lives
within our families, which once had been ripped apart.

After Ruthie left, I knew that I also had to figure out what
I would do with my life. My friends were taking the SATs to
prepare for college. Some of their parents were accompanying
them to tour schools. Lilly never mentioned our futures. Perhaps because she could never invent a future of her own, she
just imagined we were going to stay home pasted into the
house like wallpaper, like she did.

Instead of focusing on a plan for after graduation, I distracted myself with Austin. I imagined I could simply slip into his life and everything else would vanish.

It was mid-June. Austin and I had been going out seriously for nearly a month. While Mr. Cooper was out of town on business, Austin took me to his house, and I cooked him practically the only dinner I knew how to make: spaghetti, a tossed salad, and garlic bread.

"I'm going to show you something," Austin said. "I've never showed anyone, not any girl, this." He took me down the basement. There, in a separate space off the laundry room where a young boy would play, was a magnificent city made out of blocks, and Popsicle-stick houses, train tracks, cardboard boxes, intricate pipe-cleaner trees and bushes, and cutout shoe-box dioramas. Surrounded by papier-mâché mountains and towering buildings shaped from modeling clay was a huge lake made from tinfoil.

"I built this when I was a kid," Austin said. "It's a city made out of nowhere. Nothing bad happens here. Children don't get hurt, mothers and fathers stay together. No one dies. This is practically the only thing from my childhood I brought with me when we moved."

I imagined Austin as a small boy, with his jar of paste, crayons, and paints spread out on the floor of his basement working steadily, single-mindedly, so he wouldn't have to think about his mother and his father not talking to each other.

"Austin, this is magnificent." I was completely smitten.

"This is where you and I can live," Austin said. "No one can touch us here. No one can harm us." I knew exactly what Austin meant. He didn't have to explain any further.

The City of Nowhere was our own kind of heaven. It was outside the world of our families; it existed beyond Chagrin

Falls, beyond Cleveland, beyond Ohio. It was the world I was ready to venture into, that Austin made plausible. I wanted more from my life than the domesticated world I witnessed as I walked past the houses in our neighborhood, and I imagined that if I followed the tracks Austin had built, and went under the golden gate leading to the city he had fabricated from glitter, paper, and wire, I would find it.

The city we inhabited existed wherever we went. It didn't matter if we were scarfing down a pizza at the mall, or making out in an over-air-conditioned movie in the afternoon to escape the heat, or were cruising around in his car getting high. We were willing to venture anywhere just as long as a new history was being set down in the tracks we made.

That summer there were few places for a pair of teenagers to be alone. At Austin's house Mr. Cooper was almost always home in the evenings reading the paper or watching TV. After his wife had left him, he'd fallen into the routine of working to fill the emptiness of the day. It was unusual for a woman to leave her husband and kids, and Austin constantly tried to make it up to his father by spending time with him. We felt strange leaving Mr. Cooper alone downstairs while we retreated upstairs to Austin's room in the attic, but eventually, after we sat on the couch with Mr. Cooper and depleted all the small talk we could muster, Austin gave me the eye and I would follow as he made his way up the staircase.

"I always gave my mother a hard time," Austin told me in one of the rare moments when he opened up about his past. "She said I took my father's side. It's because I felt so fucking sorry for him. My mother cringed when he tried to touch her. Maybe if I was more sympathetic, she would have stayed."

"That's crazy," I said. "It had nothing to do with you." But I knew his mother's walking out had made it difficult for Austin to trust anyone. Once he felt a person had betrayed him, no matter what you said, his mind was made up. It was the end. This had happened with Peter Markson, his best friend. He'd started hanging out with Peter almost the day he moved to our town. They were inseparable. Then one day Peter didn't show up when he was supposed to. Austin and I ran into him later that night with Betsy McCracken draped underneath his arm and Austin cut him, just like that. When I tried to ask Austin what had happened to Peter, he said he didn't know a Peter. Never had. End of story.

Once, when we had returned to Austin's house after seeing a movie, we found Mr. Cooper in the dining room pumping furiously on an exercise bike, the sweat practically jumping off of him.

"Are you okay, Dad?" Austin said.

"Your mother called."

Austin turned pale.

"She wanted more money."

Mr. Cooper pedaled so fast you could feel the quick wisps of air circulating around the wheels of the exercise bike. Under his breath he muttered, "Fucking whore."

"Did she ask about me?"

Mr. Cooper stopped the bike. He paused. His voice softened. "Not a goddamn word. I'm sorry, son."

I followed Austin upstairs. He drifted into silence. I hadn't considered often enough the repercussions of Austin's mother's leaving.

"Do you want to talk about your mother?" I wanted to say something once we were in the shelter of the cheap-wood–paneled attic room, the architecture of his body solid and sturdy next to mine.

"I don't have a mother," he answered.

Usually, by the time we made it upstairs, there was still time left over in the evening to lie on Austin's lumpy bed and make out so long my lips were bruised, my hair matted, my cheeks on fire. I usually let Austin show me a few of his card tricks, and then guided his hand under my shirt, let him un-hook my bra strap. I liked to get him all worked up before it was time for him to drive me home. But that night Austin wasn't in the mood. The evening was haunted by the ghost of Austin's mother. We lay on top of his Santa Fe–style Indian blanket and stared at the slopes in the ceiling, listened to the sounds of a swarm of bees who had orchestrated an intricate hive in the crevice outside his attic window, until it was time for him to take me home.

When we pulled into my driveway, I quickly got out and said good-bye. I made sure there was no way he would be tempted to come inside. I had to have something that was all my own, that my mother couldn't taint or tamper with.

✦ ✦ ✦

When I was sick with pneumonia one winter, when I was ten, Lilly took me out to the gazebo and wrapped me up in blankets. "Fresh air is nature's cure," she said. Together we sat under the low, silvery boughs.

"A tree is protected by its bark, and you, my sweet, are armed with my everlasting love." I was attached to the depth

of beauty her eye saw in the winter trees, frozen grass, the
bleak, infectious world.

"My mother used to dress me up in fancy dresses and tell
me how beautiful I looked," Lilly told me.

I looked down at my chewed fingernails.

"When my mother was a few years older than you are, she
hid from the Nazis in a priest's cellar," Lilly continued. "The
priest told my mother's parents that he only had room for one
of their two daughters. My mother was chosen because she was
more beautiful. She later found out that her sister Edith was
killed by the Nazis the next day. My mother used to whisper
that story in my ear at night before I went to bed. So that I
would never forget that I had been blessed. She made me believe I would never need anything more than to be beautiful."

I didn't say anything. When my mother talked this way,
there was nothing to say. I remembered the story Aunt Rose
had told Lilly, that Lilly's mother died because of the suffering
she had endured in the war. If suffering had killed my grandmother, what would happen to my mother?

"Aunt Rose told me that when I was a little girl she used to
come to our house and find my mother in tears. She never got
over the death of her sister."

"What happened to your mother's parents?" I asked.

"When she made it to Switzerland, she discovered that
they'd been taken to the camps. My mother was the only survivor. I know what loss is," Lilly said hoarsely. "All I've known
is how to love the dead."

"Don't you love any of those men you go out with?"

"I wish I did," my mother said wearily.

"What about us?"

"Of course I love you," Lilly said. "You're my children."

Lilly stepped out of the gazebo. She reached above her and broke a small branch from the tree there. "I've been in mourning all my life." Her face looked toward the thick pleats of the afternoon sky. "That's where my heart is," Lilly said. "Look here, Anna." She came back inside the gazebo and sat beside me on the bench. She peeled the black bark off the branch with her fingernails. There lay the white wood, revealed, shiny and damp beneath. "Love can do this to your heart," she said softly. "It can be like a blade whittling your heart clean for you until there isn't anything left.

"Don't tell anyone our secrets," she added. "Cross your heart. People won't like us if they know we've suffered. They'd only pity us. Look at the weeping willow, Anna," she said. "When I'm missing your father, I think about those long arms weighed down by so many leaves. I think about abundance. How long it lasts, even when you can no longer see or feel it." She held out her arms as if she were embracing the air. "Sometimes all I need is to be outside, with my lovely daughter, underneath the trees. It's the rest of the world that takes the life out of me."

Like my mother I found comfort in a certain kind of feeling that would overcome me when I looked at a cornflower blue sky, or a simple wildflower, or a complicated tree. But the feeling wouldn't last long before I'd be flooded with anxiety. I knew at an early age that you couldn't live peacefully in isolation. There would always be a window to hold your nose against and wish that what was behind it was your own.

✦ ✦ ✦

*A*ustin never came right out and asked me to be his girlfriend. It was just understood after the night of his party that we were together. Austin and I worked out a scheme when we wanted to spend the night together. I told my mother I was sleeping at Maria's house, though by then Maria and I weren't even talking.

Austin picked me up and we drove out to the track. He had befriended one of the trainers, a guy in his thirties named Beep, who always wore the same plaid work shirt and cowboy boots no matter how hot out it was. His front teeth were stained with nicotine. He let Austin use his windowless cement tack room off the stables, and it was there that I let him inside me, amid the sounds of horses snorting and people walking back and forth from the paddocks to the barn, in the dirt and dust and hay.

It's funny how we enter people's lives and then realize we've walked into a deep and long history that shapes and gives form to our every moment. Once Austin graduated and began spending most of his time at the track, he began to change. After my shift at the diner, he picked me up in his noisy Mustang and popped open a beer from a six-pack he kept under the seat, and we'd drive out to the track. He began hanging out with Beep in his free time and placing bets on the races. We'd get there almost every night toward the end of June for the last few races. If Austin was winning he was high with adrenaline, but if the horses didn't perform to his expectations, he chewed the inside of his cheek and kicked the fence circling the track. Even if Austin wasn't betting, he always had a horse picked out, and if the horse didn't do well he took it personally, like he had made a bad decision. He seemed to put his whole life into it. I was jealous of it, Austin's commitment to anything beyond me.

In late June, on a Friday night, Austin put a thousand dollars on the last race. I had no idea where he got the money, and

I didn't think it was my business to ask. Maybe I was afraid to. You could only go a certain distance with Austin before he'd go silent and cold, and tighten up like an expressionless statue.

There was a feeling of desperation in the air; the crowds fired up, bystanders at the edges of their seats or pacing the platform near the fence.

The music between the races blared over the loudspeakers, and the dusty ground trembled underneath us. I watched the horses circle the track warming up for the next race while Austin studied the program.

As the horses got out of the gate, Austin was pumped. I watched him pressed up against the metal fence. I stood back, the ground littered with tickets, lit a Marlboro, and prayed for a winner. I knew that if he won he'd sweep me in his arms and tell me I was his good-luck charm. He'd take my hand and squeeze it. We might go to dinner. I was so tense my hand absently crushed the plastic cup of warm, flat Coke I'd been sipping. As the sky traveled from gray to lavender to black, I felt as if I was its sole witness.

I can picture Austin now, so vividly, and yet it's been years since I've seen him. He's still in my dreams, the recurring one where I'm trying to hold him in my gaze—I believed I could heal him—and his eyes are burning into me. His sculpted face is browned by the sun, aged not one bit, and I can see those hands, chapped and dry, with thick, hard nails. In the dream Austin and I are together, even though I'm involved with the man I'm going to marry. I'm willing to risk that all—and then Austin humiliates me. There are so many versions, but each one ends the same. Even now, no matter how I have tried to keep him out, Austin is still a ghostlike presence in my mind.

That Friday night, after the horses had made the second

turn, Austin's horse—Perfection or Electric or Wild Turkey, I don't remember, though then I said the horse's name over and over like a mantra—came up neck and neck with the horse in the lead. Austin ran up to the fence, nearly climbed it to see how his horse held back, and then he broke away. He tore up the ticket, and stomped off, not once looking behind for me. He knew I would follow. Under his breath I heard him say, "I'll kill him, the motherfucker," talking about Beep, because Beep had given him the tip.

In the dark night, in the airless tack room, I tried to console him with my body. He became calmer then. He lit a joint and got stoned. I saw what the touch of a hand on a boy's neck or along his chest could do.

The next night he convinced me to try and sneak into the Skylight Motel outside of town. I stayed in the Mustang while he went in and got the room. I'm not sure why my mother didn't try to keep me at home at night. Maybe she thought if she were me, young and in love, she'd want to stay out all night, too. It was just something we never talked about. After that first night at the hotel it became a habit. If he won big we'd go to the Skylight. We'd go first to the Brown Derby for steaks, and then back to a room that had a big, clean bed and good television and smelled of lemon-scented disinfectant and stale cigarettes. To me the dumpy motel room was no less luxurious than a room in a faraway, gilded mansion.

The first night at the motel, I lay awake all night, figuring I'd know when Austin had become real for me because then I'd be able to at least close my eyes. I hated to fall asleep and be away from him. I watched the fluorescent hands on the bedside clock. In their light I stared at his arms for hours and watched the blue veins pop out. I was glad that his chest was practically bare of chest hair—because that was the kind of boy I desired. The kind that looked boyish, not jaded and slick like Lilly's men. All night I was dying to wake him and with my hands, lure him back inside me. I liked having sex—but it was the closeness, the fierce force of it, that I craved. Sometimes, when I couldn't lose myself, I detached from my body and was like a third person in the room watching our awkward attempts to satisfy each other. But I didn't mind.

That night at the motel, I tried to tell him how I felt.

"I don't want you to be this important," I said. "It scares me."

"Don't you know I can't live without you?" When he lifted the hair from my neck and I saw in his eyes that I could hurt him, I reached out and touched his face.

"What is it about me that you love?" I wanted him to put it into words.

"Everything about you." He rubbed his hands along my arms and then over the curves of my body.

I wasn't the first girl Austin had slept with—everyone knew that—but he knew he was *my* first, and I think that was what also got to him about me. It was as if he craved the place that was pure and good at the center of my being.

I began to talk endlessly about the places we would go together, what we could do.

He told me to be quiet. My talking was giving him a headache. He kissed my eyelids and rolled on top of me, yanking up my undershirt. No matter how many times we'd slept together, I always wanted him to undress me. A rash of heat traveled up my neck and back. He kissed me again, and I felt myself falling into the warm hollow where, for a minute, I lost sight of the world. I touched the wet curls on the back of his neck and ran my finger along the creases in his forehead and listened to him say his sweet things. And before I knew it there was his touch again in the place so vulnerable it hurt.

*M*y mother roamed the house in her ballet slippers, pink tights, and a long oxford men's shirt, covered with dried paint. She was forgetful and spacey; she looked, if not for gravity, as if she might float away. My sisters and I went to the Pick 'n' Pay for groceries, emptied the garbage, and washed the laundry piled up in mounds in the basement while our mother went through the motions of painting the house.

Our neighborhood was filled with sluggish, unhappy women who dealt with the ennui of domesticity by pouring a five o'clock cocktail or popping Valium or amphetamines disguised as diet pills. Maria's mother had woken up the morning we began second grade convinced she saw Jesus looking at her outside the kitchen window when she was buttering toast. The breakdown was followed by several rounds of shock treatment. Other mothers in our neighborhood drank; ate themselves to twice-yearly visits to fat farms; or spiced up their bedrooms with affairs. But the difference between these women and my mother was that no matter how unhappy their marriages, there was the facade of a husband, and generally what came with it, financial security to protect them from sinking into the space where the mind drifts and floats untethered.

It was the Fourth of July. Austin and I planned to watch

the fireworks at the beach on Lake Erie. Louise had left early that morning with some friends for Cedar Point, an amusement park about an hour outside Cleveland, and wouldn't be back until later in the evening. My mother didn't have the energy or the wherewithal to get herself out of the house. Dust formed along the windowsills. When I pointed out the cobwebs that collected in the corners of the rooms, even whirled themselves around the wooden spoons and spatulas Lilly kept on the kitchen countertop in canisters, she looked at me like I was crazy. "I don't see anything, Anna," she said. "You're exaggerating." I knew something was off with her that day, but I didn't know what.

Lilly put down her paintbrush and went to the kitchen to fill her watering can. She watered the plants to the sound of Mozart.

I was in the house alone with Lilly. Louise had scored a summer job as a lifeguard at the community pool and spent most of her afternoons perched six feet over the pool in her lifeguard chair. The year before she had joined the high school swim team—like I did, she needed to find a way to be out of our house. When she wasn't hibernating in our room, she was submerged in the aqua blue pool, swimming obsessively, as if each stroke brought her closer to a place of safety. She lost weight. She barely ate anything all day, except a slice of toast or part of an apple. You could see every rib and muscle in her body.

Before school had let out for the summer, once I had taken the bleachers of the indoor Olympic-size pool two at a time, to watch her practice. The smell of chlorine and the humid, wet air seeped inside my clothes, warped my papers and pages from my books. It was beautiful, the way her body slipped into the water with barely a sound, and how quickly she took to it, as if her body had *become* water. I found it comforting, watching my sister glide back and forth, down one lane and up the other, pushing off with one foot, slapping the aqua blue tiles with her hands. The hollow room echoed back the quick splash of her strokes. I timed her by counting to myself. To this day it still comforts me. The sound of a body in water. I have a video of my sister when she won the state championship freestyle race. Sometimes when I can't sleep at night, I slip it into the VCR.

Once Austin had entered my life, I found it more difficult to invest in the idea that my mother could still, perhaps, change the dead-end course she was on. But sometimes I still tried.

"Mom," I asked, "why don't you come with us to watch the fireworks?" I knew she would say no, but it made me feel better to ask.

"You don't need an old lady like me tagging along," Lilly answered.

"It would be nice if you did something that you really wanted," I said, following after her while she scrubbed the paintbrushes with turpentine. Occasionally I felt the need to take her pulse, find out what she was thinking. Eventually she was going to finish painting the house, and then what would she do? She was so preoccupied painting that she barely took a shower or changed her clothes.

"It's too late for that, Anna. You know, when I was your age, a woman didn't think about herself, like you and your sisters do. My family would have considered it an indulgence."

Lilly stood poised in the middle of the living room. Her hair rested on her shoulders. She flung it back, then took a strand and wrapped it around her finger. Then, ignoring me, she got out her paint chips and pictures of cutouts from her decorating magazines and tacked them to the wall. It was no use to try and talk sense into her. It only exasperated me further. She

tacked the paint chips on different walls in each room and obsessed about which color would match the fabric on her sofa
and pillows. She preferred colors like mother-of-pearl and al-
abaster to more traditional shades.

✦ ✦ ✦

When I surmised from all the bills stuffed in Lilly's drawers
and the phone calls from bill collectors that we were broke,
I confronted my mother. "What's going to happen to us?" I
asked, as she lay in bed. It was the next night after Ruthie attempted to run away. I was in the fifth grade.

The snow had begun to fall after my sisters and I had spent
nearly all afternoon shoveling. On our block the hedgerows,
shrubs, and boulders separating one house from another dissolved under the snow. The sky was the color of slush.

"Anna, what are you talking about?" Lilly replied to my
question.

"How are we going to get the money to pay all the bills?"

"You sense everything don't you, angel? You're my alter
ego—my second self." Lilly sat up and turned on the lamp by
her bedside. She reached for a throw at the foot of her bed, and
put it around her shoulders.

"It's time we had a heart-to-heart." Lilly made room for me
on the bed. "We don't have any money left." She paused. Outside, a cascade of icicles fell against the window. "And I can't
borrow another penny. I don't know what to do." Lilly's eyes
looked like those of a cat hunkered against a door waiting to
come in from the cold. "I don't know what's going to happen
to us." None of the mothers I knew in our neighborhood
worked. My mother, as they had, had grown up to know what
kind or color of gloves to wear with a dress; how to accentuate

her eyes with makeup. From the time she was seven years old, she knew how to curl her hair. But no one had prepared her to support a family.

"We'll think of something," I tried to reassure her.

"You don't understand. I don't know how to do anything, except make a man want me." She lowered her eyes. "It scares me to have so much power over a man..." She looked off distantly and laid her head against the wall. "And such little control over my own life."

"What do men have to do with it?"

Lilly laughed nervously, almost as if she were crazy. "Why, they have everything to do with it," she said defensively. "Don't you understand? It's a man's world, Anna."

I had the creepy realization that if it weren't for the favors my mother received from her men we'd be living on the streets. But while my mother primed herself for her dates, she stuffed the bills in her drawer and dodged phone calls from bill collectors.

"Anna, promise me you won't tell anyone. If people think we don't have money, no one will want us."

I huddled closer to my mother. Her silky negligee clung to my skin. When I went to touch my mother's hand, I got a shock.

"All week I've been reckoning something with myself. I've made a decision. Your mother is going to get married. I'll make a good home for my girls, you'll see. I just hope your father will understand," Lilly motioned to the blotched ceiling where the paint had long bubbled. "Your father is watching over us, darling," Lilly said. "He's not going to let anything bad happen."

"Are you *really* getting married?" I said.

Lilly nodded.

"To who?"

"Max McCarthy," Lilly said, without hesitation. "Only he hasn't asked me yet."

"Who's Max?" I asked.

"Be patient, Anna. I want it to be a surprise."

✦ ✦ ✦

By the Fourth of July, our neighborhood was in full blossom. The maples and oaks canopied the lawns of our community, gardens bloomed with lavender, hydrangeas, and verbena. Lawn sprinklers went on and off to keep the grass from browning, nearly shutting down our water supply. And yet, though I was looking forward to seeing Austin, I didn't feel like celebrating our country's independence. There had been a heat wave the last two weeks in June. The interior of our house was so hot that it was hard to breathe.

"I've always wanted to do something grand," my mother was saying. She took the rubber plant and brought it to the kitchen sink to let the water drain from the pot. She seemed restless and preoccupied. I was trying to think of a way to get past her to go change into a pair of shorts, but she kept talking. "Study art in Italy, maybe the theater. But all of that is for you. You have your whole life ahead of you."

"What are talking about, Mom? You're living in a dream world. Art? The theater? Italy? I barely have enough money to buy next year's schoolbooks."

I was spending as much time as I could at work that summer, to avoid spending time with my mother. I tried to take whatever shifts I could manage, sometimes doubling up lunch and dinner. Clara, the head waitress at Dink's, had a soft spot for me; she made out the schedule each week. I usually made it to work a half hour early to have a cup of coffee with her before my shift started. She talked about her son, Randall, who was in dental school. She gave part of her tips to him every week.

"What's wrong with fantasizing?" Lilly continued.

"I can't afford to fantasize."

"Look at you, Anna," Lilly said, changing the subject. "Where did you get that lovely dress? It fits you like a glove." She was referring to a black sleeveless cotton shift I had just bought at the mall. "I can see what that boy, Austin, sees when he looks at you.

"I know you're in love," Lilly said. She eyed me provocatively. The crickets went at it in the backyard. The cicadas clacked. The awning over the back porch knocked and tapped in the breeze. I jumped to answer the phone as soon as it rang, made sure Austin would meet me at Dink's, rather than at home. I cherished my secret life with him, like the single rose he had given me one night, which I'd pressed between the covers of a book. I tried to ignore my mother's comment and flew up the stairs to change. Even though I was eager to have Austin see me in the new dress, I wanted to protect it from getting ruined.

Before I left that night, I looked in on my mother. She was washing dishes in the sink. She was quiet then. Subdued. In the glass I saw my own reflection. We shared the same broad forehead and widow's peak. Her nose was longer than my own, but I saw the similar arc in our cheeks, and when she went to brush a wisp of hair away that had fallen in her face, I noticed her hand, her fingers delicate and long like my own. I hadn't realized how much we looked alike and how much it scared me. Her eyes in the reflection looked swollen. Now I wasn't so sure about leaving her home alone.

"Do you want me to stay home with you tonight, Mom?" I asked.

"No, darling. You go out and have a good time."

By the lake we planted ourselves on a blanket under the umbrella of stars. Nearly every family from the sprinkle of suburbs around the center of Cleveland were squatted in their yards, next to their barbecues, or in a football field, or on the edge of the lake observing the same ritual.

The tangled smells of lake water, dried algae, and summer rain were in the air, the promise that the heat would break. As the crowds drifted to find a place on the beach, I followed the curve of Austin's back with my eyes, intuited the texture of his skin without touching it.

While we sat on the itchy blanket drinking a cool beer, I held in my mind the momentary feeling of something everlasting, like the eternal pines in the distance. The fireworks exploded overhead.

Austin got up, said he'd be right back. He was always doing that, running off in secret. I kept looking at my watch as the water lapped against the rocky beach.

As the fireworks burst into flower and rained down from the sky with their falling light, I created a picture in my mind of Austin with another girl, someone he'd bumped into at the concession stand or outside the portable bathroom stalls. He'd been gone a long time. It made me crazy, to imagine Austin with another girl. But I also knew Austin couldn't stop himself. There was a part of him that needed the jolt of attention a girl's desire could inflict.

Before the grand finale began, Austin showed up. He sat down next to me on the army blanket without explanation

or apology, and we watched the end of the finale without talking or touching. I listened to the chatter of conversation coming from a nearby group sitting in lawn chairs. A couple sitting
next to us were kissing.

"Where were you?" I finally asked. I realized I was furious.

"I saw some people I knew." In the distance Steely Dan
sang "Rikki Don't Lose That Number," on a boom box.

Austin attempted to put his arm around my shoulder as we
made our way in between the mazelike path of blankets back
to the car, but I disengaged and lagged behind, watching on
the ground as my shadow commingled with his, and moved
out again. I didn't say a word the rest of the way home. As we
pulled up my driveway, he put his hand on my thigh.

"Listen, Anna." I smelled the beer on his breath. I looked
past him to regard the stars, the incandescent blinks of light
wrapped in a sheet of darkness.

"Anna," he said again.

Just hearing the way he said my name reduced me to a place
where I could forgive him. I thought of the coolness of autumn.

"I was testing you," he said.

"What are you talking about?"

"To see whether you'd wait it out."

"That's a sick thing to do. Where did you think I was
going to go?"

"That's not important. Don't talk, Anna. Don't say another
word."

+ + +

*T*he first boy I had a crush on was Brucie Johnson. He was the
head lifeguard at one of the country clubs, and lived three doors
down from us.

The summer before I was ten, we were getting in the car to go grocery shopping when Brucie Johnson walked by.

"Good morning, Mrs. Crane," he said. "You ought to take the girls swimming today. It's a scorcher."

"My girls don't know how to swim," Lilly said soulfully. "I wish I could afford to give them lessons."

"That's a shame," Brucie said. "Hey, why don't you and the girls meet me at the reservoir tomorrow morning?"

When we showed up at the reservoir the next day, Brucie was doing a jackknife off the cliffs. His hair was in a ponytail and a rawhide choker circled his neck. He wore a black bathing suit.

Brucie saw Louise's talent in the water instantly. Over the summer he taught her how to do the breaststroke, butterfly, and back crawl. I watched his perfect, smooth strokes as he explained how to move our arms for the breaststroke—chicken, airplane, soldier—and kick our legs like a frog. When he finished our lessons, he dried off in the sun and came over to chat with Lilly.

Our swimming lessons with Brucie continued throughout the duration of that summer. From time to time, during the swimming lessons, Lilly glanced up, raised her sunglasses to the top of her head, and called out to us. Lilly sunned herself to the sound of soft rock on the transistor radio. You could smell the cocoa butter seeping into her darkening skin.

"Beautiful day, isn't it, Mrs. Crane?" Brucie called to her. His eyes sparkled, the color of a minty sky.

"Bruce, you make me feel ancient. Call me Lilly," she said.

Whenever my mother was out in the world, away from our house, she acted cheerful, as though not to disappoint people. She had a generous, open smile that accentuated the birthmark over the right side of her upper lip. Certain people, like Brucie, drew pleasure simply from Lilly's company. I noticed that Brucie looked, after a morning with my mother, as if he had caught some of her vitality, and walked away from Lilly as though his battery was now recharged.

But, after the swimming lessons, once we were driving back home, my mother's cheerful countenance dissipated. She grew dark and irritated. "Would you girls be quiet!" Lilly said. "I have a splitting headache."

Ruthie reached for the knob on the radio and turned up the volume, and Lilly switched it off.

"My head's throbbing," she repeated.

"Why do you always get your way?" Ruthie said.

"Because I'm your mother," Lilly said. She paused. "Do you think I would have *had* children, if it wasn't for your father?"

The car went silent.

Lilly backpedaled. "That didn't come out right. I meant, if I knew I was going to end up a single mother. See what I mean? With all that noise, I can't even think straight."

The rest of the day we were on good behavior. We tried to pick up the clothes scattered all over our rooms, and take our dirty dishes to the sink. As our mother began to droop like a neglected flower if she spent too much time at home, we felt as if we were responsible.

The lessons continued, and after we had mastered how to float and tread water, Brucie taught us the crawl. One day, when he was correcting a flutter kick, I caught his eyes wandering from my sisters to rest upon my mother's bare stomach and full bosom, well displayed in her fashionable two-piece. By some sort of telepathy, Lilly's head tilted to the side and caught Brucie's eyes, and she waved back at him, her smile still unchanging. My mother was perfectly aware of the spell she had over men, and had perfected a certain look, as if she were sometimes apologizing for it, peering down and then shyly raising her eyes. But in an instant, realizing that she couldn't possibly play down her effect, she smiled with a grand, open smile. Brucie sized her up the way I noticed some teenage boys looked at older women, testing their sexual power.

From time to time I ran into Brucie around the neighborhood, but I was embarrassed, quickly said hi, and walked ahead. At night, as I lay in bed trying to fall asleep, thoughts of Brucie rose to the surface from the underbrush of my mind.

Toward the end of August, Brucie sometimes stretched out on a towel next to my mother while we continued to play in the water. He was the most beautiful boy I had ever met.

"Girls," Lilly called from the water one day. "Make sure you take a rest. I don't want you getting a cramp."

I resented when Lilly tried to treat us like children, and play the concerned mother, when at home she expected the reverse: *We* were supposed to take care of *her.* I knew what was going on. Brucie was hot for my mother, and she was milking it for all it was worth.

"Mrs. Crane, I've been thinking. I know you're alone, and, if you ever need anything, let me know. I'm just down the street. I can be over in a jiffy." By then I noticed that men offered favors to my mother that I suspected married women would have refused.

"What a dear," Lilly said. She sucked in her stomach when she saw Brucie admiring her figure. Lilly had an uncanny way of making a man divine her thoughts simply by the way she smiled. When a man, even a boy, gave Lilly some attention, she became transformed from the sunken, withdrawn self I saw when she did her crossword puzzles in front of the TV.

"Oh, I wouldn't think of bothering you. I'm sure a boy your age has plenty to keep him occupied."

When I got out of the water, Brucie patted me on the head. "You did good today, Anna Banana," Brucie said. Sitting on the blanket surrounded by rocks and cliffs, I hoped that in a few years he would flirt with *me*.

The next week, after swimming lessons, I went to Maria's house for lunch, but she had come down with a fever and her mother, who spent all afternoon chain-smoking Virginia Slims in the family room, her brain fried from so many rounds of shock treatments that her hands shook, sent me home.

I walked home counting the slate squares on the sidewalk. A jet flew overhead, leaving a white slash across the heavens. Goose bumps covered my arms. My eyes filled with tears, and a peculiar feeling came over me, like the time I had stared at the back of David Oppenheimer's head in school, willing him to turn around, and he did, asking if he could borrow a piece of notebook paper. But this time I didn't know what it was telling me. I climbed the front stoop of our house, opened the door, and walked in.

I picked up the newspapers and magazines strewn all over the floor and put them away. I smoothed out the sunken cushions on the couch and removed the empty glasses and breakfast bowls from the coffee table and placed them in the sink. I opened the refrigerator, took out the jars of peanut butter and jelly, and clanked them on the counter.

From upstairs, I heard my mother's bed creaking. I walked up the stairs to tell her I was home, but loud breathing and laughter coming from her room stopped me on the landing. I sat at the top of the stairs and listened to my mother's high, silly laugh and then long, deep moans. I stared at the white walls around me, smudged with fingerprints. The bedsprings creaked and rocked. My heart went crazy. I had to take long breaths to calm myself, and to block the sounds from behind my mother's door. I focused on the white walls until finally I lifted my mind from the throbbing that seemed to have penetrated to the floors of the house and was vibrating inside me.

I ran down the stairs and slammed the front door behind me.

I collapsed on the front stoop. A cool late August wind seeped underneath my shirt, sending a shiver through my body.

Once, my mother had taken us downtown to the tenth floor of a department store in the Terminal Tower to see Mr. Jingaling and his Magic Keys during Christmas vacation. We had ridden past the dilapidated parts of Cleveland, beyond houses without plates in the windows, where paint peeled off completely, leaving only the faint remains of its pink or green color, past the Show Palace Theater, XXXstasy, Cameo, Capri. The billboards plastered over boarded windows were of naked women dancing. One marquee read BIGGEST ADULT SHOW IN CLEVELAND, and showed dancing girls in black and red bikinis with pompoms over their nipples. I studied the curves on the women's bodies as Lilly concentrated on the road. What did men like so much about the naked bodies of strange women? I had the urge to dress my mother up in baggy clothes. It frightened me, this fascination men had with stripping a woman bare.

When I was older, I realized I had rarely been exposed to the way a man might care for a woman in a daily, average way. How he might kiss the back of her neck while she dried the dishes; or tug at the sleeve of her jacket if she stepped off the curb without seeing a car whiz by. The only kind of men I saw growing up were the ones who looked at my mother's legs too long, or kissed her till she was dizzy.

I heard the front door open. It was too late to run away. I was rooted to our house like one of the overgrown shrubs neglected in the front yard.

"Why if it isn't Anna Banana." There was only one person who called me by that name. The hairs stood up on my arms. Somehow, if it were Kent Montgomery or Steve Kennedy, I could stand it, but it was Brucie Johnson, the boy who had come to possess my thoughts, who'd been locked upstairs with my mother. Years later we would learn he was killed in the Vietnam War, but what I remember about him is the look of pride on his boyish face when he came out of our house that late summer day.

Lilly came down the stairs and followed Brucie out to the front step, where I sat. As my mother spoke, I clenched my fists so tight I nearly made myself bleed.

"Anna, Brucie was helping me put in the storm windows in my room. Isn't he a doll." Lilly's face was dreamy and flushed. But as she looked at me, I saw in her eyes that she knew I understood; and in those eyes I saw the turning away, the numbness.

Later that day, as I popped a TV dinner in the oven, Lilly petted my shoulder. "What's wrong, Anna?" she said. "It's not like you to be so quiet."

I shrugged. I couldn't even look at her.

"Anna, your old mom gets lonely in this house all day. Is that such a crime? Honey, you understand, don't you?"

+ + +

After I said good-bye to Austin the Fourth of July night, I found my mother downstairs in the living room. She was staring at her own reflection in the picture window, her body moving back and forth to the sound of the radio and wearing my new black dress.

"Mom, what's going on here?" I said.

"I didn't expect you home so soon, Anna." Lilly was completely out of it. Her movements were slow and clumsy. She glanced down at herself. "I hope you don't mind. I wanted to see if it would fit, darling, that's all."

The dress was something I'd saved for and bought on a layaway plan.

I went into the kitchen. I suddenly felt ravenously hungry. But after I opened the refrigerator, I noticed a bottle of pills my mother had left on the kitchen counter and next to it an opened, half-empty bottle of wine. My mother was high as a kite.

After I heard my mother go up to bed, I took the bottle of pills upstairs to show to Louise, but she looked so tired I decided not to worry her. I didn't want to think anymore about it. Before I got into bed, I noticed that Lilly had draped my new dress over the chair in my room. It reeked of her musk perfume. I threw the dress on the floor and climbed onto my bed and peered out at the dark branches outside my window. I followed the back-and-forth arc of the sprinkler, still watering the backyard in the moonlight, and allowed myself to be hypnotized by the motion. I tried to remember my father.

I longed to know the simple things about him: his favorite food, what made him laugh, the kind of clothes he liked. My mother didn't believe in cemeteries or graveyards, or places to honor the dead. After the unveiling, she never returned to my father's grave. Instead she made a mausoleum for him in our house. I was too agitated to sleep. I got up to go out.

"Where are you going, Anna?" my mother called after me.

"Just out." I closed the door behind me. I had no idea.

I rode my bike around the brick streets of Chagrin Falls.

Without realizing where I was going, I found myself in front of the gates to the Chagrin Falls Cemetery, where my father was buried. I thought about the dead bodies buried in those graves, and the souls that must be moving in the air around me. In the trees I thought I heard the sound of an owl. A feeling of long nostalgia folded into the metallic sky.

There was one memory of my father I had carefully preserved. It was the day my grandfather, my mother's father, had died. I remember how my father came into our rooms, took Louise in his arms, gathered Ruthie and me, and sat us on Lilly's bed. I could hear my mother weeping, her chest heaving up and down.

Lilly buried her face in her pillow. "Take them out of here!" she screamed when she felt the embrace of our presence around her. "I don't want them to see me like this."

I remembered my father's soothing voice.

"This is your family, Lilly," he said or at least, that's what I imagined he might have said. He reached for Lilly's hand and forced her to look at each one of us, as if, for a second, he believed she hadn't loved us. "This is why you'll wake up each morning, how you'll endure," he said. He turned Lilly's face to his, and when she tried to turn away again toward her grief, he took her back and calmed her. Lilly fell into his arms.

A year later, after my father had died, day after day I remembered that moment. Once it was his faint smile I held on to; another time his dark eyes; his wavy hair, the secure grip of his hand on my wrist. But that night, standing at the gates to the cemetery, I understood that all those nights I had talked to my father in my head, he hadn't heard me. I knew there was no point attempting to locate my father's grave. I finally put to bed a painful lie. Nobody was going to help us. I rode my bike back through Chagrin's wilderness, and before heading back home, stopped at a pay phone by the drugstore near our corner and called Austin.

We had worked out a code when we needed to speak to each other late at night when Austin was still living with his father. I'd ring once and then hang up, and call again, and Austin would answer on the first ring. I felt that anxious feeling in my body. That if I didn't see Austin, I would die or go mad.

✦ ✦ ✦

*T*he first time we went to Nonie and Papa's house after my father died, I was five or six. During the first year, we never left our house except to go to school or to the store with our mother. Lilly was tired all the time and mostly, when she wasn't looking after us, she needed to sleep. Lilly once complained that after the unveiling at my father's gravesite, the visits from our relatives and friends grew fewer and far between.

When we knocked at the door to our grandparents' house, Nonie opened the door and demanded, in her garbled English, that we give her a hug.

She and Papa had come over on the boat from Russia after the war. They had changed their name from Kranansky to Crane, afraid that a Jewish-sounding name would mark them. Nonie was short and round and wore her hair in tight curls around her head.

"How could it have happened?" Nonie said. "These small hildren." She burst into sobs.

In our grandmother's house we were quiet and withdrawn.

My sisters and I gave one another a look. We soon got used to Nonie's remarks. Every time we'd see her, even years after, it would be the same. You would have thought that my father had just died. We were always a reminder of what she had lost, and she couldn't see us as individuals, couldn't see beyond her missing son. But we couldn't blame her.

"Nonie, please," Papa said.

"Why did God choose to punish us? Haven't we suffered enough?" Nonie exclaimed.

In Nonie's house, that first time without my father, I watched my mother slowly take off her coat. With her head raised, as though it took all of her strength to stay composed, she smoothed the wrinkles from the black skirt clinging to her small hips and entered the room. My father, who, I thought, must have once hooked his arm in hers to escort Lilly from room to room, was now a shadow next to her. Grief, I learned, was private, like a forbidden secret. And we girls were nothing but a reminder to my father's family of the past, a nightmare they wanted to erase.

After my father died my sisters and I had unconsciously slipped into the role of Lilly's protector, asking our mother about her day when we came home from school, helping zip her into dresses, accompanying her to the market and the dry cleaners, kissing her before bed.

In my grandparents' house that day, I tried to stay close to my mother. I knew she felt uncomfortable. As my grandmother asked questions about how we were making out, I watched my mother's eyes wander to the window.

"You don't look so good," Nonie said. "Lilly, you look tired."

Lilly smiled. "I'm fine," she said.

Later, when I came out of the bathroom, I heard Nonie in the kitchen, where she had gone to get supper started. I heard her talking softly to my grandfather.

"Lilly doesn't look well," she said. "Gladys Weisberg had a nervous breakdown after her husband died."

"She's fine," Papa said. "You worry too much."

I returned to the living room and looked at my mother. She was staring out the window.

Outside, the first snowfall of the year had begun to whiten the landscape. I drew a picture in my mind of the house in Chagrin Falls when my father was still alive—the five of us netted and webbed inside the walls of our home. There was a perfect quiet. Nothing wavered or trembled or threatened to break loose. I imagined so hard, I could almost feel my father then, his warm touch.

During one visit to my grandparents' house when I was older, I made the connection for the first time that I was in the same house my father had grown up in. I walked into the guest room that had been his old room and saw his high school football trophies on the bookshelf. I wanted to be locked away forever in my grandmother's house with her ancient shawls hanging on hooks in the foyer, her prayer books and menorahs from the old country lining her bookshelves. Then my father was the god I prayed to at night, the star I believed was shining over me. In my grandmother's house, I felt the warm breath of my father fill the room.

Before we left, that first night at my grandparents' house after my father died, Nonie took me and my sisters aside and thrust a crisp twenty-dollar bill into our hands. She later gave us money every time we came to visit her. When we got home that day, Ruthie took her twenty-dollar bill and threw it into the toilet bowl.

"What are you doing?" Louise said.

"We don't need them," Ruthie said.

And one by one we followed, and watched as the three bills circled the toilet bowl and disappeared.

As I grew older I learned that my father's family would always feel sorry for us. Not out of spite or lack of love, but purely because of the tragedy we were plunged into, and for the truth: If you look long and deep into my eyes and the eyes of my sisters you will notice something askew—floating lost and unattached.

✦ ✦ ✦

After I called Austin I rode back home from the cemetery. Austin picked me up in front of my house a half hour later. It was after midnight. Everything quiet except for the pestering summer flies banging and twisting against the screens. I climbed into Austin's lap in the front seat of his car, and with my back pressed against the steering wheel, I held him. The important thing was that he was there when I called him. We watched the full moon emerge from underneath a cloud before we said good-bye.

"Mom, what are those pills for?" I said to Lilly the next morning.

"What pills?" Lilly said, playing dumb.

"These," I said. I held up the vial of Valium.

"Anna, they quiet my nerves, darling. They help me sleep."

"You need to get out of this house," I said. "Maybe that will help your nerves. Mom, don't you want to go out again? To see people?" Why couldn't she take a class, do volunteer work, take an interest in something outside of her own life? I didn't know how to help my mother. I could barely get her to go to the grocery store, and yet I knew she needed help.

"Nobody wants me anyway. Even if *I* did," Lilly said, looking at her reflection in the glass. "That part of my life is over. You know I tried, Anna."

Did my mother really believe that she was no longer desired? She was only, the summer I turned sixteen, in her late thirties.

Lilly sighed. "A woman like me is used goods," she said. "Don't worry, Anna. I don't care anymore. Really I don't."

But sometimes, when my mother didn't know I was watching, I saw her in her room, holding up one of her sleek dresses to her body, regarding herself in the mirror with the look of a woman who knows she's still desirable. And then another expression would flood her, the one she had on her face when she looked at a field of wildflowers, or our lawn covered with snow. Like my mother, I was dreamy and romantic. But unlike my mother, I feared my dreams and fantasies. I forced myself to be productive. I rearranged the clothes in my drawers. I lined up my books in alphabetical order in my bookshelf. I counted the tiles over and over in the bathroom until I was convinced I had gotten it right.

It still haunts me. The thought that a woman alone is like a kind of living death—that's how it felt being my mother's witness. Perhaps it was better to die, if you knew that in life you could never quiet the anxiousness inside you. Is it possible, I wondered, to be vital without physical touch or love? How long before desire, unfed, becomes dangerous?

+ + +

Lilly came home married. I was in fifth grade. She held out her slender arm and turned her hand palm down: a big diamond ring glittered on her finger.

"Your old mom got married today," she burst out.

She'd been shopping for a husband for nearly three years, but her efforts always seemed so airless, it was hard to imagine she'd actually land a man. I never thought my mother would really get married again. It was impossible to imagine how a man would fit into our house. It seemed, since my father had died, to have taken on the shapes and colors of a house that belonged to females: Lilly's floral prints and throws draped over the couches and beds, our undergarments and nightgowns thrown all over the place, Lilly's bras and lingerie drying on the towel racks in her bathroom, her makeup and age-defying concoctions occupying all the shelves in the medicine cabinet.

I remember my mother telling me about the day my father proposed to her.

"He chose me, Anna. He could have had anyone," she'd told me. Her parents had suffered so profoundly that my mother felt she could never make it up to them. Except in the marriage she made, the children she bore—these things, she felt, could make their survival meaningful.

Lilly had often shown me a photograph of my father standing in front of the door to his office. "This was taken the day your father picked up the Lawrence Crane Construction Company sign," Lilly said. "I was so proud of him, darling.

"I ironed your father a fresh shirt every morning," Lilly boasted. "Your father loved to feel the warmth of a freshly ironed shirt on his back." I could almost smell the hot, humid, burnt smell of Lilly's iron, hear the *tsh, tsh, tsh* of the steam catching on the cloth as she spoke.

"Come give the young bride a kiss," Lilly coaxed the day she came home married to Max. "Now we're going to have a man in the house. Aren't you happy for me?" Though Lilly had told us about Max, we had never met him. Lilly slipped off her pumps, slung them in her hand, and walked up the stairs. We shuffled behind her.

✦ ✦ ✦

*A*s the roses and lilies bloomed in our neighbors' yards, and you could smell the hamburgers and hot dogs cooking on barbecues, hear kids splashing in their wading pools, Lilly disengaged from the half-finished house-painting project, and left cans of half-empty paint, wet rags, and crusty dust cloths in her wake. In the heat of July, she began going through old boxes in the attic. She came down with her arms full of knick-knacks and small mementos and arranged them around the mantel of the fireplace in her bedroom.

That's where I'd find her. Up in her room for hours. Lilly turned on the phonograph in her room, and while some romantic piece of music—often a complicated piece by Chopin—filled the room, she worked steadily, single-mindedly. Sometimes she lived like a nocturnal animal, staying up all night and sleeping in the day. Around six or seven in the evening, she'd begin her breakfast; for days, she never left the house.

Through the half-open door, as I passed her room, I spotted her stop what she was doing, go to the window, and look out, as if she were prisoner to her memory. Then she'd shake her head and become absorbed again with the reminders of her past life.

Swatches of lace and satin went down first, then two candelabras, one for each end of the fireplace. Lilac-colored candles—ten apiece. She hung crystals over the opening of the fireplace, and when the light came in, or a wind, they twinkled. She strung the crystals on a taut piece of string as though she were decorating a Christmas tree. A fresh bouquet of wildflowers from the yard filled a vase or two. My mother had a mad passion for nearly every kind of flower.

She was building some kind of weird altar in her room: a football, an autographed baseball, a letter sweater, postcards sent to her from far away. She set out a bowl of trinkets, her jewels, and matchbooks from the many restaurants my father had taken her to filled another bowl.

Once, I found her lying on her bed, in another drug-induced daze, her door wide-open, forgetting her daughters were in the house. But it was worse than I'd thought. She was in some kind of white heat, rubbing her body back and forth against the bed, trying to give herself some satisfaction, comfort.

When I realized what she was doing, I quickly left the room and pushed the image far out of my head.

On her altar there were little dolls, a teddy bear, a heart-shaped silver ashtray, a music box, a feathered pen, a necklace with a gold Jewish star, her mother's sacred menorah. Books, valentines, empty boxes of chocolate. Heart-shaped cards, a silver key ring in the shape of her initial, and a gold locket with a picture of my mother's mother inside. Even the program from the golf tournament where she had met Max. Lilly had saved them all.

She had painted her bedroom in a rose hue, and the whole thing gave off an aura of something ancient, out of its time. My eye stopped at a picture of my father that Lilly had placed in an oval silver frame on the center of the mantel. This was the first time there had been a photograph of my father displayed in the house since he died. His pictures were always buried or tucked away in boxes or photograph albums, stuck underneath mattresses or inside drawers.

Lilly caught me looking at the photograph and said, "Think of all he has lost." Her eyes softened. "The dead must be filled with incredible longing."

The room for a second was so quiet, I could hear the dust settle.

"Why, Mother?" I asked.

"What is it, Anna?"

"Why have you saved all those things?"

"To remind myself."

"Of what?"

"Of all that was once mine." She ran her finger through a lock of hair. "People don't understand that the relationship with the dead doesn't go away. Nor the love. It's just so private now. People think we've forgotten. But we don't forget."

Lilly made her mantel ornamental, baroque, like some religious shrine.

"Mom," I tried one night, when I had come home to find her still up. "You need to learn to let go. Get rid of this junk." I wanted to run my hands across the mantel and let it all fall to the floor.

"Anna, what would you know about it?" She picked up the locket with the picture of her mother inside. "My mother was so sick when she died. She had so little of me," Lilly said. "When she found out her sister was shot down by a Nazi in the middle of the street where they used to jump rope, she was made ill from all her guilt. Imagine, one of your sisters gone, so you could go on? The people who survive the dead are the ones who are cursed. I was the one that should have died. Not my mother. Not after all she had been through."

It had begun to rain outside. I felt the lawn soften.

"The war took everything out of her," Lilly went on. "Imagine losing your own sister. Your entire family. I could never make it up to her."

"It wasn't your fault she died."

"Of course it wasn't, darling," my mother said, in a voice that belied itself as she looked at her mother's picture in the locket.

$\int$ummer's nearly over," Austin said. August had come already. Dusk folded its last light into the cold Chagrin River. He started the ignition. The car coughed and sputtered until the starter caught. Through the open car window I smelled the exhaust suck out the smell of honeysuckle and lavender. Austin whacked a mosquito on his arm. "Why so sad?" he said, glancing in my direction. He lifted my chin with the tip of his fingers and turned my head toward his. I smiled and planted a kiss on his unshaven cheek. I had to work on changing my mood. "Boys don't like an unhappy, sad sack of a girl," Lilly had warned me.

Before we backed out the driveway, I noticed that Mrs. Sawyer, who lived in the house south of us, was watching me from behind the sheer curtains of her upstairs window. Her daughter had committed suicide a few years ago. She was only thirteen. I could never walk past the Sawyers' house without feeling the weight of Mrs. Sawyer's grief. I knew she was always watching us, staring from behind a window or screen door when one of us left the house, imagining the shape of her daughter in our girth as we grew older each year. I thought about my own mother up in her candlelit bedroom, and her sadness. A part of me was happy to be leaving with Austin and another part wanted to stay home with her, hoping that my presence might ignite a spark of life inside her, but I also knew if I stayed home it would barely matter.

As Austin drove beyond the weeping willows and our house receded into the distance, I took the fresh air inside my lungs. I quickly glanced at my reflection in the side mirror of the car and ran my hand through my hair, my fingers catching in a stubborn knot.

We drove through the brick-lined streets of Chagrin Falls and smoked a joint. Heat rose from the pavement at night, and we kept the windows open for a breeze. The sky fell, and the emptiness that sometimes came with the loss of light, mixed with the joint, made me dizzy. I was relieved to be out of the house and into the August night. Summer was already losing its edge to the beginning of fall.

The season's loss was on the trampled-down lawns and dried-out sprays of wildflowers, in the sounds of insects, and the light roll of heat clouds in the sky. I took a couple more hits, and together we blanked out listening to the sound of a car coming down the block, or the screech of a cricket.

At last I turned my mind back to Austin. He was wearing a black T-shirt. The veins popped up on the inner seam of his arm as he leaned his elbow out the car window. He reached for my hand, lying lifeless on the car seat, as if he knew my thoughts, and I thought how lucky I was. How calm and still the world seemed just then.

✦ ✦ ✦

"What does Max do?" Ruthie asked, the day Lilly came home married. She was eleven. Lilly was frantically packing her suitcase. They were going to Niagara Falls for the weekend.

"He likes to play golf."

It turned out that Lilly had met Max in the Chagrin Falls Open Pro Tournament, which she had attended with another date.

"Where's he from?" I asked.

Lilly thought for a moment. "Come to think of it, I don't know."

"How old is he?" Ruthie said.

"What's he look like?" asked Louise.

"What is this? The Spanish Inquisition? I married Max because I'm wild about him," Lilly trilled. "This is a new day for us. You'll see. You don't know what it's like to have a man love you." She hugged herself. "There's nothing like it in the whole world." Still, a tinge of doubt lingered in her voice, as if she didn't quite believe what she was saying.

She married a non-Jew, the enemy, the unknown. None of the men Lilly had dated were Jewish. Perhaps it was her way of preserving the memories of my father: her private, unconscious rebellion.

I told myself I would ignore my mother when she came home from her honeymoon, but I knew in my heart I wouldn't. Lilly's happiness meant more to me than that. Through the slits in the bathroom door, I watched my mother wash her underarms and brush her hair. No matter how hard I wished, I could already see that my mother was prisoner to the man who would soon be living in our phantom father's house.

She came out of the bathroom and sat us down on her bed. "From now on we have to concentrate on making ourselves happy. Enough of these sad faces," she said. "You girls have to help me." She looked up at the ceiling, as if it were a direct pipeline to heaven, and said, "Dear God, please forgive me. Please tell me I've done the right thing." She hugged each one of us hard.

Lilly reached for a bottle of nail polish and handed it to me. As she held out her long fingers, I stroked polish onto her nails. The orange-alcohol aroma filled the room. The curtains billowed against the draft in the window. After I finished one hand, Louise fanned Lilly's nails dry with a Japanese fan Lilly kept by her bedside. We were our mother's daughters.

Suddenly we heard a knock at the door. My heart jumped. Max opened it and walked in.

"How's my little women?" Max McCarthy's voice bellowed through the house like a loud warning from a foghorn.

"Girls, go downstairs. Go on," Lilly said.

We looked at one another. "Go on," Lilly pleaded. "Go say hello to Max, this instant."

This was the first time we'd laid eyes on the man who would change our lives forever. Max stood in the hallway crammed with jump ropes, roller skates, hula hoops, high heels, and snow boots. He wore a dark overcoat and brushed the snow off his shoulders once he'd stepped inside. He carried a suitcase in each hand. The room filled with the wintergreen scent of aftershave. His face was red and sunny, unlike our dark and solemn faces. It was evident he didn't belong with us; I sensed it right away.

When he saw the three of us on the landing he put the suitcases down and held out his arms. Later I realized that he never brought anything to our house except what he came with that day. How did his whole life fit into those two bags?

After Max and Lilly left, I sat back in the chair in my mother's room and opened her nail polish. Its smell poisoned the room.

Max had hired a baby-sitter to look after us while they were gone. We missed my mother, but having her gone postponed

the anxiety I felt about what it would be like when she returned with Max. Men made me uncomfortable: their loud
voices, their callused, roving hands, their unpredictable behavior. I couldn't imagine what it would be like to share our house
with Max.

Our first night alone without our mother, Ruthie opened
her sleeping bag and stretched it over the floor between Louise's
bed and mine. I felt my mind and body relax—I lost all sense of
place, of who I was—I felt only the most fundamental knowledge of my existence. It was then when I first felt my mind and
all its complicated thoughts slip away from me. I closed my eyes
and felt myself floating in the realm of everything not of the
world. It was heaven, the world of stars and air and darkness.

✦ ✦ ✦

That summer night Austin and I spent hours driving up and
down the streets as if we were the sole people on earth, as if we
inhabited Austin's City of Nowhere. As we drove past the falls
that once powered the mills when Chagrin Falls was a boom-
ing mill town, I felt the history, with its well-kept houses and
tree-lined streets in the moist air. It was so quiet when Austin
pulled into the parking lot of the golf course at the country
club.

We got out of the car and walked across the flat greens,
guided by the light from an almost full moon. The last time I
had been to a golf course was when Lilly had taken us to watch
one of Max's tournaments. Austin hopped into a golf cart and
turned the key left in the ignition. I slipped in next to him.

In early September he was supposed to be going to Ohio
State to be a freshman in college. I still had one more year left

of high school. I felt I ought to talk to him about something important, but I already knew his family story, the kind of music he liked, the drugs he'd tried, his friends. I knew the glint in his eyes when he wanted to touch me. The way he bit his bottom lip when something hurt him.

"What was it like when your father died? It must be hard not to have a father," Austin said.

I looked at him. I never considered how I must have appeared to him. It made me embarrassed. "I don't think about it," I said. "It's just how it is."

From within the stillness of the golf course, the city beyond felt artificial and gray. I carefully watched ahead, as if I was navigating, as we went over one slope and down another. The moist air, the crickets in the trees, the smell of the moist lawn reminded me that soon Austin was leaving. I motioned for him to stop the cart. I stepped out and he followed, carrying an army blanket he had taken from the trunk of his car.

Before he spread out the blanket he pressed his sweaty body on top of me in the carpetlike grass so that I could barely breathe and could not think anymore. The humid air carried the scent of the slow decay of summer. On the slope of the lawn, abandoned white and fluorescent yellow golf balls glowed under the starlight.

Austin's eyes drifted to my breasts and bare legs. I reached out and held the muscles in his forearms, and let his lips touch mine. In the distance was the swish of water going over a man-built waterfall on the ninth green, going down, down, down, in long, smooth curves, down beyond the slopes, beyond the horizon, where the sun had fallen, splintering the sky in shards of color.

Austin opened his mouth to say something, but stopped. "What is it?"

"Anna," he began again. "I know we've only known each other…"

I put my finger against his lips. "You don't have to," I said. I was sure he was breaking up with me.

"No, listen to me. There's something I have to tell you." The circle of skin in the hollow of his cheek trembled. "I didn't know until this morning that it had happened. I woke up this morning and pictured you with another guy." His eyes drilled into mine. "I can't get it out of my head. If you met somebody else, I don't know if I could take it."

I felt that I hadn't known him at all. The details of his family, his friends, the kind of food he liked, his passion for horses, hadn't said anything to me really. There was so much more in his mind, thoughts that we never talked about, so much I might never know.

✦ ✦ ✦

When Max moved into our house, he was a complete stranger. All men were to us. But this one had taken hold of my mother.

Once my mother married Max, her drawers and closets were filled with new clothes, beautiful gold jewelry, long wool coats, and soft, fluffy new sweaters. Lilly no longer needed to spend hours getting ready before they went out to dinner or to the movies. The long, affectionate kisses Max gave her when he came home from work and the way he looked at her set flame to her beauty; around her was the warm feeling of being loved and cared for.

She bustled around the house cleaning windows, scrubbing the old linoleum floors, hanging fresh, new colorful drapes in our bedrooms. She bought flowers for the dinner table each night and hired a gardener to dig a new bed in the backyard.

That spring, Max hired a painter to paint the outside of the house while Lilly ordered workmen to take away the old swing set where we had spent many of our summer days.

I stayed in my bedroom and watched from the window as the men pulled up the rusted red poles, disconnected the disintegrating chains, and took apart the silver slide. After they had gone, I ran downstairs and out to the garbage can to rescue the splintered wooden seats, as if by keeping them I could still savor a part of our lives that was disappearing. I sat outside on the lawn as clouds surged over the trees, over the rows of houses on the block, and watched the setting sun. Watched it fall into the arms of the oak tree. I threw the wooden seats back into the waste can, and wandered toward the gazebo.

I sat on the bench, rested my back against the white rafters, and closed my eyes. The sky was pure and uncomplicated. The morning glories climbed the newly painted white house. Ivy circled the chimney. The laundry drying on the line puffed with wind and then flattened again. My mother's nylons and slips next to Max's white boxer shorts flapped in the morning air.

And now, like all the other children on the block, we had to be home at six o'clock sharp for dinner. I loved the new symmetry of order and routine, of knowing what to expect. I had quickly come to depend on it.

There were strange new meals staring at us from the new china plates. We sat quietly at the dinner table while Lilly and Max flirted.

"Girls, did I ever tell you the story of the first time I laid eyes on your mother?" Max said. "I was playing in the Chagrin Falls Open…"

"Max had a difficult time keeping his eyes on the ball,"

Lilly interrupted. "He leaned over and asked me for my phone number. The nerve of him," Lilly said, laughing.

"Golf was the only thing I ever loved passionately," Max said. "The quick snap of the swing, the grace of the putt, the skill and concentration. Until I met your mother."

Lilly stood up and massaged Max's shoulders. My sisters and I looked down at our half-eaten plates of food.

Lilly had decided to become a gourmet cook; the kitchen became a complicated storm of cookbooks, exotic spices, new copper pots and pans hanging from an overhead rack. My mother ran frantically around the kitchen before Max came home from work; then she'd dash upstairs fifteen minutes before he'd open the door, to take off her old sweatshirt and put on a cashmere sweater, apply fresh makeup, and return to the kitchen, fully composed.

At the dinner table Max set the tone. If he was in a good mood, he said, "Girls, this week I'm taking you out to dinner." When Max wasn't playing golf, he invested in start-up companies, once partnered in a restaurant. If he lost a deal, or money in the market, he was irritable and moody. "You girls have got to start cleaning your bedrooms," he'd say then. "I've never seen such a pigsty. Get your goddamn shoes out of the hall." He'd start as soon as he walked in the door. My father never swore. I never heard my grandparents or Aunt Rose say God's name in vain. Swear words weren't part of our vocabulary. But we didn't care if Max swore or told us what to do. It meant someone was paying attention.

"Oh, Max, stop it," Lilly said playfully, when he squeezed her knee or reached over and bit her neck. She was never happier than when his entire attention was fixed on her. We finally had a man in our house. I hadn't realized how much I'd craved it.

One night I was making small piles of peas along the edges of my plate while Max talked, like I usually did. Max's hand left the table to reach for Lilly's knee. Lilly got up and served him another plate of Caesar salad. She filled his glass with wine. "How about another slice of meat?" she asked, as she stabbed a piece of bloody rare roast beef with a serving fork and slapped it onto Max's plate.

After dinner Ruthie came into Louise's and my bedroom.

"I wish Lilly never married Max," she said. "I don't have a good feeling about him. As soon as I can figure out what I'm doing, I'm getting out of here."

"Can't you see how happy Mom is?" I was worried Ruthie was going to ruin everything. I was nervous around Max, but I was willing to risk the discomfort if it meant my mother was happy.

Just then Lilly opened the bedroom door.

"We're a real family now," she whispered. She was dressed in a sheer negligee. With ruffled hair and rosy cheeks, she yawned dreamily.

"Lilly," Max called from downstairs. "I just uncorked a bottle of port."

"Isn't he something?" Lilly blew us a kiss and rose to leave. After she closed the door, Louise crawled into my bed. She hadn't done that in years. Everything we had known before had disappeared, except the steadfast shapes of our bodies pressed against each other. Slowly the windows filled with dark funnels of stars.

+ + +

*J*ustin traced his fingers over my nose, eyes, mouth, as if he were putting me into his memory. Underneath the stars, on the green of the golf course, where grasshoppers rustled in the shadows, I felt as if I was in my childhood room again, huddled in the dark with my sisters in a place no one could tamper with or touch. I wanted to keep that moment in the Ohio night with Austin forever, so we would never be apart. "I wish we were ten years older," Austin said. "Do you think we'll know each other in ten years?"

Goose bumps went up my arms.

"Let's make a pact," he said. "Seriously. Sit up." I sat up on the damp grass in front of him. "Give me something of yours, something you're wearing right now."

I groped at my chest for the gold Jewish star Aunt Rose had sent to me for my sixteenth birthday. I unclasped the necklace and dropped it into his open palm. He slung off his wristwatch and handed it to me. "In ten years, no matter where we are, who we are with, we'll meet here and exchange them," he said. I felt two things. First, a kind of intoxication, because what he was doing felt so intimate; and second, anxiety, because he was admitting that we would eventually split up.

Austin grabbed my shoulders and eased me into the open grass. Stars shot across the sky. He kissed me so intensely I felt myself wilt, like nightshade, into the darkness. It was misty outside, the humidity breaking into a kind of rain without rain.

"Do you think we're going to break up?" I asked. "That something will come between us?"

"You never know, Anna," Austin said. It occurred to me that maybe he was thinking about how one day his mother was in the kitchen packing his school lunch, and the next she was gone. "Just in case something happens," he whispered into my hair. "I mean, I think we should try and stay together. Don't you?" I didn't have to ask him what he meant. I knew that time could change everything, or nothing at all.

"I'm not planning on leaving," I said. "We need each other."

He pulled me next to him. "Don't you get it?" he said. "That's what I don't like. That I *need* to be with you, and to wake up next to you." He looked to see how his words affected me.

I didn't know if I should be happy, or afraid, or sad. Austin's complicated emotions confused and excited me. In the back of my mind, I was always afraid that love was as thin as a rope unraveling.

Was it emotion, in the end, that led Cathy and Heathcliff to their downfall? Did Cathy really believe that by marrying Edgar Linton she was protecting Heathcliff? Or did she marry Edgar Linton out of selfish vanity? I told myself it was because she was afraid of the dark power Heathcliff had over her. She loved him, but could she wake up in the morning and share the breakfast table with him, and be beside him when they turned the covers down each night? I didn't like to think about it too hard. Even though I wanted Austin's love, occasionally a nagging question pushed itself into my consciousness. Aside from being adrift from our families, what more did Austin and I share, outside the heat that radiated between us?

I decided, as Austin held me, that if I had to describe what love meant, really, not in the abstract or the sentimental or the way I'd imagined it before, that I'd say it was completely irrational, made up of so many opposite emotions, the kind that couldn't exist without the other: bliss and sadness, courage and fear, adoration and disgust.

*O*ne night that August we went to the movies. Under the spell *Doctor Zhivago* cast, we walked down the deserted alley behind the theater. I wanted to stay in the cold, bleak landscape of the Russian countryside, Uri's mustache covered with frost, among the white sheets and pillows of the frozen bedroom, but Austin cornered me up against the cold brick wall and gripped my arms. Something was wrong. When our eyes met it felt like the danger of looking directly at a solar eclipse. Soon he was leaving Chagrin Falls to become a freshman at Ohio State.

"You're mine," he said. "I own every part of you." He worked his hands, beginning with my face, down my body. "These belong to me," he said, touching my breasts. He rubbed up against me. He kissed my neck, and underneath my hair.

"Stop," I said. He was moving too fast, and he was acting weird. The crowd was still letting out from the theater, people slowly making their way to their cars. But he didn't want to stop.

I took his hand and began to lead him out of the alley, back to the car. But he forced me back.

"Wait," Austin said. "There's something I want to give you."

✦ ✦ ✦

In those first months when Max came to live with us, he took charge of our house with such openness and determination to make things work, I liked him instantly. Of course, we no longer had to worry about whether we'd have something besides peanut-butter-and-jelly sandwiches for dinner, or whether my mother would be able to pay the mortgage. The very fact that our fears of survival were alleviated endeared Max to me. But I didn't know what he was getting out of the arrangement. I assumed he had to love my mother, knowing three young daughters came with the package. I felt it was my responsibility to make sure we wouldn't rock the boat.

One Sunday morning Max came home from his golf game with barrels and barrels of Kirby cucumbers filling his trunk and the backseat of the car. There had been a fire sale on cucumbers, he reported. He wiped out the entire merchandise from a farmer who had set up a stand on the highway.

"Lilly," he said, beaming, "I'm going to show you how to make my famous dill pickles." Max brought the barrels down the basement, and Lilly cleaned out the sink where she washed out her nylons and lingerie. Max unloaded one of the barrels into the metal utility sink. Lilly, with a pair of blue rubber gloves over her hands, scrubbed the cucumbers with a wire brush.

"These are going to be the crunchiest pickles you've ever tasted." Max smiled. He took me with him to the hardware store and bought crates of mason jars. By the time we got home, my mother had scrubbed only the cucumbers from one barrel.

It looked like an obstacle course in the basement. It was filled with hundreds of cucumbers.

While Max was at work that week, Lilly toiled down the basement.

"The recipe has to be perfect," she said. "Altering the proportions or diluting the acidity of the vinegar can prevent the pickling process."

"How do you know what you're doing, Mom?" I asked. Once Max had brought home the cucumbers, he'd abandoned the project to my mother.

"I called Aunt Rose. She used to pickle in the old country. Now, Anna, stop pestering me. It's important that I do this right." Lilly was soaking the cucumbers in a brine solution. Our basement smelled like vinegar.

"Why?"

"Anna, don't ask silly questions."

After my mother had the cucumbers soaking in the original barrels in a mixture of white wine vinegar, sugar, salt, and garlic, she began the long process of sterilizing the jars and lids in boiling water. Every countertop and the table in our kitchen were covered with mason jars. It was amazing, watching my mother so engrossed in a project other than herself. She ignored the ringing phone. Day and night she was in the kitchen or down the basement, except when Max told her to change out of her dirty clothes so he could take her to dinner.

One day, after the pickles had fermented, Max walked in the door, dropped his briefcase in the hall, put his fingers in a jar, pulled out a plump, pimply pickle, and held it to the light for inspection. He took a bite. "Your mother's a miracle worker," he said, and laughed a laugh that was filled with forbidden, unknowable things. Max converted the basement closet into a pantry. He made shelves for Lilly's jars of pickles. They spent an entire day downstairs, labeling the jars and stacking them on the newly sanded shelves.

During the weekdays throughout golf season, Max ran the clubhouse, organized tournaments, and gave private golfing lessons. He invested recklessly in the stock market. When one of his stocks performed poorly, he cussed out his broker on the phone. My family had always been frugal. There was a sense that one should hoard things for a rainy day, for the disaster that would eventually catch up with us. The same decades-old white chenille bedspread is still draped over Aunt Rose's bed in the retirement development in California, and lining her cabinets, the familiar porcelain china passed down from her grandparents.

Max was a man of excess. He wore lime green, yellow, or khaki pants and polo shirts, a different shirt for each day of the week. Each morning he announced what color shirt he had on. "Today I feel bright red," he'd say, tousling my hair. "It's going to be a great day, isn't it, Anna?" Then he'd pour himself another bowl of cornflakes. I had never seen anyone with such appetite. Sometimes I stared at the hardness of his chest underneath the blood-red polo. The colors of his shirts were a contrast to the drab blacks and grays that my sisters and I wore. I could see what my mother saw in Max. How he loved to have a good time, not to dwell on sadness. He lived each day in the present.

On Saturdays and Sundays when it wasn't golf season, Max and Lilly stayed in bed until almost noon.

"Now she sleeps in the same bed with him," Louise announced, like some kind of grand revelation, shortly after Max moved in with us.

"What did you think?" Ruthie said. We were all in Ruthie's room, sitting in a circle and picking dust bunnies off her faded pink carpet. Ever since Max had set our house in motion, we often stayed clustered in our bedrooms. The house no longer felt like ours.

"She's acting so weird," Louise said.

"She just wants Max to like her," I countered.

My mother had sat us down the night before and delivered a lecture on our table manners. "You eat as though you haven't seen food in years," she said. "You don't want Max to think you're not well-behaved young ladies, now do you?"

"Oh, I get it," Ruthie had snapped. "You want us to put on a phony show for him, too. Maybe I should tell Max that you never used to cook before he lived with us. That we lived on Campbell's soup and peanut butter sandwiches."

"Why do you have to be so hateful?" Lilly answered. "Why are you trying to ruin my happiness?"

Ruthie stared at Lilly, and then marched out of the room and slammed her door.

I didn't mind that Max slept with Lilly. I knew their bedroom was their secret place, and what went on in there was what held them together. But there was one thought that kept bothering me. Max now slept at night in the walnut post bed my father had once slept in. But, except for Max's clothes, there wasn't one article of furniture, one book or knickknack that belonged to him in our entire house. To us he was a man without a past. Where were his things? Didn't he own any books, any papers, any souvenirs or treasures? I didn't trust a person without any need for materials to mark their place in the world, to remind them of whom they cared for, or had once loved.

✦ ✦ ✦

*I*n the alley behind the theater, Austin took out a gray velvet box and opened it. He slipped a ring with a diamond chip— the size of the point of a pen—onto my finger. "As long as you wear this ring, you have to promise that I'm the only one allowed to do this."

He kissed me and as he did so he lifted my skirt and slipped his hands in my panties. I felt his erection build against my leg.

"Not here," I said, and pulled down my skirt. I was moved by the fact that Austin had given me a ring, but I couldn't shake the feeling that something bad was going to happen.

"I have to tell you something," he said. "Something important." He looked intense. I thought maybe someone had died. He pressed my back against the wall again and worried his tongue into the hollow of my ear.

"I'm blowing off school," he whispered. "I got a job full-time at the track."

I was stunned. He had talked a lot about how he wanted to learn to be a driver. All summer he had gone on about it, like a tireless monologue, but I'd always thought it was a pipe dream. It was clear to me from the start, that no matter how wild he wanted to be, Austin would get a good education, because his father could afford it, and that one day, years down the line, he'd end up being something conventional, like a doctor or a lawyer. That's why I could tolerate his working at the track, his gambling and getting stoned—because I knew that he came from a respectable family. It pissed me off that Austin was going to get his education paid for, and that didn't even matter to him. I was worried already about my future. I was saving my tips, hoarding away money, long before I knew what for. When he would talk about becoming a driver, I humored him. I never dreamed he'd actually do it. I told myself the idea was just a phase. That Austin would eventually get bored hanging out at the track and come to his senses.

After he told me about his plans to work at the track, his face relaxed. He started kissing me again. "Let's go back to the car," I said. I didn't know what else to say.

In the next few days, when Austin told his father he wasn't going to college, Mr. Cooper exploded and threw him out of the house. "'You're just like your mother,'" Austin mimicked his father when he reported the conversation. "'The two of you have no scruples. No respect for anyone but your goddamn self.'"

"I guess he's just worried about you," I said. It was night again and Austin had picked me up from work and was driving me home.

"That's one way to look at it. The truth is, he thinks I'm a loser."

Beep let Austin shack up in one of the larger tack rooms behind the stables. I was happy that Austin wasn't leaving town. That meant I'd have him with me during my last year of high school. But I also knew that at the track Austin was too easily influenced by the lowlife there. Austin didn't see the grooms and drivers, who, for the most part grew up in blue-collar families, as any different from himself. When he was with Beep, he began to talk like him, as if he'd never been educated. I didn't consider then that Austin might be rejecting his father's wishes out of some distorted sense of revenge.

After Austin began living at the track that August, he regularly disappeared. Then, out of nowhere he'd show up, crazy to see me. He'd walk into the diner, plunk himself down at the counter, and stare at me while I finished my shift. I might not have heard from him in three days. He'd crumple up the white sleeves he tore off soda straws and leave them all over the counter. Once, he almost got me fired because he wouldn't stop talking long enough for me to get the orders out of the window during the height of dinner hour.

He forced me to do things I'd never dreamed I'd be capable of. Once we left a motel room in the early dawn without paying. We walked out of a restaurant with the check crumpled in my shoulder bag. He followed me into the ladies' room in the back of a bar, locked the stall, and mauled me. At the movies he once figured out a way to get in without buying tickets. Once we made it to the dark seats of the theater, Austin put his arm around my shoulder and squeezed my knee. He liked the rush of it, the power he felt when he was breaking the rules.

After the movies one night in late August, we went back to the tack room. We sat in the middle of the concrete floor. He lit a candle and opened a couple cans of warm beer he tore from a six-pack. From outside, we could hear the clip-clop of horses walking, the swish of a groom sweeping out the stables, a horse's long, insistent whine. At the track the trainers walked the horses from the stables into the cleared, open fields where they worked them. You could hear their snorts and sneezes cutting into the thick night air. In my dreams later I could hear it, the sound of horse hooves on soft crumbling ground; then their wildness got under my skin, the dust in my hair and underneath my nails.

"I want you to show me that you love me," Austin said.

"Why?" I said. "You don't believe me?"

"You need to show me," Austin said. Since he'd been working full-time at the track, there was a layer of dirt on his skin and in his work shirts.

"Strip poker." He took out a deck of cards.

I tried to go along with Austin's mind-fucking games, because Austin seemed desperate that I prove myself to him. I told myself that I had it under control, that I didn't need to call him on it. He acted like he was trying to pay someone back for an injustice committed against him. At home, when I wasn't with him, I justified his behavior. I studied *Wuthering Heights,* the dog-eared pages smeared with Tab stains, trying to understand Austin's character.

"I know you're going to leave me," Austin said.

Austin was afraid I was going to walk out on him. If you even mentioned Austin's mother, his hands tightened into fists. The iridescent light in his gray eyes vanished. But I think it was more than his mother's leaving that had destroyed him. It was that she did not even care enough to call or write.

But I never considered that I might be the one to let go of Austin, though the way he'd been acting since he'd decided not to go to school—unreliable, irritable, dirty—had begun to turn me off.

"Okay," he said. He held out a fan of cards in front of me. "What do you have? Loser has to take something off."

I picked three cards and ended up with a pair of nines.

"Full house," he said, with one of his devious smiles.

I started with my shorts. It was summer, and I didn't have much on, only a cotton top, a pair of cutoffs, bikini panties, and undershirt. I didn't wear a bra very often, nobody did, unless your breasts were so big you had to.

"Three aces," he said in the next hand.

I had a pair of tens.

I never paid much attention to Austin's card games. They bored me, really. I wanted him to focus on the little mole on my neck or the ankle bracelet dangling against my heel. I tried to distract him by employing mental telepathy.

He popped open another can of beer and threw the empty one in the pile in the corner with the other empty cans.

I was in my panties, nothing else. He stopped dealing the cards, and just sat across from me staring at me weirdly. I reached for my tank top. Fear rushed through my body.

Austin yanked it out of my hand. "Wait," he said. "I want to just look at you." I felt his eyes run along my body. And then he started to cry. I cradled his head like you would a small boy's.

"What's wrong?" I asked.

Austin lifted his head from my lap and pushed me away.

"Who said you could move? Game's not over."

"Austin, what's wrong with you?"

"I don't feel it yet."

"What?"

"How you love me. What you'll do for me."

His face was moist with sweat. He had drunk too much. I could hear it in his speech, the carelessness.

"Take me home," I said, and reached for my tank top again. He grabbed it away from me.

"What the fuck are you doing?"

I tried to grab the shirt back, but he pushed me down. I fell back on the cement floor.

"Goddamn it," I said. "That hurt. You're hurting me." He had his hands around my wrists. He lowered himself on top of me. I could barely breathe. Then he stopped.

"I'm sorry, Anna," he whispered. His grip loosened, and I stopped struggling to get away.

"It's okay," I said. I understood how fierce his need for me was. I also understood that he hated himself for needing me. I held him as he fell into the soundless, timeless sleep of a baby.

+ + +

After Lilly and Max's first anniversary, she began to look small and self-conscious beside him. Perhaps she feared he was losing interest. He was spending more time away from home. She let him bully her. She felt she still had to put on a show to convince him that she was worthy of his affections. I saw through my mother's forced smile.

One day Lilly cornered me when I came home from school.

"Anna," she said. "If you were Max, what would you want from me?"

"What does that mean?"

"I'm not sure I'm making him happy."

"Mom, you're worried about nothing." She was getting on my nerves.

"Help me think of what I can make Max for dinner. Would you run to the store with me? Maybe I should take up tennis or golf. Anna, get your coat."

My mother dragged me all over town while she got her hair and nails done.

"Let me tell you something about marriage, Anna," she recited. "You can't just sit there with your arms crossed. You've got to protect it like you would a little baby."

When Max came home that night, she insisted my sisters and I go out for a hamburger. She and Max needed a romantic night alone together. Max scooped Louise up in his arms, then threw her on the couch and tickled her until she screamed. "Don't you dare hurt my angel," Lilly shouted playfully from the kitchen. "Anna, fix Max a drink."

Louise screamed again. "Max, let her be," Lilly called out flirtatiously. "My daughters aren't used to your roughhousing."

Now we had to be on guard for their fights. When Lilly and Max fought, they went at it so intensely that it lasted for hours. After they'd made up Max came into the kitchen and solicited our help while he cooked up plates of scrambled eggs, fried ham, and pancakes. Fighting with my mother gave him an appetite.

"Mom thinks Max doesn't pay her enough attention," I said, picking at my hamburger. We three sat around the brown linoleum table at Dink's and conferred. Lilly and Max were at war again; they had started fighting before we left the house.

"I don't care what she thinks," Ruthie said.

"He just needs some space," Louise said. "She gets jealous that he has to go out and make a living. Mom doesn't understand that he has other interests besides her."

"I bet he does," said Ruthie.

"What do you mean by that?"

"You two are clueless," Ruthie said.

We sipped on our milk shakes and picked at our fries until

we noticed, once the busboy began vacuuming, that we were the only customers left.

Max took us out to dinner on Sundays to the Hunt Club for a roast beef dinner. He liked us to dress in identical dresses and parade us in like his harem. Of course, Ruthie was completely disgusted. At eleven, Ruthie felt she was too old to be dressed up as if she was a little kid. But I didn't mind. I liked the orderliness of routine: clothes picked out for us, my mother at the head of the table next to Max, relishing that she was finally part of a couple. I didn't care if we were playing some kind of dress-up. My mother beamed. It had been so long since she had sat beside a man she belonged to by law.

I grew accustomed to Max's strong personality, his scent—the smell of Irish Spring soap on his skin—and began to trust him. I often sat next to him on the couch in the late afternoons, while he watched *The Honeymooners* on TV. When Jackie Gleason threatened to send Alice to the moon with his clenched fist, Max laughed so loudly he made me jump. But I stayed very still next to him, afraid that if I moved or made a sound, he would leave the room. I listened as the ice clinked in his glass of scotch, and smelled the warm liquor on his breath. I watched the TV blankly. When Max laughed I looked up at him and grinned.

"I'm making a leg of lamb with mint sauce for dinner," Lilly would call from the kitchen—or whatever special dish she was working on. Max was no longer infatuated with or surprised by Lilly's fancy meals. He had grown to expect them. Sitting next to Max, I could feel my mother, restless and impatient in the kitchen, waiting for Max's attention.

Sometimes I developed stomach cramps so severe that I had to lie flat on my back until they passed.

✦ ✦ ✦

*D*uring the day I slapped down plates of pancakes, sausage, and eggs, and in the evenings in August I went to the race-track with Austin and bet half my day's take on his picks. At night I curled myself against him on his thin, rusted cot and imagined I was happy.

And then, for days at a time, Austin disappeared. There was no phone at the track. It was too far to go on my bike. There was no way for me to get in touch with him. I wrote his name over and over in my journal and drew hearts next to each letter. I rode my bike past his house, hoping I might find his car in the driveway. I almost knocked on the door and begged Mr. Cooper to forgive Austin, just so that he'd come home.

Finally it was Labor Day weekend. I'd left the weekend open, thinking Austin would eventually call, but it was already Friday and I hadn't heard from him all week. As each day had passed and it grew closer to the weekend, I'd sworn to myself I would stop seeing him. I couldn't concentrate. I'd sacrificed my friendship with Maria for Austin, and now I realized how much I missed her. I plotted how I would break up with him. I enacted long scenarios in my head, as if I were writing a play. I composed profound soliloquies where I analyzed Austin's motivations and actions, and where, through logic and reason, I came out the winner.

Then Friday, on my way to work, I ran into Brian Horrigan. He asked me to a movie with him Saturday night, and I took the invitation as an omen, as if he could see just by looking at me that I was losing Austin. For the first time I regretted turning Brian down.

In the late afternoon Louise came home from practice, her hair still wet. Her swim team had already started its workouts. Her body was long and thin. There was a time I'd been jealous of it, how she could eat and never gain a pound, but seeing how thin she was that day, I felt worried.

She looked at me, sprawled out on my twin bed, and delivered a lecture.

"Look at you," she said. "Look what you're doing."

"What are you talking about?"

"I'm tired of watching you mope around waiting for Austin to call."

I hadn't realized it was so obvious. I was embarrassed she was calling me on it.

"You should talk," I said. "You're the one we should be worried about. Look how thin you are." I took my sister's problems as a personal betrayal. "How come you're not going out with anyone? I know Todd likes you. What are you afraid of?"

"I don't think you should be giving advice on boys."

"What's that supposed to mean?"

"At least I have something I care about," she said, meaning swimming. "You're pathetic."

"It's better than pretending not to need anyone," I shot back. But her comment stung. I told myself that when Austin called, I would blow him off. Louise and I rarely quarreled, but that night we turned our faces to opposite walls and went to sleep without talking anymore.

As if I sensed he would come, I awoke as the light of dawn pressed against the window. From beneath the cracked shade, I made out Austin's Mustang in our driveway. He tapped at the windowpane of our front door. I flew down the stairs, still in my nightgown, and let him in, and we moved to the couch. "Come here," he said. "I want to hold you." I drew gentle circles with my finger on his back and told him I was glad he'd come. I didn't understand why Austin went so hot and cold, but the inconsistency in his character was a puzzle I was determined to figure out. I rationalized Austin's behavior, even though it was scaring me.

As we lay on the sofa, I tried to forget I was angry, but then I smelled liquor on his breath and the acrid stench of marijuana smoke in his hair. "Where were you?" I was suddenly fired up.

"Working."

"How come you didn't call?"

"I talked to you the other day."

"It's been almost a week."

"Anna," Austin said, his fingers gripped in my hair. "I'm here now, aren't I? It can't just be about you," he said. "I'm on my own now. I have to make some money. Can't you understand that?"

My mind went blank. All the profound and elegant ways I'd imagined I would tell him off had faded. I let him continue to touch me, just so I could go down with him to the black pond, a kind of oblivion, where time for a second stopped.

✦ ✦ ✦

On their second anniversary Max flew the family to Miami Beach to meet his mother. That he had waited two years to do this should have registered, but I was oblivious to how a man's history could shape him in the present.

Mrs. McCarthy remained seated on a leather chaise longue while the maid showed us in. She wore a pink Chanel suit that clung to her tiny, emaciated frame. Her cigarette dangled from a gold cigarette holder. When Max bent over to kiss her, she took a meditative drag from the cigarette and gave him her cheek. His very presence seemed to disappoint her.

"Max, you've got yourself quite a handful," she said, looking us over from top to bottom. Max tried to make her laugh, but everything he did, down to the way he swirled the scotch in his glass and paced the floor, annoyed her. I caught his eye and smiled at him. I felt sorry for him. Everything about his mother's house, from the nautical pattern on her dishes, to the formal Chippendale furniture, to the lime and rose colors of the pillows and wallpaper, was different from the world I had been raised in.

"What have I done?" Lilly asked, after dragging me with her to the bathroom.

I watched in the mirror as she carefully arranged her hair with her fingertips.

"I don't want to talk about it," I said. I was furious with my mother. Didn't she see that Max needed her to be supportive?

"Before you get married, promise me you'll meet his mother first, Anna. You can tell everything about a man by his mother. Don't make my same mistakes, darling." Lilly dotted on fresh lipstick and blotted her lips with a Kleenex.

"It's not Max's fault," I said. "He didn't choose her."

"I suppose you feel that way about me, too," Lilly said.

I looked away.

After we returned to the living room, Max's mother pulled out her photo album to show Lilly the rest of the family.

"Who's that?" Lilly said.

"Johnny. Max's twin."

Lilly looked surprised.

Max took another sip from his drink and looked out the window.

"Max never told you?" Mrs. McCarthy asked critically. "The boys were bumper hitching. A truck sideswiped them. Johnny was killed instantly." Mrs. McCarthy poured herself another glass of scotch. Her thin body was so brittle, it looked as if she might snap.

"I'm sorry," Lilly said. She reached over and squeezed Max's hand.

I was relieved when Mrs. McCarthy stood up and announced that she'd better start on supper.

I pushed my mother forward to encourage her to follow Mrs. McCarthy through the pink parlor into the kitchen and offer some help. It annoyed me that she hadn't thought to do it herself. The point was, whatever I thought about Lilly's and Max's marriage, I was worried that she was going to ruin the only stability we'd known since my father died.

As far as I was concerned, the world was ordered in two ways. The world of women and men, and the world of women without men. Now that Max lived with us, there was a certain symmetry to our lives. When Max had entered the picture, our world became tame and manicured. At first it was as if I had walked into a museum, I was so transfixed by beautiful objects I was afraid to touch, lest they break and shatter into a million pieces. I knew what it was like now to have balance in a house. To not feel everything was slipping into a pool of emotion. Now I thought I understood the chemistry between a man and a woman, what the combination could do.

Even though the trip had been a disaster, once we got back home, they seemed closer. Maybe Max had realized how much he needed my mother. Perhaps Lilly felt sorry for Max, once she had learned about his lost twin brother. Regardless, inside the walls of our house was the smell of my mother's perfume, mixed with the liquor smell from their breath, the damp smell of sex—I felt the warmth of their bodies over my sleep all night long. I stopped trying to shut out their sounds in their bedroom. Now, deep in the night, through the walls, I listened for Max's snoring, the great dark voice of his sleep that rose and fell in my dreams. The house echoed with the almost horsey gasps of air going through his thick nostrils; his snore was a deep hum, a music box whose song I never tired of.

✦ ✦ ✦

As Austin grew more involved in the insular world of the track, and less attached to the world outside, I began to worry. I told myself I had to try harder to understand him. One Saturday afternoon I told him I wanted to spend the day with him at work and arranged for someone to cover my shift at the diner. I sat on a stool in the corner of the stable as he brought in fresh hay for the horses and began to pick his brain.

"So what's the goal?" I said. "I mean, what are you trying to get out of this?"

"What do you mean, Anna?"

"I mean, is it just to have the fastest horse? To win the most money? I thought it was the horses you loved. But from what I can see, it's really all about commerce." I had been studying the owners as they came by, how they studied the program, then cussed out the grooms and trainers if the horse the night before hadn't lived up to expectation.

"Sometimes passions don't make any sense. I didn't think you'd understand."

I thought for a moment. "I just don't know whether you'll be happy here in the long run," I said, listening to the horse in the stall go at a salt lick with his tongue.

"I might not be. But I have to give it a try. I'm not a shirt-and-suit guy, Anna."

Jane Smart poked her head in and said hello. Austin went out to bring in another bale of hay. I overheard the two of them talking outside about getting together to go riding. When I confronted Austin about it later that day, he shrugged it off, but I sensed the chemistry between them. Maybe Austin was right. Maybe the track life wasn't so bad for him. After all, he was only seventeen.

That night Austin had money on a horse called Silver Lightning. We sat next to each other and held hands. All that day after I had given up on trying to discourage Austin from staying at the track, I felt closer to him. I watched how seriously he took his job, how patient he was as he rubbed salve on the raw sore on the leg of Midnight Magic, the barn's prize horse, and then wrapped it with a bandage. He knew the peculiarities of each horse in the barn—which one preferred an apple, or a sugar cube, how gently to tap the whip on a trotter's back, how to cool a horse down just right before bringing her back to the stable.

We sat by ourselves away from the crowd, in the dim corner of one of the bleachers. Austin put his arm around my shoulder and told me he was glad I had spent the day with him. "Do you want to make me *really* happy?" Austin said playfully. He placed his hand on the back of my neck and lowered my head into his lap. During the race, just as Silver Lightning was neck and neck with another horse around the last turn, I sucked him off. Austin dared me. He said it would bring him luck. And he was right. That night, for the first time in a while, he had a winner.

*T*his is where everything falls into place, like water absorbed into sand. Every story has a point of no return, where something irrevocable happens, where events unfold and spin out of control and determine each character's fate. In *Wuthering Heights* it is the moment Cathy marries Linton. For me, it was when I refused to see the signs of trouble that were staring me in the face. I wanted to have control over my emotions, but my body and mind were at odds. I listened to the way the wind spoke to the leaves, to the sound of water rushing over the falls, crushing the pebbles and rock, but I could not listen to myself, because every thought and feeling changed from one moment to the next, depending on what Austin had said or done. I saw nothing I did not want to see. I ignored the intensity throbbing in a boy's neck, the movement of a woman's body when she was restless, the repetition in our histories. I decided to see, feel, and hear only what was in front of me, like a horse with blinders on raging toward the finish line. I just didn't know what I was racing to or from.

The first week in September, just as school had begun, I woke up in a cold sweat. I developed an acute sensitivity to smells. The sour odor of an open refrigerator brought me lurching to the bathroom. I was nauseous all day. I knew Austin and

I should have been using birth control, but we'd gotten care-less. I wanted to believe that what was between us—curvy and complicated as an endless road—was so strong that none of the rules mattered.

I knew about the womb, shaped like a pear, which sheds its lining every month. That blood is food for a baby. I knew that all it takes is one of thousands of sperm to put a pinprick in-side an egg, and then the cells would multiply. That Septem-ber I waited for the feel of my womb contracting, releasing the egg that ripened inside me that month. I waited for the feel of my womb's lining shedding the way you wait for the wind on a humid day.

Soon Aunt Rose called long-distance to wish us a happy New Year. It was Rosh Hashanah. Eight days later it would be Yom Kippur. "What do you want God to forgive you for?" Aunt Rose asked. She asked each one of us this question every year.

There was only one thing I could think of, but I couldn't dare tell Aunt Rose. Since my grandfather passed away, Aunt Rose had become active in charity foundations. She had a small pension from all the years she'd worked at the bank. Nothing seemed to rattle her solid constitution. But I believed if I told her I might be pregnant, she'd think less of me.

"Put your mother on," Aunt Rose said finally. "Maybe this year will be her year. When God closes a door, a window opens. Your poor, poor mother," Aunt Rose said.

Before I handed Lilly the phone, I spoke briefly to Ruthie.

"How are you guys doing?" she asked. "I miss you two."

"We miss you, too," I said. I didn't think I could confide in Ruthie either. I was afraid to say out loud what was troubling me, what was happening, not only to me, but to my mother and Louise. I was the kind of girl who always hoped to catch someone's eyes, to hope someone else might fish out what was wrong with me, but never dreamed of offering it. And a part of me still believed that if I could deny what was happening to my body, I could make the nut-sized embryo attaching to my womb disappear. I handed Lilly the phone and went into the bathroom for the tenth time that day to check my underpants for blood.

On Yom Kippur, which fell in early September that year, I fasted. I thought that maybe if I repented, restored my covenant with God, he'd void the secret buried inside me. But there wasn't going to be a miracle. If God worked in mysterious ways, his plan hadn't revealed itself to me, though I tried to look for meaning in the pattern of the stars in the night sky, or the map of fading daisies in the field beyond our house. My period was faithfully regular, and I was already two weeks late.

✦ ✦ ✦

The leaves had begun to turn color and were falling off the trees. It was a bright, crisp autumn, late afternoon. Ruthie was fixing her bike in the garage. I was reading in the gazebo.

"It's a goddamn beautiful day for baseball," Max said as he came out the back door into the yard. He put his can of beer on the ground. His face looked flushed and puffy, but it wasn't the kind of red you get from a suntan. Every day, the moment he came home from work, before changing his clothes or saying hello to us, Max took a beer from the refrigerator or made himself a cocktail. He'd continue to drink throughout the evening, sometimes substituting a glass of red wine, or an after-dinner port.

With a phantom golf club in his hand, he practiced his swing.

"Let me give you a hand, sweetheart," Max called to Ruthie, where she was working on her bike.

"You don't have to," Ruthie said, yanking out a lock of hair that had gotten tangled in the spokes of her front wheel. She was in that awkward stage where a girl is no longer a child, but not quite a woman. Her sweater crept up when she raised her arms, and revealed a sliver of her stomach. Her nose was covered with uncountable numbers of freckles.

"What do you mean I don't have to?" Max cleared his throat and walked toward her. "Of course I don't have to." He knelt down and pinched the tire with his fingers. "This looks beat. When's the last time you put air in the tires?"

Ruthie glared up at him.

"I'm on to you," Max said, his voice bouncing off the garage walls. "Don't think I don't know what you're trying to do."

Ruthie's dark hair had been tinted red by the sun, and was brushed behind her ears. "I don't know what you're talking about," she told him.

"You're wasting your energy. There's no way you're going to sabotage this thing. There's no goddamn way in hell."

Ruthie gave him one of her famous I-can-see-through-you looks.

"I'll make a deal with you," Max said. "If you don't want me to be your father, I can accept that." He paused. "But I think we ought to manage to be friends." Max waited for a response. When he got only a blank face, he added, "You're upsetting your mother."

"That's too bad," Ruthie said. She flung back a lock of her hair.

Max grabbed her wrist.

"I don't ever want to hear you talk about your mother like that. She's been through a hell of a lot."

"You're not my boss," Ruthie said. "You can't tell me what to do. Let go of me."

From the gazebo I was watching them as if I had been stopped still in a game of freeze tag. I swatted a fly that was buzzing around my face.

"No one asked you to live here," Ruthie said. She jerked her hand away from Max. "This is our house, not yours."

I stepped out of the gazebo and walked across the lawn.

"Is that right?" The red in Max's face spread, like a complicated rash, to his neck. The muscles in his jaw tightened. "I married your mother, and whether you like it or not, you're stuck with me. You better learn to like it, is that understood? I love your mother," Max continued. "Is that so terrible?"

"That's between you and her," Ruthie said. She threw out her chest, which had just recently changed from small, swollen-looking bumps to bosoms, and began to walk away.

Max kept after her. "I need this like a hole in the head," he called. "If you think I'm going to stand for this, coming from a snot-nosed brat, you've got another thing coming." Max caught up to Ruthie, grabbed her by the wrist again and twisted it. "Don't you walk away when I'm talking to you!" he said. "You're screwing things up, do you know that?" Ruthie struggled to pull her arm away. "What you need is a good kick in the pants."

I tried to catch her eye, hoping she'd back off.

"Let go of me!" Ruthie shrieked. "You're hurting me."

Lilly, in the new yellow sports car Max had bought for her, pulled up the driveway. I was relieved. She stormed out of the car. "What do you think you're doing? Don't you dare lay a finger on her."

"Now I'm going to get it from you, too?" Max took Lilly in with his piercing ice-blue eyes. "No sir. No sirree, bob." He turned away from Lilly and walked down the driveway toward his car, which was parked on the street.

Lilly tripped over her heels as she ran after him. "Max, where are you going? Don't you dare leave." She tugged on his sleeve to pull him back. Max drew up his arm as if to hit her and then stopped himself.

"Don't touch her!" Ruthie shouted. She flew down the driveway after them. Max slapped Ruthie across the face so hard she couldn't talk.

Max got in his car and slammed the door. Lilly banged on his car window. "Roll this down. I want to talk to you." He ignored her. "Max, where are you going?"

"None of your goddamn business." He revved the engine. Lilly clung to the car door by its handle as he began to pull away. "Please, Max, I beg you!" she called. She was still standing at the end of the driveway as his Lincoln screeched around the bend. "Don't do this to me," she said, more quietly. "Don't you dare."

✦ ✦ ✦

For days I hid the truth from Austin about the embryo growing inside me, its cells multiplying and dividing secretly, independent of my will. I sequestered myself in my room and spent hours staring out the window, trying not to think about the sensitivity in my breasts, which felt as if they were being pricked from the inside. Instead I thought of Austin and me lying in the grass in the fields outside the track, the little wombs of light from the fireflies coming out in the darkness, blinking on and off like some indecipherable Morse code. But the memory quickly vanished, and I grew anxious again. I paced the carpet in my room, wondering what I was going to do.

A few days after Yom Kippur, I finally confessed to Louise

that my period was late—I thought I would go out of my mind if I didn't tell someone—and she accompanied me downtown to the free clinic to get a pregnancy test. We'd heard that Nancy Newby had gone there to get an abortion. I took out the robin's egg that I had found months before with Austin, wrapped it in tissue paper, and put it in my shoulder bag for good luck. I was like a mother who keeps her kids' tiny drawings tucked in her back pocket, as if the thin piece of paper might keep the children from harm. But I didn't have to wait until the pregnancy test was confirmed. I knew I was pregnant. I knew almost the morning after it happened. The embryo had clutched onto my uterine wall like a desperate hand, unwilling to let go. And yet, like everything else that summer and fall, I tried to push away what I didn't want to see.

Meanwhile, my mother was absent from us. Not even the sun filling our living room in midday could coax her out of herself. Lilly occasionally came downstairs to prepare a plate of food, get the newspaper, or inquire passively where we were going, though once we told her, the details slipped from her mind. She took up the painting project haphazardly; then, as if she'd grown bored staring at her color samples, she retreated to the solitary cave of her room. It never occurred to me to ask for my mother's help. She was so incapable of handling her own life, I didn't dream of complicating her worries with mine.

"You should tell Austin you're pregnant," Louise insisted. We were on our way home. The downtown smog stretched before us. I listened to the sirens wailing, the low rumble of the Rapid once we'd gone underground, the dull sounds of a car backfiring when we reemerged into the bright light from the subterranean depths. It was early September, but during the day the temperature was still in the eighties, though by then I was tired of it, the heat and humidity, the summer's lost promise. The birds were restless in the trees, waiting to leave.

"He should know," Louise repeated.

"He can't handle it," I told her. The train screeched around a turn. "He's got enough of his own problems."

Austin had been going on drinking binges. He guzzled down beers, bit into a lime, knocked down shots of tequila or peppermint schnapps. He could drink steadily all day, and you'd barely notice he was drunk. Then, at night, he'd crash. Sometimes he slept for twenty-four hours at a stretch. He looked like he was going to jump out of his skin. Since he'd been living at the track, he barely washed his clothes. When I'd first met Austin, I saw the effort he made to spend time with his father. When he was living at home, he rarely cut classes, was always on time to pick me up. He cared about how he looked and what he wore. I was sorry he and his father were not speaking. I thought that maybe, if his father were in his life again, he might be able to turn himself around. I rationalized that Austin was in a funk. That once the season broke and classes had started he'd get serious about his life and wish he was going to college.

I put my hands over my stomach, as if I was protecting my baby. I had never done anything exceptional in my life, and carrying this baby, even though I was only six weeks pregnant, felt exceptional. I wondered how Austin would react when he learned I was pregnant. The sun slowly sank into the horizon, coloring the sky with an intensity so original and fundamental, I felt immobile watching it.

"Well then, maybe we should tell Mom," Louise continued.

"Are you crazy?" I said. "What good would that do? I don't want to worry her."

I listened to the sound of metal against the tracks as the Rapid made another turn. I thought of the anonymity of the city as we rode beyond the maze of buildings at the edge of downtown. I thought of all those people who lived in cramped apartment houses, and ate meals in tiny kitchens and didn't even know one another. Didn't even feel they had to nod when they passed on the street. I thought of all those men and women dressed in suits on their way home from their offices, sitting with us on the Rapid, and I longed for that feeling of being unknown as I watched the birds skit from tree to tree outside the transit window. I sensed that years from then I'd be able to read the situation I was in. But then I hadn't a clue what I was doing.

Louise and I were sitting behind two women whose overflowing shopping bags from Halle's crowded the aisle. I hungered for the simple pleasure of shopping.

"If Mom finds out she'll blame it on Austin," I said, still trying to convince myself I was doing the right thing.

"So what," Louise said.

"Louise, promise you won't tell Mom."

"You know I won't, Anna. I'm just worried about you."

"Nothing's going to happen to me." I began to feel nauseous and opened the window.

"Anna, take it easy," Louise said. She pulled the hair back from my face. "Sit back. You look pale as a ghost." Below the tracks, rock crumbled under the motion of the iron wheels. By the time we arrived at the end of the transit line and boarded a bus home, the birds had quieted.

✦ ✦ ✦

It was essential for Max to feel idolized, adored, and in control. It pissed him off that he had no persuasion over Ruthie. That even his simple gesture of offering to fix her bike had seemed to her a violation. But, unfortunately, Max was not the kind of man who was able to look past his own hurt pride, and consider that Ruthie's behavior might have nothing to do with him, that she was simply not willing to give up our father so easily.

To apologize for slapping her, Max went out and bought Ruthie a brand-new, top-of-the-line ten-speed bicycle. "I didn't realize the strength of my own hand," he told her. But Ruthie could not be bought. She kept the new purple bike in the back of the garage and continued to ride her old one.

The war between them escalated. One day Max asked her to answer the phone. He was fixing a stopped-up drain in the downstairs bathroom. She turned up the volume on her stereo and pretended she didn't hear him.

From down in the cool basement, where Louise and I were playing cards, I heard Max yell up the stairs to Ruthie. Lilly was out running errands. "Goddamn it, Ruthie, I said answer the goddamn phone." His temper shook the house.

Max stormed up the stairs, opened the door to Ruthie's room. Louise and I heard a blast from her stereo, then instant quiet, except for the incessant ringing of the telephone, and the sound her body made on the hard wood as Max dragged her into the hall.

"Next time you goddamn answer the phone when I tell you to, do you understand?"

"You can't tell me what to do!" Ruthie hollered.

"You bet your pretty ass I can," he said. "I'm sick and tired of your prima donna routine. Who do you think you are?"

"Ruthie Crane," she said. "No relation to YOU."

"As long as you live in this house, you do as I say, do you hear me, young lady? I'm not standing for any more of your bullshit, understand? It's about time you girls were disciplined."

"Take your hands off of me!" Ruthie shouted.

The phone rang and rang.

Ruthie's screams were piercing. The phone continued to ring until Max kicked the stand where it perched and it fell to the floor.

When Lilly came home Max was in a foul temper.

"I'll talk to Ruthie," Lilly said. "She's having a hard time adjusting."

"A good slap in the face would teach her a thing or two," Max said.

"Please, Max, don't," Lilly said. She caressed his back. "She's just a kid. She needs a little more time."

Lilly went to sit in his lap, the way she used to when they'd first gotten married.

"Get away from me," Max said. "I don't feel like it now."

"Please give Max a chance," I heard Lilly plead to Ruthie, after she went upstairs to console her.

"He's crazy," Ruthie said. "Just because you like him, doesn't mean I have to."

"Ruthie, you have to look at it from Max's side. He's not used to a house full of girls," Lilly said.

Louise and I opened Ruthie's door and plopped down on her floor.

"Ruthie, please forgive me," Lilly said. She tucked her face in the palm of her hand and began to cry.

"He's no good, is he?" Lilly said.

"He's not so bad," I countered.

"Mom, maybe you shouldn't have married him," said Louise.

Lilly wiped the tears from her face with the sleeve of her sweater. "Don't worry, girls," she said. "I'm going to make this work. I'm not going to let you down." She gave each of us a kiss.

"I have to go," she sighed. "I have to go make Max happy."

After Lilly went back downstairs, we heard occasional loud wails of laughter break the silence in the house. Max was downstairs with a six-pack of Canadian ale and bowl of the big salty pretzels he liked, watching *The Red Skelton Hour.*

Later that night, before I drifted off to sleep, Lilly came back upstairs and wandered into our room like a restless child. She sat down at the foot of my bed.

"Is everything okay, Mom?" I asked.

"Louise was right, Anna," Lilly whispered, glancing over at her. Louise pretended to be asleep. "I didn't want to admit it in front of Ruthie because she's having such a hard time. But I never should have married Max."

I didn't want to hear what my mother was saying. "He doesn't know how to touch a woman," Lilly said. "He's always so rough. My mother never would have approved of Max. She didn't trust anyone who wasn't Jewish. Can you keep a secret, sweetheart?" Lilly said.

I felt a knot form in my stomach.

"When my mother was in hiding from the Nazis, the priest forced himself on her. He made her sleep with him once a week, after Sunday Mass. My mother whispered the story when I went to sleep at night. She wanted me to make sure I understood how important it was to tolerate a man's needs."

Did Lilly mean that Max was forcing her to have sex with him against her will? I don't think my mother really understood what she was saying. All I knew was that she'd gotten in over her head with Max, and she didn't know what to do or how to handle him.

"My mother never told my father what she'd done in hiding. She was afraid, if he knew, he wouldn't want her. She told no one. Until she couldn't keep it quiet anymore."

"Mom, you're not in hiding," I said. "You can escape."

Lilly just looked at me.

"You have my mother's eyes," Lilly said, like there was no fleeing our history.

Despite my mother's confession about Max, I had begun to form an attachment to him. Their marriage wasn't perfect, but my mother was functioning. She wasn't living in a dream world. That night my loyalty began to shift. I harbored fantasies that Max would take me away with him. We'd move into our own apartment, without my mother or my sisters. I hadn't been around men very much in my life, except for the parade that had come in and out of our house, and Max fascinated me. I liked the way he could take me out of myself, make me forget who I was or where we came from. Even when Lilly tried to distract us or console us, you could still feel the weight of her troubled history in every word she spoke. There was always a dark undercurrent of feeling when we were with our mother.

When we were younger, Lilly had taken us for long drives in the car. As we drove along the Chagrin River, I smelled the rusted scent of the Ohio wind through the windows. In the winter it was too cold to walk barefoot in the high, scratchy grass, play in the fields, feed an apple or a handful of sugar cubes to the horses that ran in the fenced-in yards we would pass on the way to school; they were mostly under blankets, boarded inside the barns. But no matter what season, there was always the river—I tasted it in the drinking water, felt it in the damp air as I bathed. I felt blessed by it when there was nothing else, and came to think of the river like a lost father—a soul or spirit. I loved the richness of the countryside, the acres and acres of wooded land, the falls and the river; I felt them in my flesh and bones, their freshness crept into the color of my face and folded itself inside the clothes I wore. I used to dream of following the creek, moving through the brush and pine, using a branch as a walking stick, until I arrived at the great heart of the river. On the other side I imagined a secret paradise different from what we could glimpse of the river from the gazebo, built on a small incline in our backyard, where I kept watch. Sometimes I imagined our white house, with its black shutters, to be a marooned boat, flooded and warped, rocking in a turbulent sea. I'd pretend that my family was stranded, then I'd make up stories about what we did, how we lived, and when we would be rescued. I'd imagine the house, a private sanctuary, floating along the water in good weather and bad, to the other side of the river, where we'd all be welcomed by a tall, handsome man with outstretched arms.

From the backseat of the car, I watched my mother's eyes in the rearview mirror. She always got nervous on the way to Nonie and Papa's house. To calm herself she filled the drive with small talk.

"Girls," she told us, "the Indians came up the river in canoes expecting to find a waterfall the size of Niagara, but instead, they found just the little waterfall in the middle of town, which wasn't nearly as grand."

"What does this have to do with anything?" Ruthie asked.

"Let me finish, Ruthie, and you'll see," Lilly said. "Your father told me this story once. I want you all to hear it. I have so little of your father to share." She gazed off for a second as if she were lost in a deep reverie. "When the Indians went back to the reservation to tell the chief of their disappointment, he insisted upon seeing the falls for himself. So they all got into canoes and paddled back up the river. When the chief came upon the falls, however, he was so overcome by their beauty, he let out a cry that rang through the trees, and shook the black leaves and the pines."

"You're making this up," Ruthie said.

"The chief made the Indian braves drink from the river until their stomachs almost burst, because he thought they had been blinded by vanity." Lilly rapped her nails on the steering wheel as she talked.

"What's vanity?" Louise asked.

I watched my mother adjust her shoulders and straighten her back. "Vanity means caring too much about appearances. The Indians didn't appreciate the humble beauty of the tiny falls. The river of shame," Lilly said sadly, as if her mind had drifted to something else entirely. "That's how Chagrin Falls got its name."

"It's easy to feel ashamed," she said, when we reached a stoplight. "Especially around people who are more privileged. But it's much more difficult to look for the beauty in things. Come on. Let's get out and stretch. Follow me," she said. She pulled the car over and parked. She reached out her arms, lifted her chin, and closed her eyes, as if she were praying to the open sky.

She was trying to tell us that we shouldn't feel ashamed at Nonie and Papa's just because our aunt and uncle had lots of money, our cousins had expensive new clothes and the carefree attitude of those who have never felt out of place and alone.

"Why do we have to go to Nonie and Papa's?" Ruthie said. "They don't care about us."

"Because they're your father's family," Lilly stated.

After the visit she spoke to us again. "Girls, I have to tell you something," she said, once we were back in the car. "It's not because Nonie and Papa don't love you that they rarely call or come see us. When they came over on the boat from Russia, they wanted your father to marry one of the rich girls, like Evelyn Horowitz, whose father owned a dress factory. I was just a poor bank teller's daughter. Nonie blames me for your father's death," she continued. "She's never approved of me."

I didn't understand how Nonie and Papa could blame Lilly. It wasn't her fault that our father had died. Sometimes I didn't know what to believe. I tortured myself, trying to decipher the truth, when there really wasn't any single truth to be found. Truth was in the eye of the beholder.

With Max, I could forget that we had this strange, uncomfortable history behind us. As a girl I just wanted to be like everyone else. I craved normality. I didn't want to feel singled out or special because something bad had happened to my family.

When Max took us on car rides, he popped in a Frank Sinatra or Burt Bacharach tape. He bellowed and rocked in his seat, and we all started singing with him. As the car filled with our voices, we were taken to a place not compromised, still salvageable, and the sun bounced off the windshield until we could see nothing ahead or behind us.

On the car ride to the Hunt Club, I remember exactly what Max wore: lime-green pants, a navy V-neck sweater, and polished loafers. "Move over here, sport, there's nothing to be afraid of," he said as he ruffled the top of my hair. "I would never hurt my princess."

The day after Lilly had confessed her reservations about Max, I went alone with him on a father-son weekend to his Hunt Club to take part in a hunting trip. As we settled in the car, Max pushed the recliner button so that his seat went back, then turned on his Frank Sinatra tape and began singing. *I'm king of the hill, top of the heap....* He grinned from ear to ear. I sat pressed against the passenger door and opened the window. The smell of the new leather seats in the long silver Lincoln made me nauseous.

"When will we be there?" I asked. I was twelve.

"In less than an hour. The club organizes this father-and-son trip every year. This is the first year I've been able to go," Max said. "Since I don't have a son, Ed O'Brian suggested I bring one of my daughters." Max squeezed my knee and beamed. He opened the glove compartment and reached for a flask of whiskey and took a long swig.

I watched his Adam's apple move up and down as he drank heartily from the flask.

When we pulled into the lodge a family of deer sprang over the fence of the parking lot into the fields. I listened to the sound of their footfalls until they'd made it to safety. After we had changed into our hunt clothes, I set off with Max and his three friends, Fred, John, and Ed, and their sons. I was dressed in jeans tucked into black rubber boots, and a red-and-black CPO hunting vest with a hunt cap to match, which Max had bought for me at the club's supply store before we headed out. Max wore a rough jacket of beaten brown leather with a leather strap slung over his shoulder where he carried his shotgun, and boots that reached his knees.

He handed me the duck call and said, "Here, sport, this is

your territory—you be in charge." He pulled down the brim of my cap. I felt proud next to him. I felt his hand pat my head, grip my shoulders.

We walked for what seemed like miles, deeper and deeper into the trees, until we came to the part of the woods where there were tall, strangling reeds and the ground was soft and muddy. The clouds hung down in the dirty, overcast sky.

Among Max and his friends and their sons, I felt lonely. The boys grew restless. "Where are those damn ducks?" they kept asking, watching the ominous sky.

Overhead I heard a clatter. Two large Vs of geese traversed the sky.

From the other direction three ducks came in close to the ground. The men raised their shotguns. The ducks came down, one after another.

I listened to the thump, thump, thump and imagined pieces of their souls falling bit by bit, like feathers to the ground. The boys squinted at the sky and shouted loudly, after each crack of the gun.

How was it possible that the ducks were dead, when an instant before they'd been free to roam the large sky? I stayed back as the men fetched the birds. A swarm of mosquitoes circled like a dark halo over my head. I admired the strength and nonchalance of Max and his friends. Men, from my perspective, did not grapple with feeling, sort, dissect, obsess, as I did; men took action. When Max walked into our house at the end of the day, my sisters and I stopped fighting over what TV program we wanted to watch, and Lilly, who had been chatting with Aunt Rose long-distance, immediately hung up the phone. Max was a man of limited conversational gifts, but when he spoke he was definite and decisive. We stood back and waited passively for Max to take charge.

And yet, being with Max, I wanted nothing more than to be strong and in control. I had seen firsthand what kind of life was in store for anyone passive and without purpose.

The hunting troop stopped at Squaw Rock—another smoke. Max said it was a ritual they followed after each hunt. The huge rock, large enough to lean against, bore carvings of birds, animals, and Mother Eve guarding the serpent. Max said that the etchings on the rock were the hand of an Indian, before the white man had inhabited the wilderness of Ohio. A particular Indian brave had wandered from camp to the banks of the Chagrin River, where he'd met an Indian maiden to whom he gave his heart. The sculpted rock was his valentine.

"I might just do the same for your mother," Max said. He laughed so loud the leaves shook on the trees. It made me happy to think that Max was thinking about Lilly.

"Come, here, Anna," he said. "Boy, it's good to have you here." He gave me a big squeeze.

When we got back to the lodge, Max told me to go upstairs, shower, and change. He was going to the bar to have a couple of beers with the guys. "Put on that pretty new dress I bought you," he told me, like I was his date. He planted a kiss on my forehead, and a feeling of warmth traveled through my body. I felt as if I were the object of someone's pride. I tried to enjoy myself, even though my fantasy of being alone with Max wasn't working out the way I imagined it.

I picked the dried leaves and mud off my boots in the little bathroom off our small room with its two double beds. I took a long time in the shower. When I looked in the mirror after getting dressed, all polished and primped, I wished only to be in my dirty jeans, work shirt, and work boots.

Max and his friends were drinking shots of whiskey and chasing them with beers when I came downstairs. Max sat next to a tall woman with a pile of frosted hair on top of her head and a pair of pastel earrings dangling to her neck. He straddled his arm against the bar and leaned over her as he talked. She wore a tight sweater set that stuck to her body like static.

When Max caught a glimpse of me, he put down his glass and whistled between his two fingers. "A Shirley Temple for the young lady," he ordered. I sat on the bar stool next to him.

The woman with the frosted hair uncrossed her legs, took a last sip from her drink, and opened her leather pocketbook, the shape of a long envelope.

"It's on me," Max told her.

She snapped her pocketbook shut.

"Anna, I'd like you to meet my secretary, Crystal Martin. She keeps me honest."

"You look just like your mother," Crystal said. Then she turned her eyes to Max. "I'll see you Monday," she said, nuzzling up to Max's ear and practically kissing it. She used a voice meant for men, a voice I knew by then.

After she'd left Max and his friends continued to knock down more shots, and order refills for me.

"Max, I'm tired. Do you mind if I go back to the room?" My stomach was feeling queasy from drinking so many Shirley Temples.

"When are you going to start calling me Dad?"

"Dad, can I?"

"Anything for my princess. I'll have room service send you up a plate of food. Give me a kiss. I'll be up soon." He squeezed me to his chest so forcefully I thought I was going to stop breathing.

I walked upstairs, wishing my sisters were with me. Without them, I felt as if I were missing an essential organ. I longed to look into their faces and burst into giggles over the sound of a fart, or to catch one of them roll her eyes at me the way we did when our mother snuggled up to Max. The part of me that, earlier, had been happy to be alone with Max had disappeared.

I took off my dress, slipped into my nightgown, and stared at the wallpaper, covered with dogs, rifles, and figures of men dressed in old-fashioned hunting clothes, wearing black riding boots. Above the bed was a stuffed deer's head. I pulled the covers around my neck and made myself fall asleep.

I woke near dawn. Max was sprawled next to me, his face buried in the pillow, wearing only his boxer shorts. He smelled liquored up and smoky, so drunk, I guessed, he couldn't find his own bed. Like the times I used to watch Jackie Gleason sitting next to him on the couch, I was afraid to move.

Then I felt him rub up against my body. My heart began to pound so loud I thought it would wake him. I held myself as stiff as a corpse. Max's mouth hung open like a window letting in flies. He began to snore loudly through his nose. He mumbled and turned his head toward me. What if he'd gotten himself so drunk that he could lose consciousness completely?

I shook him by the shoulders. "Max, are you all right?"

"Sweetheart," he moaned. His hand crept up my thighs. "Come here," he mumbled. "Crystal, sweetheart." He hadn't a clue where he was, that it was *me*, Anna Crane, his wife's daughter, in bed with him. Max's body was drenched with sweat and burning hot. He was in another universe. I stared at the wallpaper and counted the little hunting dogs as Max's body rubbed harder against my leg, his penis hard as wood, burning through my skin like a hot coal. A spray of his hot, warm cum rushed over my thigh. Then Max rolled over, mumbled, and fell into a hard sleep.

I tiptoed to the empty bed and turned my body into the wall. I told myself he didn't know it was me. I know he didn't. But I hated him. For the rest of the night I was kept awake by the coarse pull of Max's mucus-filled snores, vibrating the bed and rattling my half-finished glass of water on the nightstand.

By the time Max woke up, I was already showered, packed, and dressed. On the car ride home, I closed my eyes and pretended I was asleep while he sang "Strangers in the Night," to the tune of the radio.

When we stopped for gas, Max turned to me.

"I'm so glad to have you here," he repeated. "I've always wanted to have kids." He put his hand on my leg. "Ever since I lost my brother, I've never really had a family until I married your mother," Max said. "Can you keep a secret, Anna?"

I nodded as he dug into the pocket of his khakis to pay the gas station attendant. Outside the window the sky was a pure, translucent white. You could smell the autumn air in your clothes. "I wasn't sure how things were going to pan out when I married your mother," Max continued. "But I think we're going to make it." I felt as he said those words that they were what he wanted to believe, but not what was true. Maybe secrets are only told when you're trying to protect the real truth from coming out.

The minute we got home I changed into my blue jeans and walked out back to the gazebo. Behind me, the late-afternoon lights of the house dimmed, leaving it a cloak of darkness against sky and trees. There was no wind. No movement. I didn't even hear a bird. My soul felt flat. I imagined a blade of grass in an open field slaughtered by the sunlight. What was my relation, I wondered, to my mother, to Max, to my sisters, to this strange world? I didn't know, but I felt my existence wrapped up with all of them.

I scratched my arms, and then my legs. I saw that my skin was covered in red bumps and raw patches of sores. I must have rubbed up against some poison ivy. I couldn't stop scratching. It was as if I had to shed my skin, any memory of that night.

+ + +

During the lull after the lunch rush, the morning after I'd been to the clinic, as I was refilling the sugar packets, I thought about how I would break the news to Austin that I was pregnant. I was angry that I felt I had to protect him— after all, he was part of why I was in this situation to begin with. Perhaps there were things about Austin that I knew nothing about. I began to doubt him, to find fault with everything he did. I racked my brains, thinking back to each encounter, trying to figure him out. I remembered how strangely Austin had acted the first time that summer when I introduced him to my mother. She was curled up on the couch doing one of her crossword puzzles when we walked in the house. I could smell the burning odor of chemicals in her hair. That morning she had dyed out the gray in the bathroom sink, leaving an auburn ring around the drain.

"So this is Austin." She stood up to greet him, and as she did, smoothed her hair with her fingers as if she were a Clairol model. "The one who's taking my daughter away from me."

She wore a pair of shorts and a tight sleeveless shirt. Her bare toes peeked out from her sling-back, open-toe sandals. Austin ran his eyes along her body, slow and careless, the way all men did.

"I can see where Anna gets her looks." He reached out and shook my mother's hand.

Lilly perked up.

"Anna, why don't you get Austin a glass of iced tea?" Lilly said. "I just made a pitcher."

"That's okay, Mom. We're not staying."

"I wouldn't mind a cold glass," Austin said as he flipped through a magazine on the coffee table. I could barely pry him away.

Once we were in the car, he bombarded me with questions. "What happened between your mother and your stepfather? Did he walk out on her? I just don't get it," he said. "The way people think they can just get up and leave. I feel sorry for your mother. It must be fucking hard raising three daughters."

"I guess," I said. But I didn't want Austin feeling sorry for my mother. I didn't really like to talk about her past. Once I had mentioned to him that years after my father died, my mother had remarried but the marriage didn't last. I lit a cigarette, even though Austin hated when I smoked in his car.

"I don't know why your stepfather left your mother," he continued. "He must have been out of his mind."

"Same reason your mother left your father, I suppose. Wasn't your mother having an affair?"

Austin stepped on the brakes. The car came to a crushing halt. "Fuck off, Anna," he said. "Unless you want to walk." Then, without looking at me, he floored the gas. What I didn't know was that a letter he'd recently written to his mother had come back unopened, address unknown. I found it a few days later in the tack room, between the wall and his bed, where he must have stuffed it, when he got up and went outside to take a leak.

On the way to the track that night we went to the liquor store. Austin bought a bottle of vodka and a carton of orange juice. In the car he spilled out half of the juice from the carton on the ground and then poured in the vodka. He took a swig and passed it to me. I took a long swallow. We spent the better part of an hour that way, in the parking lot, passing the carton back and forth, like a tonic. By the time we got to the tack room, I could barely feel the weight of my body. I lay on the cot and watched the room spin.

"Austin doesn't look me in the eyes when he talks to me. Have you noticed that, Anna?" Lilly said, when I returned home the next day, queasy and hungover.

"Mom, that's absurd." I felt an almost innate urge to defend him. If Austin was ashamed, he had reason to be, I thought. Austin's shame, I convinced myself, like Heathcliff's, came from feeling helpless and abandoned. I didn't mind it. It endeared him to me, the complex range of feeling.

"I have a lot more experience, Anna," Lilly continued, in the all-knowing voice she adopted when she attempted to be maternal. She picked at the chipped nail polish on her fingers.

That night Austin and I had plans to go pool hopping with a group of friends and, as if to exacerbate my mother's suspicions about Austin, he stood me up. I waited in the living room, leafing through a magazine, ears listening for his car. I tried to hide my anxiety, but my eye kept darting to the window every time a car sped by.

After some time my mother came downstairs for a cup of tea.

"You can't let him treat you that way," she told me. She

knew what was going on without my having to say a word. It was close to midnight. "Don't answer when he calls. Let him think you're doing something else. A man knows when a woman wants him too much."

"It's not like that between us," I snapped. "He's not like Max."

"He's going to take advantage of you, Anna," Lilly warned. "I don't want to see you get hurt."

I told myself before clocking out that now that I had my own problems to figure out, I had to be harder on Austin. I was tired of thinking about him. I sat down in the booth in back of the diner and counted my tips.

There was this game Austin and I liked to play. Under the dim light of a candle, we sat on the cot in his tack room and fantasized about how we were going to make our escape from Chagrin Falls. Austin undid the end of the long braid in my hair, as if coaxing the mane loose on a horse's back.

"I'm going to Kentucky," Austin would say, "and work on a horse farm. That's where they breed the best trotters. And after you graduate you'll come out and go to school out there."

I'd always been fond of reading. The characters in novels felt closer to me than my own relatives or friends. I would imagine I was inside Emily Brontë's head on a foggy moor or wrapped inside an elegant, velvety room in one of Henry James's pristine mansions. I had consumed Ruthie's philosophy and poetry books. Once her boyfriend Jimmy had been sent away to boarding school, she would spend hours in her room reading passages from *The Stranger*. Knowledge will save you, Miss Hockenberry, my high school English teacher, had told us; I ingested books and savored them like a tonic. Miss Hockenberry repeated the last lines of the Frost poem we were reading: "Two roads diverged in a yellow wood / . . . . / and I— / I took the one less traveled by, / And that has made all the difference." I imagined Miss Hockenberry's life had been

structured around the ideas behind those words, and I was
going to be the same way. I wanted to devote my life to something beyond myself, to follow a path unlike all I had known,
even if it meant I had to consult a Ouija board in order to find
my direction.

"I'm going to Paris," I said. "I'm going to study at the Sor-
bonne, and you'll come and live with me, and cook for me."

We laughed.

"Is that all I'm good for?" Austin said. "To be your cook?"
He tackled me on the bed. "I think I'm worth more than that,
don't you?"

The tack room was damp and hollow. From the crack underneath the door, we could smell the horses and, if there was a
summer wind, the steam from hot dogs turning on their spits
in the concession stand. I felt alive and buoyant in that tight,
filthy box of a room, even if I had to walk halfway across the
stretch of barns to get to the girls room. The track became
my second home. My mother stopped questioning me about
my whereabouts—so different from other mothers. I stayed
away as much as I could.

I watched the girls who cleaned the stalls and trained the
horses. They had lockers in the girls room, where they'd go
after a long day to shower. They'd boast about the horse they
had rubbed, or what driver they were grooming for. Then
they'd sit around at night drinking beer and whiskey. Sometimes someone would go out and get a pizza. One girl must
have been sixteen or seventeen. She was eight months pregnant
and still hosing down the stalls. I didn't know whether she had
a boyfriend, or any family. I wondered what would happen to
us if Austin decided to stay at the track and learn to become a

driver. After a good race, freedom and possibility, like an urgent rain, pressed against the cement walls of the tack room, but if the horses Austin trained weren't racing well, it was a different story. I feared, as we spent most evenings together, that I would no longer feel Austin's love for me.

There was another game we played, in the dark, without even the bare flame of a candle; we'd lie beside each other, not touching. The point of the game was to try and seduce each other without touching.

"I'm on top of you now," Austin would say. "I'm whispering in your ear, my tongue is inside now. I can hear what you're thinking. I'm licking you."

"My hands are on your back," I'd tell him. "I'm kissing down each bone of your spine."

We went on like that for hours, until we couldn't take it anymore. The point was to see who would give in first. Who would have to grab the other person, because it hurt too much not to.

"We've moved to a Caribbean island," I said to him a few days after the trip to the free clinic in mid-September, stroking the inside of his arm. "All we have to wear all day long are bathing suits and shorts. We get jobs at one of the resorts, and go to the beach all day. And make love." I paused. "And then I'm pregnant, and we decide to have a baby."

I shot him a meaningful look. He turned around and stared at me.

"You're not pregnant, are you?" He balled up the single sheet on the cot in his hand.

I nodded.

"Anna, how did that happen?"

"What do you mean, how did it happen? How do you think it happened?"

"I thought we were being careful."

"What difference does it make now? It happened," I said. "You don't have to worry. I'm taking care of it."

My eyes turned from his and rested on the Northfield Track poster taped on the cement walls. In the half light of the candle, you could barely make out the figure of the horse, bold and beautiful, a study of power and desire.

I wanted him to tell me to keep the baby. I didn't care if it meant we had to stay in Cleveland. But when I looked into his eyes, he looked back, and shook his head.

+ + +

Not long after the duck-hunting weekend, Lilly sat us down and told us she and Max were having a baby. In Lilly's arms was the kitten Max had brought home for us one day. "A baby is sacred," Lilly said. "It's made out of the love between a man and a woman. This baby is a blessing to our family. Why do you look so worried? It will be our very own living doll."

"Congratulations, Mom," I said dutifully. Even though I was too old to be babied, I still longed for my mother to hold me in her arms and stroke my hair, but Lilly sat there, oblivious, stroking our kitten.

Around this time Max began going out of town on business. Once, when Lilly hadn't heard from him for a couple of days, she called his secretary. But she only got a recording. "Crystal must be on vacation," she sighed. She waited up all night for Max to call—I could hear the restless springs on her bed every time she turned—and was anxious and needy the next day.

I resented knowing something so formidable about my mother and Max's private life, and not knowing exactly what it meant. Did Max's flirting with Crystal Martin that night at the Hunt Club mean he didn't love my mother anymore? I didn't know then whether my mother had the constitution to withstand Max's indiscretions. She seemed to need Max's undivided attention. Should I have told my mother that we had run into Crystal at the Hunt Club that weekend? I felt as if I were carrying around an explosive I had to be careful not to agitate, and silence seemed the best way not to.

That day I was on the porch step reading *Jane Eyre*. I'd read the pages over again the entire fall. I imagined myself growing up in an orphanage, sleeping on a cot with other orphan girls, and then falling in love with a blind man. I pictured myself driving away in a carriage to become a governess, and suddenly I knew I'd miss having staring contests with my sisters when we couldn't fall asleep at night, or raiding the refrigerator if we were hungry.

A police car pulled up the driveway.

"Is this the McCarthy residence?" one of the officers asked, when they came to the door.

Lilly nodded.

"Ma'am, your husband was in a car accident last night. The Ohio Highway Patrol found him just outside of Cincinnati."

"A car accident?" Lilly repeated.

"He was pretty banged up. His car veered into the guardrail off Interstate Seventy-one and spun out of control. Miss Martin got a couple of fractures in her leg, and some facial scratches. They're lucky they're both alive. They flew your husband in this morning to the Cleveland Clinic. They're operating this afternoon."

"Why didn't someone phone me last night?" Lilly said.

"Your husband was unconscious, and Miss Martin didn't mention a wife and children," the officer said.

The wind went out of Lilly. You could practically blow her away.

Not only was she shocked by the accident, but she just found out that Max had been having an affair.

The officer gave Lilly a lift to the hospital. Lilly held the bottom of her womb with both hands, climbed into the back of the police car, and from behind the metal grate, gave us a small, defeated wave.

Max was in the hospital for nearly three weeks. Lilly dutifully went to see him, with near-heroic devotion. She held her hands over her growing stomach, still believing the baby was her trump card, and while he was convalescing in the hospital, she carried in her arms magazines, cookies, and cakes. She brought pillows from home for his hospital bed, but there was a private sadness perched inside her.

The day Max came home, I didn't recognize him. He was black-and-blue around the eyes; his jaw was wired closed, and a bandage crowned his head. He turned his head slowly, like a robot would; his face was swollen, his posture rigid, and stitches were sewn across his forehead and along his chin. It was as if he had turned into the reincarnation of his darker self, the mysterious, reckless creature that I had begun to sense underneath his happy-go-lucky nature.

"How are my princesses?" He forced the words out his wired jaw. They sounded flat and hollow.

"Give your father a kiss," Lilly said, motioning us forward.

"Are you okay, Dad?" I asked timidly.

Max nodded his head, but without his big smile and confident disposition he looked sadly diminished.

After the accident everything changed between my mother and Max. Lilly was reserved around him, less anxious to please him. She now began to demand things she had in the past been afraid to do. Instead of wearing fancy negligees and silk robes, she wore old T-shirts around the house. In the morning she plugged in the coffee pot and wandered back up to bed before Max had finished reading the paper.

"Get dressed," I said one afternoon when I came home from school to find Lilly still in her robe. I threw her magazines off her bed. "Can't you at least change your clothes?" I was angry that my mother did not know or even care how to win Max back.

After Max went back to the hospital to have his jaw unwired, he slowly returned to his former activities. When he came home late one night, Lilly cornered him before he had a chance to pour himself a scotch.

"I called your office five times today," she said. "Where were you? I'm your wife, I have a right to know."

"Is that right?" Max tore down the basement. We could hear jars breaking and smashing. All Lilly's pickle jars, one by one, came down from the shelves in the pantry and crashed to the linoleum floor.

My mother screamed down the stairs at him.

"Max, what are you doing! You're crazy."

But he came up newly restored. Calm. "I didn't get married to be cross-examined," he told her.

As the weeks of her pregnancy crept on, Lilly had trouble holding down food, and complained of feeling light-headed,

and of cramps. Even though the doctor assured her that everything was fine, Lilly believed something was wrong, and she
quarantined herself in bed.

During the week, Max snapped at Lilly if she didn't have
supper waiting for him on the table when he came home from
work. At dinner, Lilly and Max rarely spoke. If she complained
that she was tired, he said, "Quit your goddamn bawling," his
rage like a cork about to blow. Then he went outside with his
putter and practiced his swing. When he came back inside, he
grabbed me and tickled me until I screamed. It was the kind
of tickling that hurt.

Lilly looked so agitated and worried, I prayed things would
soon return back to normal. I was beginning to feel sorry for
my mother again, and angry that Max had humiliated her.
Maybe I was protecting him for no reason. What good were
men anyway? I wondered. Brontë's Mr. Rochester was a saint,
but Max, as far as I could tell, had none of his characteristics.

Max was basting a roast for dinner. Sometimes on Saturdays
he liked to spend the day roasting a turkey or simmering an
expensive cut of beef. Lilly was upstairs napping, and Ruthie
came into the kitchen.

"Dad, can I help you?" she said.

It was the first time Ruthie had ever called Max *Dad.* My
stomach tingled.

"Of course you can, sweetheart," Max said, and kissed
Ruthie on the forehead. "You can peel the potatoes."

Even Ruthie couldn't bear to see Lilly in so much pain.

After Max had regained all his strength, he sometimes
didn't come home until midnight or later. Lilly grew increas-
ingly angry.

"Where the hell were you?" she'd shout when he came in. She was in full throttle.

"None of your goddamn business," he'd tell her. Sometimes he'd turn around and leave the house again.

Once, in the middle of the night, when Max still hadn't shown his face, Lilly called to me. "Bring me an aspirin, darling, I can't lift my head." Lilly was furious that Max had betrayed her, but she still ached for him to love her. Louise rubbed Lilly's feet while I held out a glass of water for her to take her pills, and Ruthie navigated the windows to see if Max's car was approaching. We all wanted him to come home.

Then one day my sisters and I found Lilly hunched over the bathroom toilet, holding the small mound of her womb. She was into the fourth month of her pregnancy. Tears were smeared across her face. We got the next-door neighbor to drive her to the hospital. Hours later Max stormed into the waiting room. He had finally been located at the Hunt Club.

"Your mother's going to be all right," he told us, but he looked concerned. I smelled liquor on his breath.

When the doctor came out to report that Lilly had miscarried, Max had already, in his impatience, exited the waiting room for the gift shop. He returned to Lilly's hospital room with his arms filled with a dozen red roses and a box of Lilly's favorite chocolates to find us surrounding her. Her face looked tense, and engraved at the corner of her eyes were a few new lines. She had lost a lot of blood and developed an infection. When Lilly saw Max her lips opened into a small, sad smile. She held out her arms for him and began to cry. Then, quick as the snap of a rubber band, she pulled back and stared at him. The room was empty and white, filled with trapped, stale air.

"Where were you?" Lilly shouted. "How come you're never here when I need you?"

"I'm here now," Max said gently. He took Lilly in his arms.

"Don't touch me," Lilly said.

"We'll have another baby," Max said.

"I don't want another baby. I wanted this one." Tears filled her eyes again. "I lost my baby," she sobbed, pounding her fists against Max's chest. "How could you do it to us? How could you? I was carrying our child." She paused. "The doctor said it was a blessing." She covered her eyes with her hands. "It was God's way of telling us that it wasn't meant to be."

Max tried to hold her. "Get away from me," she screamed. "Everything you touch turns to evil."

"Go get the nurse, Anna," Max said in a tempered, desperate voice. "Your mother's hysterical."

"My poor baby," Lilly cried. "My sweet, sweet baby."

That evening Max took us home without our mother. The doctor wanted to keep Lilly in the hospital for observation. We all piled into the backseat of Max's Lincoln.

"Isn't anyone going to sit in the front with me?" Max said. I peeked over at Louise and Ruthie, then got out of the backseat and slipped into the front passenger seat. Max wore the sheepish look of someone who felt ashamed at what he'd done. I felt sorry for him, but I stared straight ahead into the pigeon crap splattered on his windshield.

That night I looked up *miscarriage* in the dictionary: "failure to achieve a proper desire or result." *Like my mother's marriage,* I thought. I closed the dictionary and planted myself against the window. Polaris, the North Star, the brightest, was the star navigators depended on to find their way in the dark, but the sky was filled with so many stars I couldn't make it out.

✦ ✦ ✦

At seventeen I wasn't ready to have a child. My mother had had her first child when she was not more than a few years older. One day that fall I stared out the window of my bedroom into the yard thinking about what I was going to do. I thought about what it would be like to keep the child. But any life I imagined, the image of the pregnant girl at the track, the home I grew up in, didn't seem right. I never considered giving the baby up for adoption. It wasn't something anyone I knew had done. I tried to tell myself that none of this was happening.

I worried that my mother would be able to tell I was pregnant just by looking at me, but she was too preoccupied. By the time I discovered I was pregnant, my mother's attention was elsewhere. It happened, as such things do, long after we had given up on it, that toward the end of that summer, the perfect man for my mother had moved into the neighborhood. Joe Klein had left an opulent home with three acres his wife had groomed and manicured and moved to a spare, modest Tudor two houses north of us. He came by one Saturday in August, when we were pulling in the driveway, to ask my mother if she knew of a neighborhood boy who could bring in his newspaper and check his mail when he traveled.

"I'd be happy to keep an eye on the house," Lilly said. "It would be silly for you to pay someone." My mother asked Mr. Klein in for a cup of coffee.

Shortly after Lilly met Joe Klein, I came home one day to

find him at the table with Lilly. "I'm not used to being in this situation. My wife took care of the house," I heard him say.

"Your wife?" Lilly said.

"Cancer," Joe Klein reported, like it was an evil word that needed no other explanation. He snapped his fingers. "It took her just like that."

"I'm sorry," Lilly said. "I know what it's like to lose someone you love."

"Esther was organized and energetic," Joe Klein continued. "She was president of Hadassah. I really don't know how she did it all." He diverted his eyes. He was the first Jewish man my mother had been interested in since my father had died. "I can't get over it," he said. "I don't know if I'll ever get over it. One day the sun is shining, and the next your entire world has changed."

Lilly patted his hand. "Oh, Joe," she said. They were already on a first-name basis.

I quietly retreated upstairs so as not to disturb them.

When Louise and I came downstairs later that afternoon, Lilly and Joe were still talking. On the coffee table in the living room were two plates filled with remnants from their lunch.

"I was in the army during the Korean War. Watched my best friend get his brains blown out..." It was clear the way Joe Klein blathered on to my mother's willing ear that he hadn't talked to a soul in ages. "Our family lost everything in the Depression. But this...," he said. "I don't know how you get through it."

"You girls don't have to hang around here," Lilly said. She gave us the eyes that meant she wanted some time alone with

Mr. Klein. I hadn't seen those eyes in a long time. Not in the years since Max had left us.

Things moved quickly, and Lilly was in heaven. They had become friends. Joe Klein often sat with Lilly on our front steps that August drinking iced tea with mint that Lilly had picked from the garden. He talked my mother's ear off about complicated business deals, or reminisced about his dead wife. Lilly patiently endured his endless conversations, but after he scuttled off to tinker in his yard she talked about him as if his wife had never existed.

One day Joe Klein was out of town, and Lilly was sorting through his mail.

"How's it going with Mr. Klein?" I asked her. He wasn't Lilly's usual type. He wasn't flashy or slick; he was what Nonie would call a *mensch.*

"Anna, he reminds me of your father," Lilly said. "He's the first man I've felt that way about in a long time."

On Saturdays Mr. Klein mowed his lawn. "This will only take a second," he said, as he rolled the mower across the driveway and sheared down the square of our front lawn after he'd finished with his own. "No use in letting leftover gasoline go to waste."

He was easy to get used to.

"You must be in the middle of thinking about colleges," Joe Klein had said to me one weekend. I was sitting on the front steps at the house. "I'll help you with those applications. My two sons both went to Ivy League schools, and they're not half as smart as you." I wasn't going to break the news to him that there was no money for college. There was barely enough to pay the bills.

The next time Lilly came back from collecting Joe Klein's mail, she was excited. "This one is from Merrill Lynch," she said. She held up an envelope to the light. "He must be worth millions."

"If he's worth millions, do you think he'd be living almost next door to us?"

"He wanted a clean break," my mother stated confidently. "He couldn't bear all the reminders of his past life. Look at all these," she added. She held a stack of condolence cards. "He's well liked," Lilly summed up. "He's been getting four or five a week."

On the night of my seventeenth birthday, a week after I discovered I was pregnant, I came home from an afternoon shift at the diner to find my mother had invited Austin for dinner. It was Saturday night. I really didn't expect much of a birthday celebration. Birthdays were never big in our house. And all my thoughts were on the baby growing inside me, and what I was going to do about it. I'd been hoping the day would pass by unnoticed.

When I came into the kitchen, Austin was helping my mother set the dining room table.

Since Joe Klein had entered the picture, my mother had become energetic and talkative. Lilly had her makeup on, wore one of her slinky dresses, and had musk perfume pressed against her pulse points.

I was still wearing my stained waitress uniform. I smelled like greasy French fries, ketchup, and spilled Coke. My hair was pulled back in a ponytail. On my feet were dirty tennis shoes.

"Anna, aren't you going to offer Austin a drink?" Lilly mused. "Since it's a special occasion, I thought we could all have a glass of wine." She opened the refrigerator and took out a bottle.

"Let me help you, Mrs. Crane." Austin took the corkscrew and bottle from Lilly. I should have been flattered that Austin was working hard to win my mother's approval, but I was pissed off that he could carry on with his life as though nothing had happened, while my world had hit a dead end.

Austin wore clean blue jeans and a crisp white oxford shirt. He smelled like Irish Spring soap. Usually he wore the same Grateful Dead T-shirt and pair of ripped jeans I watched him pull on day after day.

The kitchen table was covered with Lilly's color swatches and magazine clippings.

"Your mother's a closet artist," Austin said, looking at the table.

"What do you think of rose for the bedrooms?" My mother held up one of the swatches.

"Where's Louise, Mom?" I was hoping Louise was going to join us.

"There would have to be a war going on to drag her out of that pool. Sit down, Anna," Lilly said. "Why are you so jumpy? I don't want you to lift a finger. This is your day."

"I'm going upstairs to change."

When I came back down, Lilly and Austin were talking by the stove. I quietly walked into the hallway by the kitchen and listened.

"Anna thinks I should work. All my girls do. But what would I do?" Lilly said. "I've never been good at anything."

"I'm sure Anna understands," Austin said.

"Why should she?" Lilly was stirring a skillet of sauce on the stove. "My family was wrong. They all were. They thought it was enough to expect a man to take care of you."

"You're too hard on yourself, Mrs. Crane."

As soon as Lilly's divorce was finalized, she changed her name back to Crane. "I don't want to think about Max every time I sign a check," she offered as an explanation.

"My daughter is seventeen today. I wish her father could see her."

It was impossible to make sense of what my mother was doing. Why she felt she needed to explain herself to Austin. It made me sad to think she didn't fit in with all those couples she used to socialize with before my father died, or later the friends she had made with Max, as if she'd been expelled from the world of country clubs, cocktail parties, and aqua pools just because she was a widow. When I stopped to think about it, I didn't know who would be her friends or confidantes. She was like a castaway on a desolate, uninhabitable island that belonged to birds and vegetation.

At dinner Lilly drank too much. She picked uneaten mushrooms off Austin's plate.

"Anna, you didn't tell me Austin is training to be a driver," Lilly said. "Your father used to love to take me to the racetrack. I think it's so romantic. I'm glad Austin is going after his passion. Anyone can be a lawyer or a doctor."

My mother was making me furious. How could she encourage the sleazy track life for Austin? I was getting tired of going to the track every weekend night, worrying about how much money Austin was losing gambling, and then having to walk through the barns with him, watching the track hands gape and stare. I was hoping that his attraction for the track was wearing thin. By the time fall had come, I longed for the geography of my life to expand, wanted to be consumed by something outside myself and my family.

"Your father used to get us seats in the clubhouse, and we'd drink chilled champagne with the Moskowitzes and Shapiros," Lilly went on. "In our day there was dancing at the clubhouse. We'd wear our cocktail dresses, hats, and white gloves. Before I married your father, I went out with a different boy almost every week. The world has changed so much since the time I was a young woman. I told Anna that at her age she should date. But nowadays everyone just wants to hunker down with one fellow. I don't understand the modern world."

"You're still young, Mrs. Crane."

Lilly laughed. "I've got three grown daughters."

Austin was falling under Lilly's spell. It was so clear, I felt as if I had stepped back and was watching a movie. My mother was animated and suddenly vital now, with Austin's attention focused on her.

"Austin, I'm so proud of Anna," she said. "She's the strong one in the family. I don't know what I would do without her. Happy birthday, darling."

"Mom, thanks for dinner." I rose and motioned for Austin to follow. I was tired and cranky. My breasts were tender. Pregnancy hormones had suffused my body. I could practically taste them.

"Where are we going, Anna?" Austin was still pinned to the chair, no longer playing our game where no one else in the world mattered. He was awestruck, glad, I could see, to be taken out of his own life for even a brief time. He was so starved for any kind of maternal attention. I assumed he was comforted simply by the fact that my mother had made him a home-cooked meal.

I reached for his hand and pulled him up. He reached over and kissed my mother's cheek. "Thanks for the dinner," he said. A smile half budded on my mother's face. And then as we turned to leave, her eyes were flooded with that familiar look of abandonment.

Once we were in Austin's car, he turned to me. "Anna, I like your mother," he said. "She's different."

He held me in his eyes and between a catch of breath I could read his thoughts in the expression on his face, in the long curve of his cheekbone. And looking at him, I felt a glimmer of what I'd lost, because the loss of his mother seemed so powerful just then. Both of us had lost a parent— in a way that's what bound us, what we had in common. He pulled me next to him, so close I hit my hip on the gearshift between the two bucket seats of his car, turned my face to his, and with the other hand he rubbed the inner part of my thigh. I thought we were good for each other. I had convinced myself that we were so much alike that we never had to talk about it, that we could see the lost parts of ourselves in each other.

We made it to the track for the last race. In another week the track would close down for the season. After the photo finish we walked past the scattered trash, beyond the bleachers, where the roar of the crowds siphoned off, and then we were in the tack room, with its empty sound of trapped air. I was sure Austin would bring up my pregnancy, and we would talk about what we were going to do. Finally I blurted it out.

"What are we going to do?"

"Anna. I'm bad news. You should get up right now and walk away and never see me again. I'm warning you."

I hugged him. It was always an effort to pull myself out of his long, cool embrace and into the shock of morning, and I remembered, then, that in the morning he'd be driving me back to my mother's house. I buried my face in his shirt and inhaled his smell. I didn't want to think about the baby anymore.

Austin said he had to go back to the barn, that one of the horses needed to be rubbed down, and like a fool I sat on the rusted cot and waited until he returned.

During lunch at school on Monday, I called the free clinic from the phone booth and scheduled the procedure for the following Saturday. I was relieved. I didn't want to have to spend another day sitting in class knowing I was pregnant. I tried not to think about the stories I'd heard. That if something went wrong, you might not be able to have another baby. The rumor was that Nancy Newby had had an abortion. I had run into her at the grocery store, and scanned her body and face for any residue of damage. She was tan from having spent the summer on a dude ranch in Arizona, and her personality was as bubbly and vacant as ever. I rationalized that if she had come through it, seemingly unscarred, so could I.

It wasn't until the Friday night before the procedure that I told Austin what I had decided. By not telling him, I thought I was getting back at him—it bothered me that he didn't press me, that he was leaving it up to me to decide. I was always putting him under these kinds of tests to see whether he loved me.

On the floor of the tack room were balled-up, dirty T-shirts and heaps of unwashed clothes. Socks and old towels hung over his only chair. He raised his head in the casual way boys do, and nodded when I told him that the next morning he needed to take me to the clinic. He was relieved. Outside we could hear the sluggish clip-clop of horse hooves. It was dark, save for a sliver of light from underneath the door. Austin held me, and for a brief second I felt the quiet, steady sound of my heart. It was going to be okay. I was going to get past this.

Someone pounded on the door. Austin jumped. I was still inside the cool heat his body gave off. It was Beep. The sharp, overpowering light from the overhead lights in the barn blinded my eyes when Austin opened the door. I heard them talking in heated whispers outside the metal door. I heard Beep say something about his big horse, a euphemism I'd picked up that meant it was the horse the owner had the most riding on, the horse that was winning.

Austin came back in and paced the tiny floor of the room. He was pumped up, ready to explode. He cracked his knuckles on each hand. He'd gotten himself a tattoo a few days before, a snake that coiled around the muscle of his upper arm, and as he walked, I stared at the intricate, flashing colors.

"What's wrong?" I said. "Are you in trouble? What did Beep want?" I pulled the sheet up over my chest.

"You have enough to worry about," Austin said. The muscle in his jaw popped. He took a coin from the top of the TV, where he kept his change, and threw it in the air. Caught it. Threw it up again. He was agitated. "Come on. Get dressed. I have to take you home."

I was sitting up on the cot, my back against the cement wall.

"I don't want to be alone tonight." I wanted to sleep next to Austin so I wouldn't have to think about the next morning. I had it in my head that we would hold each other all night as if we were performing some kind of sad ritual for our baby.

I don't remember what I had told my mother about where

I was that night. By then I wasn't making excuses anymore for when I didn't sleep at home. My mother must have known Austin and I were sleeping together. Looking back, I probably would have gone ahead and slept with Austin anyway, even if she had attempted to stop me. I had no limits, and didn't think twice about being too young to lose myself in a boy.

At times, when I've completely forgotten about Austin, when I feel squarely planted inside my own life, it catches me unaware, the reality that, if things had gone a different way, my child would be three, four, five....

I had no idea what was going on with Austin that night. Maybe Beep was trying to con Austin out of some money, or maybe he wanted Austin to come out and party with him. Or maybe Austin was dealing drugs. And then I remembered what I had heard Beep say, and thought maybe he was involved in some seedy scam at the track.

"You can't take me home," I said again. "Who's going to take me tomorrow?"

"It's your problem," Austin said. "Don't give me a hard time, Anna." He threw my sweater and my jeans in my lap. "Let's go," he said. "I mean it, Anna. Let's boogie."

My back felt tense. The room spun, like that feeling of drinking too much, only I was dead sober. I thought I was going to throw up.

Then, when I was in his car and we had started toward the gate, he pulled over, stopped the car, and turned off the ignition. Then he went into Howard White's office and came back with the next day's marked-up program. I sat facing the window to hide my emotions.

On the ride through the dark, nearly trafficless streets, we were silent. We followed a trail of endless back roads. Austin barely stopped for stop signs. He ran a light. In the past, when Austin drove recklessly, I'd panic and tell him to slow down. This time I was quiet.

Austin reached for a warm Budweiser from underneath his seat, popped open the can, and guzzled it down. When he pulled up the driveway of our house, he said, "Go on, now. Get out. Don't give me a hard time."

I mustered all the strength I had into a look that said he was crazy. I followed with my eyes the telephone wires running from one house to another and felt trapped, as if they were barbed wires surrounding a prison and not simply lines we depended on to make our town function.

"This is it?" I said. "You're just going to leave me? You're not going to take me in the morning?"

"Anna, you don't know a thing about what's going on."

"Tell me. I want to know."

"I don't have time for this, Anna." He barely looked at me. I tried to reach for his hand. He revved the engine. He practically pushed me out the door, he was that anxious to get rid of me.

After I'd climbed out, heard his car race down the street into the half light of the horizon, I stood motionless on the front steps, sure he would come back for me, until the sound of his tires faded away.

✦ ✦ ✦

How dare you humiliate me?" Lilly asked Max. They had just come home from a party. I thought she meant when Max wasn't around when she miscarried. Or maybe it was the affair. She tipped against the wall and began to sob. We had experienced this scenario so many times, doors slamming and windows rattling, it was nearly casual. After my mother's miscarriage, their relationship plummeted further. It was months before they finally split up.

"Girls, your mother isn't feeling well. Go upstairs to bed. You'll see her in the morning."

I didn't know Max well, not the way you know a friend you have shared life stories with, seen through tragedy and joy. He came in and out of our lives so quickly. I'm not sure exactly what happened the day Lilly threw him out. All I knew was that my mother was not the kind of woman who could live with a man's betrayal. I do believe Max loved us, in love's simplest form. Because he saw how much we needed him, and because he felt sorry for my mother, he let his love for her redeem him, give him a purpose for a short time. Max and Lilly were an ill-fated pair. And yet I understand it, the way we are drawn to what threatens us.

Doors slammed. They had stormed up to their bedroom. Something, maybe a vase or Lilly's perfume bottles, crashed to the floor.

All night through our bedroom walls, my sisters and I could hear Max and our mother fighting.

"How could you betray me when I was carrying our child?" Lilly shouted. In the last year their fights always circled back to this one issue.

"Lilly, she meant nothing to me." Max pleaded with her.

"How could you?" Lilly yelled again.

"Why don't they stop?" Louise asked. She snuggled closer to me in my bed.

"Try not to listen."

"I can't."

"Then put your pillow over your head."

In the next room I heard my mother turn and sigh, and then the stops and starts her breath made as she tried to hold back sobs.

The next morning, a cold November day, Lilly came down the stairs with her hair flyaway and her face swollen. A small brown bird was perched on the windowsill, leaning its feathers against the glass for warmth.

A black-and-blue bruise surrounded my mother's eyes and stretched to the bridge of her nose. My sisters and I were eating Froot Loops at the breakfast table. Our kitten had filled out to the elegant shape of a cat, and was perched on the kitchen counter. Lilly took a dishrag and shooed him off.

"Mom, what happened?" Louise cried.

"I had too much to drink last night, sweetheart. I bumped into a door."

I looked suspiciously at my sisters.

Max pushed open the front door with a bag of fresh bagels in his hands. Their smell of steam and flour filled the stale house.

"How are my princesses?" he bellowed.

Lilly took one long look at him. Her body contracted. "This is it, Max. I don't want you in this house ever again. Go upstairs and pack your bags and get out of here, or I'm calling the police."

I was proud of my mother. She was standing up for herself. I could see clearly now that things were not going to return to normal, that my mother had been hurt too deeply, and worse, that Max seemed to have lost all respect for her. I got up from my chair and stood beside my mother.

Max's face went pale. He stepped back and breathed deeply. "What the hell are you talking about, Lil?"

"I mean it, Max. This is it."

"Lil, we had too much to drink."

"I don't love you anymore."

"That's rubbish."

"I don't want you in my bed. Don't you understand? It's over. Now get out of my house." Lilly's body quivered; she rested her hand against the kitchen counter to steady herself. "I don't love you," she said again, as if to convince herself.

"You're damn right, I'll get out of here," Max said. "Take one last look." He pointed to his face. "Because you'll never see it again."

Max marched up the stairs. He threw open drawers. He swore loudly. Something crashed to the floor. It was as though a wild animal had been set loose in the house. Lilly continued to make breakfast, but her hands shook.

"Drink your juice," Lilly said to Louise, who looked like she was going to burst into tears. "Did you hear me?"

Max came down and set his suitcases in the hallway. They were the same suitcases he'd come with the day he walked inside our house for the first time.

"Please, Lil, don't do this," he said. His shoulders crumbled and he wept. No one moved an inch to comfort him. I went back to the breakfast table. My sisters and I sat stiffly in our chairs. Our allegiance was with our mother. I tried to focus on the crook in the tree I could see in the backyard from the breakfast room window. I imagined curling inside its bark like a caterpillar.

Max grabbed Lilly by the arms and pleaded with her. "I'll change, I promise," he said It looked like it took all Lilly's strength not to comb her fingers through his boyish hair.

Max took the suitcases from the front hallway. He shut the heavy door first gently, but when the lock didn't catch, he opened it again and slammed it so hard the panes of the windows shook. This time, Lilly didn't run after him, begging him to come back home. She buttered a piece of cold toast with fierce strokes.

Louise and Ruthie and I sat there, stunned. I don't think it had occurred to us that Max would actually leave. We just thought we'd go on with the perpetual state of tension Lilly and Max's relationship sent through the house.

"Don't look at me that way," Lilly said curtly. "I had to do it. You must never let anyone humiliate you. If I didn't do this, I would never be able to look at myself again."

Lilly leaned over in her chair and began to cry. A small part of me was sure Max would come back the next morning, that my mother would soften and forgive him. But I was wrong. Lilly tightly closed the door on that chapter of her life and never looked back. Even though I wanted him to leave, I felt abandoned.

+ + +

After Austin's Mustang peeled into the distance, I went into the house and prayed Lilly was asleep. I went directly up to my room and closed my door. Still, I listened for the sound of his car. I knew its cough and purr so well. Louise returned nearly an hour later. Why wasn't I like her? Why didn't I have something I was good at, a talent or skill or passion, something to calm me, other than the shape of a boy's body next to mine?

Louise took one good look at me and said, "What happened? What's wrong? Anna, you're scaring me."

It amazed me that my stomach was still flat as a board, while internally everything about me announced that I was pregnant. "Austin blew me off," I said. "He can't handle it."

"I'll take you to the clinic," Louise said. "We'll get up

early, before Mom wakes up, and we'll call a cab." I listened to the whippoorwills in the yard repeating their same tiresome song. I no longer rose to its fine and definite trill, its cry of hunger, as if it were calling out my name. I no longer imagined a future I could unpack like freshly washed clothes from a suitcase and try on and feel instantly hopeful. The calendar had stopped. The dependable trees protecting our roof faded into shadow.

But when I awoke, the first Saturday in October, it was to the sound of a handful of dried mud thrown against the window. I looked outside. Austin leaned against the house, the heel of his cowboy boot tearing a chunk out of the matted-down lawn. The sky was half awakened. "Come on," he called. "Get dressed. I'll take you."

I was so glad to see him, I woke up forgetting for a moment that I was pregnant. I pulled down the flowered seersucker sheet Louise clutched in her fist when she slept, and told her that Austin had come for me, and tried to blot out the scribble of concern in her eyes.

"Let me come, too, Anna," she said, as she rolled onto her back, fully cognizant. But I shook my head. This was between Austin and me, I foolishly thought, still believing that the intimacy we shared, incarnated in our baby, could ensure his love.

We arrived at the clinic at eight o'clock, and an hour later the doctor had sucked out the little nut I had grown to treasure with a machine that sounded like a vacuum cleaner. The force and quickness confounded me. All those weeks I had carried the emotional gravity of being pregnant, and then, like that, it was over. The nurse gave me a glass of orange juice, graham crackers, pain medication, antibiotics, and something to contract my uterus. There was no look of regret in her eye, no elegiac turn to her lip. How many other girls had she waltzed through this lonely initiation? She reeled off her instructions by rote, suggesting I have a good meal, preferably red meat, since I had lost blood and needed the iron. Austin took me to the Brown Derby for lunch, as if we had something to celebrate, and I ate a bloody sirloin steak—I've never again eaten meat since then—baked potato, and a salad with pink dressing, as ferociously as I could, so I wouldn't have to think about my empty uterus shrinking. Afterward, I went to the sherbet-colored powder room and threw it all up. My whole body felt like it had been evacuated.

Austin got us a room at the Skylight Motel, where I noticed for the first time that the bed linen was filled with dust balls and itched, and the ceiling was blotched with water stains. I drew the sheets over my chest and held them tightly in my fist. I slept the rest of the afternoon and when I awoke we silently watched TV. After we shut the television off, I listened to the sound of the ice from the ice maker in the hall outside our room crashing in the bin. I don't remember if we touched.

When Austin dropped me off the next morning—it was Sunday—I dug in my closet for my waitress uniform, stuffed it in my knapsack, got on my bike, and rode to work. It was sunless. Quiet, except for the chime of church bells. A bird flapped her wings in a tree overhead, the only hint of the ordinary world.

In Dink's bathroom, before I began my shift, I put the toilet seat down and locked the stall. I sat there, numb and drained, and thought about that glimmer of possibility I had felt in that baby, that small window on a future I would not inhabit. I longed for that moment upon waking, before it is light, before you remember what's done. All day I worked like a dog. I chatted it up with the customers, made sure to give re-fills of coffee. It didn't bother me if they wanted to change their orders. The tips I collected in my apron—as soon as I came home I carefully unfolded each crinkled dollar, counted every quarter—felt like the only essential thing in my life.

I stayed after school, holed up in the library, rain pelting against the windows, and randomly flipped through college catalogs filled with color photographs of sophomores and freshmen conversing on the college green, and tried to imagine myself a coed. To see whether I'd qualify for scholarships or financial aid, I had made an appointment with my guidance counselor. In a carrel in the back of the library, I studied the practice questions to prepare for the SATs. A spider drew a web between the spines of two oversized books. I watched how carefully she protected herself from harm.

My breasts had shrunk back to their normal shape. I looked at them closely in the bathroom mirror each morning for any signs of transfiguration. I touched the lower part of my stomach involuntarily, the way your hand automatically goes to pick at a scab. I knew there were scars, but I couldn't see them.

On my way home one day, two weeks into October, I ran into Maria, and instead of waving and walking on, I stopped to ask her if she wanted to go to a movie. We smoked a cigarette as we walked home. She didn't ask about Austin, and I didn't offer anything. Walking next to her, I felt the stem of my being toughen and root itself further into the earth. And I thought then how much I had missed her without ever really knowing it. About how much of my life I had been missing.

+ + +

*A*fter Max evacuated our lives—there wasn't a trace in our house that he'd once lived there, not one tie or abandoned sock—I was thirteen. Lilly's unhappiness hung over the ceilings and eaves. She floated in an unconscious pool where nothing, not the sound of frogs in the yard or the chirp of crickets, could reach her. Some days she got dressed, put lipstick on, and tried to appear happy, but I knew that as soon as we left the house, my mother resumed her life in bed. It was only in the solitary world of the unconscious that Lilly was free—I wondered what it was like to live inside her mind, all the what-ifs and regrets tangled up like intricate twine.

Dirt and dust collected in the corners of the floor near the walls of the house; spiderwebs hung at the edges of the ceiling; the windows were smudged, and the couches in the living room had frayed and yellowed. The walls needed to be painted, our ceilings were marked with water stains from the upstairs toilet leaking; grease dried and hardened on the stove and along the kitchen counters. You could almost hear the sound of the wood as it began to splinter and decay. The image of my mother recoiled against the wall near her bed was lodged inside my brain.

When I came home from school, I turned on the lamp on the nightstand next to my mother's bed. I could see the veins over her temples, a weave of them I had never noticed before. Lilly was sedentary; hard and unmoving.

After Lilly signed the divorce papers, she withdrew inside herself. She spent days wandering from room to room, picking up a magazine, throwing it down again, attempting to mop the floor, and then leaving a bucket of soapy water in the middle of the kitchen floor and drifting back up to bed. Two years passed by without any change in our mother's disposition. By the time I started tenth grade, Ruthie was cutting classes and getting high with Mark Zion and Jimmy Schuyler in Hippie Hall. If she wasn't smoking a joint, she was huddled in the corner making out with Jimmy. She had grown so far removed from us that when I passed her in the halls at school, we looked at each other like strangers. I knew she was getting high a lot, but there was an unspoken sibling code of honor between the three of us that I could not violate by telling my mother. At least a year went by, and Lilly hadn't a clue that Ruthie was in trouble. One night Ruthie came home with a school of painful-looking hickeys on her neck. Other times, I saw her pressed against Jimmy's jacket so tightly, it looked as if she were part of his body. She drifted in and out of the house wearing Jimmy's army jacket; she even slept in it. In the mornings she sat on the edge of the beige tub in the bathroom, smoked a joint, and stared at herself in the wall-length mirror as if she were trying to locate a lock of hair that had fallen out of place.

The night before Ruthie got busted, I waited for Louise to finish swim practice and we walked home together. The sky was slowly shifting from blue to black. It was usually dusk when my mood would darken, as if the soul were sensitive to shifting light and weather.

"What do you think's going to happen to Ruthie?" I said to Louise. Before school that day, dressed in a gauze skirt and tie-dye shirt, she'd done a bong in her room. She took a hit before she came downstairs to grab something to eat. We often heard the bubbling of the bong water in her room after she strolled in past midnight, ignoring Lilly's curfew. Over the past year the pot had stained her teeth; little seeds were buried inside the carpet in her room or sometimes stuck underneath her nails.

Louise and I were in a bind. Worrying about Ruthie felt like the same hopeless conversation we'd had about our mother. The question hung there between us like a long, impenetrable afternoon.

When we got home Lilly and Ruthie were at it again.

"You can't stay out all night with *that* Jimmy, and that's final," Lilly said. "I'm your mother, whether you like it or not. You're stuck with me."

"You're ruining my life!" Ruthie shouted. She was so stoned that she could barely open her eyes.

She disappeared into her room, and the faint and soothing sounds of James Taylor singing *Sunny skies sleeps in the morning, he doesn't know where to be found* vibrated behind her door.

Ruthie's boyfriend had hair that reached the middle of his back. The shirttails from an oxford shirt hung beneath his sweaters. He took his German shepherd, Nietzsche, in desperate need of a bath, wherever he went. He chained him near the bike racks behind our school. I could hear the oversized dog panting outside our house when Jimmy was with Ruthie, doing God knows what, sequestered behind her bedroom door. As they walked to school, Ruthie's head was perfectly cradled in Jimmy's neck as if it were carved into a stone statue.

That night, after we were in bed, I heard Lilly get up and go into Ruthie's room.

"Why, that little sneak," she said. "God must be punishing me."

Ruthie had slipped out of the house to meet Jimmy. I wished that I had a boyfriend who could take me away, as if love were simply a way out, and not a way of being.

Ruthie and Jimmy Schuyler were busted by the police that night. They were found smoking a joint in the parking lot of Dairy Queen. The police confiscated a dime bag of pot from Jimmy's coat pocket. Later, his bedroom was searched. Turned out he was supplying the entire neighborhood with pot. Since it was Ruthie's first offense, she was given a warning. Lilly called Aunt Rose, and when Aunt Rose found out Ruthie was smoking pot, she made the decision. Ruthie would go to live with her.

As Ruthie sat in the backseat of the car that came to take her to the airport, Lilly's face looked as if a little piece had been torn out and then pasted back. Heavy snow spun in the shapes of haystacks into the night and early morning. Ruthie caught the last plane before the blizzard. It was one of those weeks of winter when temperatures in Ohio fell to zero and below with wind chill, and no one went out to work, or to plow, or shovel. It was no matter; our house was always in a state of winter, waiting for someone to dig us out. Ours was like a house under snow, frozen since the day our father died.

In spite of the snowstorm, Louise was determined to go to the pool to swim her laps. Like an aquatic creature, her body depended on the feel of water to survive. On the way downstairs one morning, we passed our mother's bedroom door ajar. Lilly slept soundly, her face pale and peaceful, buried in layers of blankets and quilts. If the house was quiet, she'd sleep till noon.

Once Louise had left, I went back to my bedroom as the snow continued to fill the backyard. I could barely make out the gazebo, so covered in snow, but I felt the lost outlines of it and its shadow. The tree branches, burdened with snow, looked as if they'd snap. The furnace kicked on again. The sky was a blue lake of frost.

Later, I walked into town through the deserted, private streets, off Main Street, past the bank, the pharmacy, the liquor store, over the ramp of the crashing falls, stuffed my hands in my pockets, and walked along the river. I didn't know what to do with all I was feeling. My fingers began to numb inside my gloves. The trees seemed to have grown tall and erect over the winter months, in their effort to reach more sunlight. A gusty wind echoed through the bare treetops. I trudged through the snow, now up to the tops of my boots. I could barely feel my toes. Two birds tore at a carcass of a dog, no doubt hit by a car. As I drew nearer, they rose up and flew away. With my boot I covered the carcass with snow. As I walked on, in the sky's whitewash, the birds flew back to feast on the dead.

The bare birches bent and sighed as the wind ripped through them. I listened for the sound of snow falling. All around me everything was dying. It was winter break when Ruthie went to live with Aunt Rose, and when I returned to school after winter vacation to begin the new term, Austin Cooper opened the heavy doors of our school for the first time.

In the middle of my walk in the blizzard, I decided I was going to make it no matter what the cost. I had to be strong now that Ruthie was gone. Maybe because I saw more of the world beyond my home, saw that people even less fortunate than my mother could piece together a life, my tolerance for my mother's way of living was quickly disappearing.

When I returned home from my walk, Lilly was outside, in an old man's overcoat, wearing rubber boots and with a scarf wrapped around her head, shoveling out chunks of snow from behind the tires of her buried used Chevrolet. Once Max had left she sold the sports car, bought the Chevrolet, and pocketed the difference to help pay her bills.

"Anna, how in the world did you go out in this winter storm? Where's Louise?"

"She's at the pool."

"In this snowstorm?"

"It's indoors, Mom. Here. Let me have the shovel."

Lilly was so out of touch with the world that she hadn't a clue what was going on with her children. "I don't think it's good for her to be swimming so much. Can all that chlorine in her system be good for her?"

"What's wrong with it? At least she's doing something productive."

"Look down the street," Lilly said. "It's so untainted." She brushed back a few locks of hair and scraped them underneath her scarf. "On a day like today you can hear the spirits."

"Spirits?"

"According to the Hindus, a spirit is captured, bound to the flesh, sorrow, and pain," Lilly said, as matter-of-factly as if it were her religion. "Spirits begin a pilgrimage away from the material world, desiring never to be captured in the flesh again."

"Is that what you're trying to do?"

"Sometimes I think I hear the wind talking to me, but then I realize the voices are in my head." Lilly laughed. "Sometimes I think I'm half in the other world already."

"Maybe you want to be," I said. I took off my gloves, and attempted to bring life back to my hands with my breath.

I leaned against the shovel, which was propped against a hard brick of snow. A brittle branch cracked overhead. Our gutters creaked with the weight of the snow. Sparrows scattered in the trees. All around me the landscape was white; an arctic sheen of ice buckled against the side of our house.

"Mom, sometimes I wonder. Do you miss Max?" The question had been on my mind for years—but for some reason I hadn't known how to ask it. Lilly never mentioned Max. Like everything else, she had wiped him from her mind. But the ways in which he'd humiliated her had formed a hard, brittle crust over her heart. Everything was stationary and static—it was as if, if we looked hard enough, we could see the water slowly crystallize and freeze into the icicles that hung from our gutters.

"I knew when I married Max that it wasn't right," Lilly said. She wandered toward the front stoop of the house. "I was trying to punish myself. I didn't want anyone to take your father's place."

"Now you can put it behind you and start over," I said. It really did seem simple, if only my mother would try to step out of herself. I had ideas that she could go back to school, train for a profession, but then I looked at her staring into the sky as the snow began to fall again. The sun had come out earlier, before the last snowfall, and melted some of the snow hanging over the roof and gutters. A cascade of icicles made a chimelike sound as they fell to the ground.

But it wasn't simple.

"It's not letting up," Lilly said, drifting. "Between you and me, I'd like it to snow forever. It's so warm and cozy at home when it snows. The world barely matters."

She pulled nervously on the fingertips of her gloves. "Your father was the only man I've really loved. Now I've lost Ruthie. I don't want to lose you and Louise."

"You haven't lost any of us," I said.

+ + +

*A*round the time Lilly met Joe Klein, Aunt Rose found a job counselor that was willing to help my mother get a job. For one day Lilly treated herself and went shopping. She came back home with a new beige suit and a red silk blouse she was planning to wear for the interview. But weeks passed, and the suit remained behind its plastic sheath in her closet. Even so, I remained a hopeless optimist. I believed that like the heroic characters in the novels I read, my family would overcome our setbacks.

When late summer came, Joe Klein gave my mother reason to hope again, and I was grateful for the timing. Maybe it was because he didn't seem to latch on to her sexually, the way her other men had, that my mother felt she could trust him. Still, there was a part of me that wondered: How could a sane man like Joe Klein really fall for my mother?

When Joe Klein was out of town, my mother built fantasies around him. "He's got a huge master bedroom," Lilly said. "What it needs is a canopy. One of those big, romantic, cherry-wood or iron beds with an eyelet comforter and silk sheets. I'm sure Joe Klein wouldn't bat an eye spending money on silk sheets."

"What if he doesn't want to get married again?" I said. "His wife has only been gone a few months. It could take years for him to get over her."

"Anna, why do you always have to be so negative?" Lilly said, flipping through *Better Homes*.

By mid-October, the sky, the trees, the row of stores in our town were bleached out, like fabric that had lost its original color. The week after the abortion, Austin called a few times, but I told Louise to tell him I wasn't home. But that didn't stop him. One afternoon his car was in our driveway when I came home from school. My heart raced for a few moments, and then slowed.

When I opened the front door, he was on top of a ladder in the hallway, replacing a lightbulb that had been burned out for months in a ceiling fixture.

"Hey, Anna," he said when he saw me. He perked up. Gave me his signature wink. "I've been waiting for you."

"Austin offered to change the lightbulb," Lilly said from behind. "He changed the bulb in my upstairs bathroom and sanded the upstairs doors so they won't stick so badly next summer."

My mind flashed to my father. I wanted to stand close to Austin to make sure he wasn't going to fall. I did not very often consider the reasons my father died. I didn't believe his life was taken to instill some larger meaning in my character, or make me a better person. I preferred to believe that a person might be taken for no reason other than the random winds of chance, the same forces that could create a brilliant sky after a terrible storm.

Austin put the stepladder back in the hall closet and stood not an inch away from me. He sniffed my hair. My whole body reacted. I was certain my love for my father must have been so immense that I could not contain it. It free-floated toward a necessary object. How else to explain why, with the brush of Austin's arm against my own, I weakened.

"What's gotten into you?" I said.

Austin looked surprised.

"It's not like you to sign on as my mother's handyman."

"Can't a guy help his girlfriend's mother without his girl-friend thinking he's got ulterior motives?" Austin said.

"Who said anything about ulterior motives?"

"Why don't you two come in the living room? I'll make us some hot tea," Lilly interrupted.

"No thanks, Mom." I spoke softly. I was tired. "I have to get ready for work."

"Just for a few minutes?" Joe Klein was out of town again, and Lilly was anxious. I looked at the coffee table, where Lilly had placed a bouquet of fresh roses Joe Klein had given her. I looked at the stain on the wood floor, at Austin cracking his knuckles.

"I'm going to be late," I said again.

"I'll drive you to work," Austin offered.

I took the stairs two at a time to get my uniform. When I returned Lilly and Austin were talking intensely on the couch.

"I think it's terrible that Mr. Cooper won't support his son's decisions," Lilly said as I approached.

Why was Austin telling my mother about his father? He rarely talked to *me* about anything.

"He has his reasons," Austin said to Lilly. "He thinks I'm a loser."

"Austin, I'm late." I grabbed his arm.

"It won't kill them," he said.

"I can't afford to get fired."

"They don't deserve you."

"And you do?"

He had no idea how much I needed my job. When you grow up with financial security, you don't know what it means to be without it. You don't realize that without money there is no freedom. As Austin drove me to the diner I gazed at the monotonous road. The sun faded slowly behind a stand of elms. The heating vents in the Mustang blew out hot, dusty air. Five o'clock and it was near dark. The Indian summer had evaporated into the crisp shock of autumn.

"What's up your ass?" Austin cranked down his window.

"Nothing."

"How come you've been avoiding me? I'm not good enough for you anymore?"

"What's that supposed to mean?"

"I saw you talking to Brian Horrigan yesterday."

"You were following me?"

"I thought you'd want a ride. When I saw you with Brian I took off."

"He's in my Shakespeare class." I paused. "At least *he* talks to me."

"What's that supposed to mean?"

"He isn't always ditching me to hang out at the track."

"So you're into him?" Austin drummed his hands on the steering wheel. "Does he do it for you?"

Brian Horrigan was so different from Austin. I could find nothing in which to compare them. I wasn't sure what I felt for Brian, but suddenly the fact that he seemed less complicated, that we didn't have so much history together, was appealing. Maybe it was his ordinariness that felt attractive. But I let the question hang there.

Austin stared over at me. "When did you get to be such a little cunt?" he asked.

I looked at my hands, folded in my lap. Austin pulled over. As we were talking we could feel the thrust of a small animal, maybe a squirrel, underneath his car. Injured, it limped to the side of the road and moved away into the long grass.

"So it's true? He's poking you?"

"Oh, right," I finally said, disgusted.

He turned his head to the windshield and floored the gas. Once we were in front of Dink's, he pulled up to the curb and shifted into park. He held me by the wrist. "I'm sorry, Anna." He took both of my hands. "I know I let you down." I saw him in my mind standing at the curve of my driveway as he did the first time he came to pick me up. I loved that image of Austin, open and confident, that hunger in his eyes.

"I'll come by and pick you up when your shift's over," Austin said, looking at me vulnerably.

"Tonight's not good. I'm tired," I heard myself answer.

"Fuck you, Anna." He turned his eyes to the windshield and took off. I called after him, regretting what I'd said, but it was too late. But, later, when I saw my reflection in the round mirror of Dink's bathroom, I liked what I saw.

My mother was busy in the kitchen. She was baking chicken cutlets. A fresh almond cake was cooling on the counter.

"What's all this?" I said.

"Joe Klein is coming home tonight. I thought I'd surprise him with a home-cooked meal."

The rest of the afternoon Lilly spent sequestered in her room. When she came downstairs with her hair curled and nails newly polished, she looked ten years younger. She wore a red A-line skirt that showed off her curves, and a strand of

black pearls around her neck. She packed up the chicken, potatoes, salad, cake, and a bottle of red wine in a picnic basket
and exited the house with Joe Klein's key in her hand.

She came home an hour later, hysterical.

"What's wrong, Mom?" Lilly sat down at the table. "Is Mr.
Klein okay?"

"That bastard," Lilly said. "He was using me. All those
days and nights I listened to him go on about his dead wife.
All the pain he was in. Joe is moving to St. Louis. I can't believe what a sucker I am."

I was in shock, too. "I'm sorry, Mom. Maybe he just needs
to get out of Cleveland."

"Oh, Anna. You're so naive. He's just like the rest of them.
I bet she's in her twenties." And then, just like that, a picture
formed in my head of how Lilly must have appeared to him. A
woman who spent all day and night painting her house, who
had lost complete touch with the outside world, who barely
left her home. While Joe Klein was busy creating a new future
for himself in St. Louis, my mother was building a fantasy.

My mother had convinced herself, day after day, that Joe
Klein was going to be hers, and this is what had kept her
going. I watched her face collapse and diminish.

"What's wrong with me, Anna?" Lilly said. She looked
suddenly tired, and years older.

"What's going on between you two?" Lilly asked me a few
days later. Since Joe Klein had taken the wind out of her sails,
my mother had spent the days tending to her garden. It was
nearing the end of October and since it had been warm all
September, Lilly was preparing the garden for the winter.

Sometimes I'd see her kneeling on the ground, garden shears still in her hand, staring at the sky.

My mother told me Austin had stopped by again looking for me when he thought I'd be home from my last class.

I shrugged my shoulders. "Why? What did he say?"

"It's not what he said. It's just something I picked up. Are you two fighting?"

"Why don't you ask Austin? You seem to know more about what's going on with him than I do."

My mother looked like the cat that ate the canary.

"I made him lunch, Anna. I couldn't stand to see him moping around. I was trying to help."

In a small voice I said, "That's not your job."

"He needs you to give him some attention," my mother said. She was sitting near the corner of the couch with our cat on her lap, stroking him.

"I don't need you to tell me how to handle my boyfriend, Mom." Then I thought for a second. "What happened to the job counselor you promised Aunt Rose you were going to see?"

Lilly stared at me.

"She told me I have no skills to get a job," my mother said. But later that afternoon, when my mother was outside in the yard, the job counselor's secretary called to say that Lilly had missed her appointment.

I hung up the phone and went upstairs. I was furious with my mother. I had lost faith in the idea that my family could sustain me. Our pristine neighborhood, with its beautiful homes and raked lawns, had little to do with security, comfort, and love. Even the street names—Elm, Maple, Walnut—were neither interesting nor profound. I longed for a place where no one knew me or my history. Where I could reinvent myself. I was determined to depend only on myself. But that night I knew nothing of what I would become.

I couldn't sleep well that fall. I watched the hand on the clock. Once, by the time I fell asleep, it was four in the morning. When the alarm clock blared, I was so tired I could barely pull myself out of bed. Paint fumes snaked through the house. Our mother had resumed her house-painting project. By now, the walls in each room were each a different color. That morning she was scraping the paint from the downstairs hallway, peeling away years of old paint that had cracked, buckled in places, and yellowed. She seemed to believe that if she found the right shade to paint each nook and cranny of our house, she would redeem herself. She knew she had failed her children. She never had to say it. But could she mentally repaint the walls of our rooms for the rest of her days?

"Anna! Louise!"

"Mom, we're right here." We had grabbed Pop Tarts from the kitchen and were nearly halfway out the door.

"I've ruined my house!" Lilly shouted.

The paint for the living room hadn't mixed right, and its walls were streaked the color of muddy water.

"It's ruined!" Lilly said. "Everything's ruined."

She looked unbalanced and anxious. She was popping pills again. I could see the vacancy in her eyes, the way she stumbled when she walked. "Nobody wants me. Nobody will ever want me."

In the last few weeks, school had become the focus of my life. I threw myself into studying and books. When I was consumed by my studies, my own worries and inner turmoil receded like the world at night. I loved history and literature, subjects where I could see the drama of human nature acted out on the page. I was mesmerized by the repetition of sounds, of words, the rich substance I garnered building like layers of protective skin inside my body.

"Girls, please stay home and help me," Lilly said.

"We'll help when we get home. We can't miss school. Go upstairs and get some sleep." Louise took the paintbrush out of our mother's hand. "Mom, you look so tired."

"Don't you care what happens to me?"

"Of course we do." I paused. I looked at the mess, at the dozens of paint cans stacked in the room, the spilled paint that had dried on the floor where the drop cloth had come loose. "You need to sleep now, Mom. We'll help you when we get home," I said slowly. I glanced at my watch. We were already late. "We have to go now."

"Austin must be waiting for you," Lilly said. She was slurring her words.

I tried to remain calm. "Mom, we're going to school."

"Please, girls," Lilly begged. "Please stay home and help me." Paint was splattered in Lilly's hair. "I'm lonely, girls."

"Mom, please don't do this." I wanted to try and comfort her, but my body had begun to build up resistance. I forced myself to reach out my hand, but my mother backed into the ladder. It fell against the piled-up furniture, sending a can of paint splashing against the wall. Our cat ran across the room and stood pressed against the front door. As I opened it, he shot past.

"Don't desert me. Please, girls," Lilly said. But we couldn't stay.

We saw her through the picture window as we walked past the front of our house.

"What are we going to do?" Louise asked. She looked at me and gestured toward the window, where we could still see our mother watching us. I thought of Lilly later retreating upstairs to her bedroom, wanting, like a small animal, to dig a hole lined with features and twigs, where she could nest, safe and warm.

When I came home from Dink's that night, Lilly wasn't around. The cans of paint were stacked neatly against the wall, and the ladder she had knocked down that morning was now standing upright; the wall she had splattered the paint against was freshly painted an eerie blue-green. Draped over the floor, her white canvases were speckled with fresh paint. I walked into the kitchen looking for her, and in the side window, parked near the garage, I recognized Austin's Mustang. Since I had cut across the front lawn and entered the house from the front door, I hadn't noticed it. It had been almost a week since I'd seen him after the day I had blown him off when he drove me to the diner. Sometimes, when Lilly was home, Austin and I used to get high in the gazebo, and I ran out the door, assuming that's where I'd find him.

I realized how despondent I'd been, because once I saw Austin's car, I felt awake and alive.

There was no moon that night, only a canopy of stars. It was still warm enough that October that you only needed a light jacket, but the wind carried the decaying smell of autumn. I was familiar with the dark, uneven path to the gazebo, aware of the dips and curves in the grass, the large rocks. In the gazebo I knew the places where the white wood was beginning to splinter, where the floorboards creaked. How to scare the bats that liked to rest in the rafters. My body felt queasy with excitement. It was always like that with Austin. No matter what he had done to me, I was ready to be possessed by him all over again.

As soon as my eyes adjusted to the darkness, two shapes slowly came into focus, and then disappeared. I heard my mother's voice. And then something occurred to me. Maybe it wasn't Austin after all. Maybe Joe Klein had changed his mind.

I crept closer. I stopped at the big oak tree about fifteen feet from the gazebo. Two thick candles, one on each side of the gazebo, gave off tiny flames of light.

I stopped dead. I stared toward the gazebo.

Then, as I inched closer, I saw, next to one candle, a joint burning in the blue-and-green–tiled ashtray I had made one year for Lilly at school. Usually the ashtray was in the center of the coffee table in the living room. And then I knew, just as I knew the feel of his skin against my hand. I stopped, stunned, like a deer trapped in front of a headlight, not knowing which direction to run.

It was my mother's laugh, and Austin's quick-throated breaths, the sound he'd always made as he eased into me. I saw that he was on top of her, on the bench, and she was in his arms with the skirt of her robe hiked up. I saw how small my mother looked under him, pressed against the wooden bench, observed the slow motion of her body. My eyes fell on his arms, propped against the wood. I saw his face as he was about to lose control.

I saw their lips. They were kissing. I saw his hands over hers. I saw the way he looked, heated, almost angry, furious and fast, and determined.

The blue needles of the pine above fell, with a brush of wind, and nettled over them, and a cry went into the wind that was like the sound of someone released, momentarily, of suffering.

And then I took off. I ran through the backyard and into the yard of our neighbors, and I kept on running. I ran down the street and through the neighborhood until I reached the high school. I sat on the steps in front of the building and worked on controlling the sound of my breathing that had accelerated, and just sat there so shocked I couldn't cry. Then I got up and walked to the pay phone in the school parking lot and called Maria.

I spent the night at Maria's house. I told her Austin and I had broken up, because I didn't know what else to tell her, and out of respect she didn't push me to say more. I curled into the wall of the twin bed next to hers listening to the cold sound the wind makes when fall has come into the air, and pretended I was asleep. But, as it always is when you come upon something so shocking, so unreal you wonder how you'll survive it, I woke up the next morning the way I always did, only I woke up with dread, and didn't feel as if I had slept at all. I counted the little panes of glass in each window of the room, and then the number of fringes that dangled from the blanket on the chenille bedspread of the twin bed across from me. I looked at the bulb in the glass fixture on the ceiling and wondered how much pressure it would need to break.

Later I learned that Austin had come to our house that morning, after Louise and I had left, to give me a ride to school, because he couldn't stand the fact that I was refusing to see him. And when he discovered I'd already left, Lilly had cornered him into helping her paint the living room. I don't like to think about how it started. How, at the knock of the door, Lilly must have come down the stairs, defeated after her outburst that morning, barefoot, still high on pills, dressed only in her silk robe. How they must have teased each other throughout the day. I don't want to think whether it was my mother who started it. After all these years it's still so hard to remember it. Afterward I became numb and distant. It was as if a shade had come down on that part of my memory, and whited it out. But eventually even the things we don't want to remember come to the surface. Every fall, just as the summer is ending, and the air takes on that hair-raising chill, I remember it, the sound of the trees containing the wind, holding it between the branches just before it lets go.

Eventually, I had to remember how my mother had begun to fall into that place where she was responsible for no one. She must have been desperate to make sure she was still desirable. To make sure even her own daughter's boyfriend would still want her. Perhaps I was naive not to have suspected. After all, my mother had seduced boys before.

Did she lure Austin, I wondered, first with her helpless routine, the way she had gotten the men she had dated to fix her leaking roof, buy her jewelry, or mow her lawn? Did she look closely into his eyes, or did she stare off into the air, all the while willing him to pay attention?

After a long day's work of painting, he would have been tired. Intoxicated by the paint fumes. I imagine my mother played music for him, maybe one of our James Taylor or Cat Stevens albums, as he scraped down her walls and mixed the paint. As he rolled the roller in the pan, I wonder, did he think he was doing me a favor, that once I saw that he had helped my mother I'd give in. We had rarely talked about my feelings

toward my mother. I had never broken the silent covenant between mother and daughter, had never revealed my mother's
secrets or strange behavior to anyone outside of my sisters. I
mentioned Max in passing, but I didn't dwell on that. Instead,
I built a rainforest with big trees and wet, humid air in my
mind, where I could wander free, without being suffocated. If
there was evil in the forest lurking there, like exotic unknown
animals, I always chose to see beauty. Because without beauty
or goodness, I did not see the point in living. Having seen my
mother and Austin together, I felt for the first time the presence of evil in the world.

I can see my mother smelling the underside of her scented
wrists before she came down the stairs. Then, as she poured
him a glass of water, I can see her lean in close to him, raise her
wrist near his face. I can see the glistening of the sweat on
their skin.

Austin always flirted with my mother. He flirted with most
women, especially if they were attractive. I used to burn with
jealousy when he did it in my presence. Like that time at his
party with Rita Fox, or at the track when I saw that killer
glimmer he turned on in the presence of Jane Smart at the
stables. Sometimes when she wasn't working, she came by the
stables after one of their horses had raced, dressed in white
boots and a white leather coat, her blond hair bouncing down
her back, and her breasts jiggling in his face. It drove me
crazy. Sometimes, if we were in a fight, I used to think to myself, she's the kind of girl he should be with. A girl who was
light and bubbly and obsessed with horses. But I knew Austin
had never crossed the line—had never betrayed me.

It was only later, when I began to put the pieces together,
that I realized how much Austin needed me, how he couldn't

stand my pushing him away, and how he felt abandoned again. I could not have imagined, that first day I saw him walking down the halls of our school, that he was capable of cruelty.

For years I hated my mother for betraying me, but she was so lost that continuing to think ill of her would be like hating a small, helpless child. Even when you think you've stopped loving someone, one day, watching rain fall against a window, or catching the whiff of the approaching autumn air, it seizes you, the remembered touch of a mother's hand on your cheek, or the look of adoration in her eye. Maybe you never stop longing for the love of a parent. But I couldn't forgive my mother then. I couldn't even look at her. It took years before I would even talk to her on the phone.

I still remember. Because once you know something, it can never be forgotten. His body against hers; pounding into her is how I imagine it. It cannot be gentle. In my mind it has to be cruel.

She would have gone to the kitchen and taken out the bottle of whiskey she used to keep underneath the sink and offered him a drink. Austin was good at making a woman feel special. She would have sat down at the kitchen table with him. Maybe ran her fingers through her hair, perhaps bent down so that her robe would have opened slightly, so that he could see the top of her breasts, the space between them. Suddenly her entire body would have come alive and dangerous as a bare electrical wire. I've seen it happen. She would have said something about how tired she was, how she was getting old. And Austin would have reassured her.

"You don't look a day older than twenty, Mrs. Crane," I can hear him say. "You and Anna could be sisters." He would have been touching the stubble on his cheeks, running his fingers along his chin, staring her down in that sexy way he had when he was studying every inch of my body.

"Oh come on, Austin. You don't have to flatter me," she would have flirted, and laughed, and moistened her lips.

Maybe my mother would have gotten him to talk. She could do that sometimes. Find a way to enter a man through a soft spot, as if she had found the room in the heart that had been empty and vacant. I had learned from her. I used her method, later, on many other boys. She would walk, at first cautiously, lovingly into that complicated place. And then she would find a way to make it hers, as if she had sensed there was something incomplete, something still childlike she could make dependent upon her. It seems wrong to know this about your mother.

She would have gotten him to talk about his mother. She told me that once. About getting a boy. "Find where he hurts, honey. That will make him yours."

A strange feeling would have come out of him, colored his eyes. I saw it every time his mother's name was mentioned in conversation. A wave of loss or loneliness washed over his face—perhaps they are the same feeling—the way the willow tree in the yard sometimes looked so vulnerable covered with frost that it would send a chill down your spine. And then his body tensed. He chewed the inside of his jaw like a cow working at his cud. He picked at the dried skin around his fingers. When he did that I always wanted to take his hands in my own and quiet them. Kiss each long finger. And she might have consoled him. Told him how she knew what it's like to be abandoned, to lose a mother. My mother was good at that kind of talk.

I have spent too many years turning it over the way you might worry a stone in your hand, sitting by the river on a winter's day, watching a sheet of ice float with the current, the trees bare and vulnerable, while above you the sky is a sly white light, stealing the truth from you. I have spent all this time, so many hours, so many days, bargaining with my soul, trying to forgive. What is lust? I've wondered. Can it be forgiven?

＊ ＊ ＊

A girl never marries the boy who makes her heart ache, the one she might have risked her life for. She always marries the Edgar Lintons of the world. I have read *Wuthering Heights* on many occasions, and each time I see things differently. It's the age-old question of passion versus tranquillity. I see the sky turn dark, blue and then bluer, the most insanely exquisite color I have ever seen. I want to look at it forever. I don't want to take my eyes away for fear the sky will break or disappear. But if I look so intensely, I can't see or feel anything else, not the swaying of the branches of the willow or the pinpricks of wildflowers or the singular sight of a tall white pine, or the sound inside the body listening to a calm wind. In a softer light I can see further into the horizon.

I only saw Austin again once after that night. He came to Dink's looking for me, plunked down on a stool, and ordered a cup of coffee from Clara. I can still remember her full girth in her starched white uniform, the smell of her hair spray, her hair pulled back in a hair net. She came into the kitchen to tell me Austin was at the counter. Everyone at Dink's knew I was crazy about him.

Austin tried to catch my eye when I went to the window to grab an order, but I wouldn't look back. I don't think I was capable of ever looking at him closely again. I was such a fool to have romanticized him, to see him as *my* Heathcliff.

Austin sat at the counter while I did the closedown. I refilled the ketchups, finished the setup on the tables, wiped down the sugar bowls and salt and pepper shakers. I felt Austin's eyes burning on my back. When Toby, our overweight manager, saw that I didn't want to see Austin, he asked him to leave. He pointed to the sign next to the clock that said NO LOITERING ALLOWED. I felt pain in my chest watching him go.

I wished I could turn back the clock and still lie beside Austin on the grass, and read each pore and blemish on his face, but I knew it was impossible. I would never smooth the veins on the insides of his arms with my fingers, or let my hair fall over his chest when we made love.

That night Austin waited for me in the parking lot of the diner. Hearing the stamp of his Mustang's engine sent fear through my body.

He pulled out of the parking lot and drove beside me as I began walking home.

"Come on, Anna, just get in. I have to talk to you."

"Go away," I said. "I don't want anything to do with you. I saw you last night in the gazebo." I looked at his face, at the color rushing out of it.

"Just give me five minutes. You owe me that."

"I don't owe you a thing."

"Anna, if you don't get in this car, I'm going to drive into that wall." He started to pump the gas.

"Five minutes," I said, because looking into his eyes, I knew he had the guts to do it.

He reached over and opened the passenger door.

"I'll give you five minutes."

"You don't understand." He grabbed me by the shoulders

once I had gotten in the car and he had pulled back into the parking lot and parked. "I can't live without you, Anna. What I did was wrong. I thought I was losing you. Beep said if I didn't get him the money I owed, they were going to kill me. I borrowed money to place on a horse Beep was sure was going to win. I racked up twenty thousand dollars' worth of debt. I was coming to find you. To take you away with me.

"And then your mother said you weren't coming home after school. I pictured you with Brian. It was stupid. I just did."

"That's bullshit. Nothing is going on between Brian and me. You're crazy. And how could you let yourself get in that kind of debt? What's wrong with you?" I stared at him with contempt. "Did you think she was going to help you?"

"I don't know what I wanted," Austin said. He looked down and cracked the knuckles on each one of his fingers.

"It looks like you got the money somewhere," I said. "You're still here, aren't you? You're still alive." His fingers were white from where he'd been squeezing the steering wheel. I watched as he loosened his grip and opened his fingers. I looked at the thick calluses and his hard nails. I continued to stare at his hands, which I could feel, even when he wasn't touching me, reading my body.

"You don't believe me, do you?" he said. "You're not going to come to Kentucky or anywhere with me, are you?"

"Does it matter if I believe you? It's been done."

"Anna." He gripped my wrists as he said it. "Come with me. We'll get married."

"You're out of your mind," I told him. "There's no reason for us to get married now." I thought about our baby and the future that was never to be. It was wrong and I knew it, but I blamed Austin, because I couldn't forgive myself.

"My father said he would pay off my debts if I moved out

of the track and agreed to go to college next fall. My father likes you. He'll help us out."

I would be lying if I said I didn't consider it. But I knew that I was too young to be married, and if I married Austin it would only be because I wanted escape and not because I'd chosen to. I wasn't sure Austin and I could ever be together anymore, even if nothing had happened with my mother. It hadn't bothered me before that Austin and I rarely talked about anything that mattered. That we lived in a kind of dark hinterland beneath words. But I wasn't sure that the silences, in the end, would be enough. As the summer had disappeared, not emotion, but concrete words and ideas seemed the only source of sustenance.

When I'd first read *Wuthering Heights,* as a child, I was devastated when Cathy marries Edgar. Her betrayal of Heathcliff was unfathomable. But reading it again, I saw what comfort she found in Edgar. Cathy and Edgar are counterparts. Cathy finds security in that which is solely different from her own nature. And Edgar finds temporary bliss in the presence of someone capable of such passion. Austin and I were too much alike. I knew that what was between Austin and me could only exist in brief flashes, like the flame of a match before it is extinguished.

He reached over and took me in his arms, and I was pulled again, into his aura. I smelled the horses in his hair and on his clothes, a smell that to this day makes me ache. I allowed him to hold my face, and he pressed it into his chest, where the wool from his sweater burned me. I felt his lips on the back of my neck and in my ear.

"Don't you understand?" I said. I shrugged him off and

pulled away. "Every time I look at you, I see my mother. How could you?" I slugged his chest with my fists.

I gathered my shoulder bag, opened the door, and took off. In the parking lot of the diner, I felt his steps coming after me. He was practically nipping my heels. I heard the busboy open the back door to the diner to throw out the trash in the bin. And then I heard the sound of the door as it slammed shut.

"Please come back to the car," Austin said. "Please let me explain."

I followed him, more because I was afraid the people I worked with would overhear us. Once we were back in the car he tried to hold me again. He pressed his face into my neck. "You're still mine," he said in my hair. "You'll always be mine, Anna." I was despondent. I let him turn my face to his so he could kiss me. I heard nothing, only the sound of his breath. And then I snapped. I hit him until I had no strength left. I was out of control. "Get away from me," I told him.

"Anna, listen. I'm trying to tell you something," he said. He grabbed my arms like you would a crazy person to calm me. "I'm asking you to forgive me." He was crying.

I was listening with my body, the way you listen for the sound of the river, or the *swish* of the wind through the trees, but I couldn't hear my heart anymore, it was no longer reliable. I looked at him. "You know I have to leave," I said.

As I walked home that night I felt the last hint of the summer in the autumn air.

There is little redemption in Emily Brontë's world. Evil and goodness exist simultaneously within her characters. They do not apologize for what damage they've done or what heartbreak they've caused. They are flawed, imperfect.

Though I once drew comfort from the parallels I saw between Heathcliff and Austin, I did not allow my mother the same kind of indulgence. I could not understand her.

"My nerves were frayed," Lilly said when I told her I knew. I was in my bedroom packing.

"I was working day and night on the house. I hadn't slept in weeks."

I didn't say a word. I had no mother.

"I hadn't realized how much Joe was beginning to mean to me," Lilly continued. She paced the room. She walked to the window and raised the curtain. "Anna, you know I would never deliberately hurt you."

I couldn't bear to look at her. I stared inside the open dresser drawer. When I said nothing, Lilly waited a few moments, then in a huff walked out of the room and shut the door behind her.

Outside, the snow had begun to fall. It was early November by now, and had grown colder as the day went on. In Cleveland the weather was always drastic. It could be a sunny autumn day, and then out of nowhere the snow would begin to fall. I used to love being inside our house most when it snowed. You could feel the snow falling on the boughs of the pines, on the roof, covering the house in a protective blanket, falling on the windowsills, the ledges. They say that each snowflake is a different shape, that not one crystal is exactly like another.

The wind picked up. A gust whipped leaves across the yard. A sound fierce enough to send tremors down your spine. The wind took a branch off a tree. Whirled it back. It was beautiful, the way the snow began to fill the backyard. How light slipped carelessly into dusk. And then the smell of wetness, loss in the cold air; the weight of another history sealed in the frost settling on the earth's floor. A promise of a new future when all the ice and snow thawed.

"Anna," Louise said. She dumped her books on her bed. She had just come back from school. "Do you think Aunt Rose has talked to Mom yet?"

"I don't know."

"Don't you think we should tell her?" Louise said.

I had told Louise what Lilly had done the morning after, when I ran into her at school. We sat on the school green and smoked a cigarette. No more needed to be said. Louise must have weighed ninety pounds. Finally I saw what I should have seen long ago—my sister needed help. When you love someone, see her so closely every day, it's so easy to delude yourself, not to see what's staring you in the face. It was clear to both of us what had to be done. From the pay phone at school, we called Aunt Rose and arranged it.

"I'll tell her," I said.

"What will happen to her?" Louise asked.

Neither of us had an answer.

I went downstairs to find my mother. Lilly was outside, wearing an old coat and a scarf around her head, sipping a cup of tea. She watched the snow begin to fall over her lawn of autumn-flowering crocuses. In her face was that look of wanting to become one with the landscape, to dissolve. The air carried the smell of someone burning logs in a fireplace, of burned wood and ash.

"I'm over here, Anna." Lilly threw up her arms. Dusk was just beginning to steal the light from the sky, and Lilly looked almost consumed by it. She breathed deeply, inhaling the smell of wet leaves, grass, trees. "It's so magnificent. The first snowfall," she said. "Come sit with me."

"I can't now, Mom. I want to tell you something."

"Hear that?" Lilly said. "It's a nightingale. It's such a sad cry. I heard it all day. It was as if she were speaking to me."

"That's ridiculous," I said, because, whatever my mother felt, I was going to feel the opposite. She yawned long and languidly, still as if she were entitled, as if no one else had felt anything or mattered.

"I have to tell you something," I repeated again. "And then I'm not going to talk to you anymore. I'm not going to talk to you for a long time."

"I spoke to Aunt Rose this afternoon. She told me you and Louise are going to live with her. I know you're both leaving me," she said. "All my children. Gone."

"I don't want to talk about it. I just wanted you to know."

"I warned you, darling," Lilly said. "I told you Austin needed you."

"You don't know anything about what he needs. You don't know anything about me and Austin."

"It was a mistake," Lilly said.

"No, Mom." This time I didn't turn my eyes away. I wasn't going to forgive her. "It was more than a mistake."

"How can you and Louise leave me now?" she demanded.

It was so twisted. In my mother's eyes, I was at fault for wanting to leave her.

My rage against her was useless. No matter what I felt she wasn't going to be accountable. It gives you a particular strength, a coldness, having to bear another person's weakness. It is amazing to me, the burden of love, the weight it must bear.

That day, I took a walk around the house. I wanted to make sure it was planted deep in my memory. For months my mother's purpose had been to repair and salvage, to clean the house of everything that lay dormant all those years with fresh coats of paint. The house sparkled with her efforts, but underneath the layers of paint I could still make out the outlines of each painted-over shadow.

She had carefully taken up the canvas from the living room, den, and dining room. Each room had been painstakingly planned, one an extension of the other. Each stroke of paint allowed her spirit to come alive inside her house, until she owned it completely, until there wasn't a trace of our childhood fingerprints on the walls. Our childhood pictures, paintings—all those she had stuffed in drawers, tucked away.

The walls in the living room were painted a forest green, giving an eerie texture to the room. My eyes followed the walls into the dining room, painted in burgundy. The mauve alcoves, low ceilings, and her carefully tended plants at the windows made the house look as austere as a dense wood.

I felt the trees outside beating their leaves against the roof. The wind, still in full force, whipped and whirled the falling snow in gusts.

That's how I always imagine my mother, alone in her sanctuary—like a house cat, shut in, watching a bird perched on the limb of a tree, but afraid to step outside—among her memories, living like ghosts in the creaks and crevices of our house. That day the snow was building a white layer around the house in drifts and swirls, falling over the roof, covering the branches, windowsills, lining the gutters and eaves. I wish I could say she had changed. There was a time I might have written it that way.

After Louise and I left that night, I didn't talk to my mother. Louise, Ruthie, and Aunt Rose gave me occasional reports. I no longer understood what my place was in her life. When I open the newspaper and read about mothers who abandon or harm their children, husbands who murder their wives, I am terrified by how complicated we are, and the terrible weight our pasts exert on our future. What freedom there is in realizing one cannot shape or mold another person. Sometimes I see the outline of a leaf, or the black center of a sunflower and feel the uniqueness of each thing. On occasion now I visit, and sometimes my mother's out in the garden or tending to her houseplants, and for a brief time I can forgive her.

The first time I called Lilly, I was fully established in my own apartment, where I no longer had to worry about pasting together a life. It was from a place where I knew who I was and understood that what I had built could never be taken from me. For years I had dreamed of creating a home in a place that had nothing to do with any home I had known. And that's eventually what I did. I created a home in a city full of skyscrapers and millions of people. Just a few hundred square feet of studio apartment, painted all white, with room for a sofa bed and bookshelves for my books. It had to be small and inexpensive, so that when something needed repair, I could afford to take care of it. I didn't care if I had to wait tables, bartend, wash people's clothes, and clean their houses to support myself. I promised myself that I would never be like my mother. Still, in the back of my mind there's always that threat of an avalanche in the distance, reminding me that everything can be wiped out in a single instance. To quiet the feeling I sometimes have to walk outside in the middle of a snowy day, or stand at the edge of the ocean and inhale as much air as I can in my lungs and hold it there.

I don't try and change my mother anymore. I no longer wonder what is in her thoughts and prayers. It's enough to make sure she's comfortable. I always have my antennae up— we all do—to make sure she can't hurt us. We visit. We speak. We try and love her when we can.

On the day of my wedding, I plan to wear the antique wedding dress my mother wore when she married my father. Months ago she had it dry-cleaned and sent it to me. It fits as if it were made for me.

The day I left my mother, I moved to the front window to have one last look. The entire lawn was covered—a snow-dusted field of violet, yellow, and baby blue autumn crocuses my mother had planted. There was no grass, just flower after flower. Many of the crocuses had dried out, though some still shimmered with vibrancy, even in the cold. And the snow fell on top of the crocuses, covering them so that you could only see the tips of their leaves, the tiny bits of color. My mother was so proud of her crocuses. She had planted them at the end of the summer, when she found out how easy they were to care for. How with a lawn full of crocuses, she wouldn't have to pay one of the boys down the street to cut the lawn.

"These are autumn-flowering crocuses," I hear my mother say to me now, just like she did the day after she'd planted them. "If you plant them in late September they will last until October or even November. Just when you think the summer is over, they bloom again. Baron Van Brunow are the dark ones. The dark, lilac-colored ones are called Early Perfection; the sweet purple are Pupera Gradafolia. The most splendid is the Queen of the Blues, the pure lilac ones. They remind me of you, Anna. You're so strong, darling," she said, reaching out to me and stroking my hair.

At last the house itself, from a distance, seemed almost invisible in the snow; it stood as if in memorial to something no longer of the earth.

It kept growing colder as the day went on. You could feel inside your throat the snow's damp mist, in your bones its cold beauty. By evening, before the car came to take Louise and me to the airport, the snow was nearly three inches high. On my finger was the ring Austin had given me that night behind the movie theater. The diamond chip was impossible to see under the dim light, but I felt the weight of the gold strand on my finger. I don't need to see him anymore. I prefer to remember him as we were together once that summer so many years ago.

The snow softly settled on the roof, on top of the gutters,

the chimney; it draped over the branches of our trees. As the car pulled out from the driveway, our house receded into the frozen whiteness. By dawn the snow, pure and untouched, covered the bushes in front of our house, every crocus, until there wasn't any green left, any color, not a trace.

Acknowledgments

For their support and friendship, I would like to thank Helen
Schulman, Cheryl Pearl Sucher, and Diane Goodman. Im-
measurable thanks to Lelia Ruckenstein, who patiently read
more than one draft and offered insightful suggestions and
comments. This book improved under her careful scrutiny.
Sandra Bragman Lewis had faith in this project even when
I didn't. Thanks to Elizabeth Gaffney for her good eye
and perceptive suggestions. I am in debt to my editor at
Harcourt, André Bernard, for his care and expertise; to Sarah
Chalfant at the Wylie Agency for her wise counsel and con-
viction; and to Jin Auh. Thanks to Marian Ryan for her
thorough copyediting. Thanks to Alice Mackenzie for her
expertise regarding harness racing and track life. Lee Abbott
read a portion of this book years ago, when I fled the halls of
law school for the English department at Case Western Reserve University, and saw something in it worth pursuing.
Frederick Busch read an early draft and offered invaluable
suggestions. David Schwartz, my husband, stood beside me
through it all. Special thanks to my son for his patience. I am
forever grateful to them all.

I would like to thank the Western Reserve Historical Society Library for supplying research on the history of Chagrin Falls and to Starling Lawrence for his insight about colchicum, the fall crocus. And if Emily Brontë were alive, I would thank her for writing *Wuthering Heights,* a novel that has continued to enchant me.

Reading Group Guide

Reading Group Guide

1. Themes of abandonment—whether by death or design—
   run throughout this book: Lilly is abandoned by her
   mother, her husband, and finally her children; Austin is
   abandoned by his mother and rejected by his father; Lilly
   emotionally abandons Anna and her sisters. How are these
   themes carried out, and how does abandonment affect the
   life of each character?

2. Anna's memories of her early childhood include regular
   observation of the Jewish holidays and traditions. After
   her father dies, though, Lilly rejects the faith. How does
   this affect Anna, in light of the stories Lilly tells about the
   death of her mother's sister and parents during the Holocaust, and the death of Lilly's mother, after living with her
   own survivor's guilt?

3. When Lilly marries again, she marries an Irish Catholic.
   Consider the differences between Max's behavior and
   world view and that of Lilly and her daughters. Why does
   Lilly marry outside her faith? How does this decision affect
   her daughters?

4. After her husband dies, Lilly's whole identity is in question—she lived for (and, possibly through) her husband. On page 24, Anna observes, "[Lilly] needed a different kind of love to make herself feel alive." How does this manifest itself in Lilly's behavior toward her daughters? How does this observation—and Lilly's behavior—affect Anna's own sense of identity? How does it affect her relationships with the various men in her life—Austin, Max, and the memory of her father?

5. Anna's childhood occurred during the 1960s and '70s, the Vietnam era. What affect does this have on her, and how much of Lilly's behavior is reflective of those influences?

6. Throughout the novel, Anna describes Lilly's habit of cutting out hundreds of magazine images and storing them in boxes. What is Lilly doing with these pictures, and why does she do it? Does this behavior foreshadow her deteriorating mental state? What does the novel say about grief and its aftermath?

7. When Anna and Austin go horseback riding, Anna's horse gets spooked, races off, and then throws her. Austin, frightened that Anna's been injured, and also frustrated by her inability to help herself out of the situation, asks, "Can't you for once be in control?" What does he mean by this, and how does it seem that Anna is out of control in other areas of her life? Why is Anna so seemingly passive at the outset of her relationship with Austin? How do her feelings change as the book progresses?

8. As Anna and Austin's relationship develops, Austin shows her a model he'd built as a child, one they refer to as his "City of Nowhere." What does the City of Nowhere mean to each of them, and why do they fantasize about living there?

9. On page 84, Anna observes, "I knew at an early age that you couldn't live peacefully in isolation." What does she mean by this? How did this realization affect choices she made in her adult life, and her relationships with those around her? Anna may be the only character in this novel, however, to have reached that conclusion. How are the other characters isolated—her mother, sisters, Austin?

10. When Lilly builds the shrine in her bedroom, Anna asks why her mother has saved these particular objects. Lilly tells her, "People don't understand that the relationship with the dead doesn't go away." This seems to have both positive and negative ramifications for Lilly and Anna as individuals. What does Lilly's statement mean as it relates to each of them?

11. At the conclusion of the novel both Lilly and Austin betray Anna. How does Bialosky foreshadow that climactic scene? Did you find it believable that a mother would hurt her daughter so cruelly? Why does Austin betray Anna?

12. On page 206, there's a reference to the novel's title— "Ours was like a house under snow, frozen since the day our father died." What does Anna mean by this? Snow

appears frequently throughout the novel—how does the author use this metaphor?

13. Throughout the novel, Anna refers to Emily Brontë's *Wuthering Heights* and compares herself and Austin to Cathy and Heathcliff. What parallels can you draw between Brontë's characters and Bialosky's?

14. How did you react to Bialosky's use of flashback to convey Anna's story? What affect did that have on you while reading the book?